PRAISE FOR *THE TEN*

What can we give up to save that which we cherish most? This is one of the questions posed by this absolutely gripping novel of a family on the verge of breaking apart. The characters here are as vivid and real as people we know in life...and just as captivating and mysterious. I was enthralled.

> — Ann Packer, author of *The Dive From Clausen's Pier*

We need more novels like *The Tenderest of Strings*, realistic but sympathetic depictions of ordinary men, women, and children trying to get through their days and nights with their dignity intact. Because Steven Schwartz's characters are people we are sure to care about, we're likely to turn this novel's pages as quickly as we would a thriller. But in *The Tenderest of Strings* we read to learn how the mysteries of the human heart will be resolved. This is a remarkable novel, wise, well-written, and evocative.

> — Larry Watson, author of *Let Him Go*

Fast-paced, unpredictable, and thoroughly absorbing, this is a beautiful and touching story of an American family, who, in a fractured, confusing world, try to remember how to be loyal, and how to love.

> — Ann Cummins, author of *Yellowcake*

The acuity of Schwartz's gaze is matched only by the enormity and suppleness of his writerly heart. He is a maestro of the humane, a brilliant chronicler of the many barely forgivable ways we approach and avoid the mirror of our essential selves. *The Tenderest of Strings* is at once a superbly compelling page-turner and a subtle, complex investigation—make that celebration— of the ties that bind.

> — Robert Cohen, author of *Amateur Barbarians*

Also by Steven Schwartz

Madagascar: New and Selected Stories

Little Raw Souls

A Good Doctor's Son

Therapy

Lives of the Fathers

To Leningrad in Winter

The Tenderest of Strings

A novel by

Steven Schwartz

Regal House Publishing

Published by
Regal House Publishing, LLC
Raleigh, NC 27587
All rights reserved

ISBN -13 (paperback): 9781646032211
ISBN -13 (epub): 9781646032228
Library of Congress Control Number: 2021935997

Interior and cover design by Lafayette & Greene
Cover images © byKyle Spradley Photography/Shutterstock

Regal House Publishing, LLC
https://regalhousepublishing.com

Printed in the United States of America

For Zach and Marissa
and Elena and Sarah

PART 1

1

In the emergency room, Reuben's son Harry, fourteen years old, sat on the end of the examining table. His new sneakers were caked with mud. He had his head down and a wad of gauze in his mouth where his tooth had just been knocked out.

When Reuben walked in, Harry looked up.

"You okay?" Reuben asked him.

He took the gauze out of his mouth. "What?"

"I said are you okay?"

His son's hair fell loosely over his forehead, his eyes hooded in fallen grace, the single left dimple of his infrequent smile nowhere to be found. He had gorgeous olive skin, a wide sculpted mouth like his mother's, and a strong angular nose of Semitic nobility, even if he'd been kicked out of Hebrew school in Chicago.

"Which one is it?" Reuben asked.

Harry pulled down his bottom lip revealing a somber black gap. He was supposed to get braces soon. An orthodontist back in Chicago had advised them to wait until he was at least thirteen. That was more than a year ago, before they moved to Welton, Colorado, and now Harry had entered his teenage years with a windy hole in his mouth. Braces would have to be deferred until they fixed this breach.

Wade Mitchell, Welton's police chief and Reuben's sometimes lunch companion, came in. He'd been in the waiting room filling out paperwork at the reception desk. Twenty minutes ago, he'd called Reuben from his squad car to say that he'd found Harry, who was supposed to be in school, walking along the old Welton highway and holding his hand to his mouth with blood gushing out between his fingers. That was all Reuben knew before he sped out to the Greeley Emergency Room after giving permission for Harry to be treated.

The ER doc had stopped the bleeding, cleaned out the hole, given Harry a pain killer and a prescription for antibiotics. The next step was to see a dentist. With its dangling roots, the lost tooth floated in a preservative solution on the metal hospital cart. Fortunately, Harry had had the presence of mind to pick it up and bring it with him.

"Harry told me he tripped on a rock," Wade said.

"Why weren't you in school?" Reuben asked.

Harry avoided eye contact with either of them. "I was sick. Mom said I could stay home."

"How come I don't know anything about this?" His son dabbed at the hole with the gauze, saw that the bleeding had stopped, and then wadded the cotton gauze up in his fist. "Are you in pain now?" asked Reuben.

"I'm fine," said Harry, his bottom lip swollen and bruised the color of a plum.

"If you were sick, why weren't you at home?"

"I started to feel better and I left the house for a walk."

"A walk?" Reuben turned to Wade. "Where did you say you found him?"

"Out on East County Road 30."

"That's about three miles in the opposite direction. What were you doing there?"

"Can I just go home, please? Doesn't it matter to you that I got hurt?"

"Of course, it matters, but you're lying to me. I know when you're lying."

"It's not my fault, all right? Punish me or whatever you're going to do." Reuben looked at Wade, who had cleared his face of all partiality. Used to domestic abuse, robberies, and suicidal threats, he no doubt found this assignment an insignificant nuisance. It was a real kindness and favor, Reuben knew, for him to drive Harry the twenty-five minutes all the way out to the Greeley Hospital.

"I'd rather know the truth," Reuben said, staring at Harry's sneakers. "Why are your sneakers so muddy?"

"Just leave it, okay? Please don't ask me anything else. I feel really, *really* shitty."

"This isn't going to get us very far," Reuben said, knowing he had "locked on," as Ardith would say. And indeed, in some acutely tender place surrounded by his own calcified anger and frustration, he ached for his son and had no sternness left to berate him.

Harry slid off the table. "I'll walk home if I have to."

"What did you say you tripped over?"

"A dead body."

"I don't find any of this funny."

"Ditto," said Harry.

"What's that supposed to mean?"

"It means I just lost my fucking tooth!"

"Gentlemen, please," said Wade. "Perhaps you should work this out in private. I need to get back."

"Sorry," said Reuben. He felt miserable, weak with a brittle spite born of too many mishaps with his unhappy and difficult firstborn. And yet part of him wanted to gently remove the ball of bloody gauze that was wadded in Harry's hand and put something hopeful there in return, a smooth stone that would remind him *I'm your father and I love you.* But the gesture seemed impossibly naive. "Thanks," he said to Wade. "I'll take it from here."

Harry grunted at the idea.

2

Ardith's reaction put Reuben's to shame. As soon as they walked in the door, she swooped down on Harry with maternal wings. She chose not to cross-examine or confront him as Reuben had done. Instead she sent Harry up to his room with an ice pack to lie down for the moment. She'd speak to him later. She exhibited a perfectly rational response to your child losing a permanent tooth, focused primarily on his welfare and not his behavior, and Reuben wished he'd shown the same grace. But his anger at Harry had been out of guilt: What had *I* done wrong? What had *I* missed that led to this (and this and this before it)?

Meanwhile, Ardith had called the dentist—there were two of them in Welton—and made an emergency appointment to have Harry seen right away. The dentist told her to put the tooth in milk, while conceding it might be too late to save the tooth. No one knew, and Harry wasn't saying, how long Harry had lost the tooth before Wade found him. Still, there was a small chance it could be replanted.

"I'll call you as soon as I know anything," Ardith said to Reuben. All business. She grabbed the car keys, her bag, and the glass of milk with the tooth somewhere at the bottom like forsaken coral. She was still in her running clothes from this morning. Reuben said he would pick up their younger son, Jamie, from school if Ardith got held up at the dentist. At the foot of the stairs, she called for Harry to come on. He did so, clomping down still in his muddy sneakers. Ardith chose not to comment, if she'd noticed at all. She was pulling him by the hand to hurry, the life of his tooth at stake.

3

Jolie Mattson came back and plopped down in the chair in front of Reuben's desk. One of his only two full-time employees (Rosa Morales, his office manager, was the other), Jolie handled local reporting and helped with selling ads for the weekly. Every issue included her "Little Maddy" column and her restaurant reviews. Last week she'd reviewed Taco John's. Before that it had been Burger King and Subway. "These are not quality restaurants," Reuben had informed her shortly after he took over the *Welton Sentinel*, thinking he was stating the obvious. "Surely we can dispense with evaluating fast food that's the same everywhere." Jolie's bottom lip had quivered: "I guess you'd just as soon I left then, Mr. Rosenfeld." He'd hesitated a moment before telling her, "Of course not."

In truth she was perfect for the paper. The town loved her reviews: *Arby's brand-new laminate tables are SO classy! The restaurant's décor features a knotty-pine motif that complements the sultry ambiance of lush artificial foliage and emerald eyeshade fixtures...*

The big hit, though, was a column about her baby daughter, Maddy. "HAVING A BABY IS A LIFE-CHANGING EVENT!" the breathtaking lede of her opening column screamed. From then on, every nuance of Maddy's short two-and-a-half-year-old life, from cradle cap to potty training to her first Barbie, had been documented in excruciating detail.

Yet, when readers did post comments on the paper's site and Facebook page, those rare positive ones, they invariably singled out her column: "As a new mother myself, I laughed my head off hearing about Maddy's 'fun' with her father's shaving cream. Sorry about your new couch!" Or: "My husband and I held our breath reading how Clement saved Maddy from crawling out that open window! He is *truly* her guardian angel."

The column about Clement had caused a sensation and

generated a flood of reaction praising the arthritic eleven-year-old lab who had supposedly saved Maddy's life. Supposedly, because a week later, when Reuben was at Jolie's house to pick up the keys to the office—he'd locked himself out—he asked to see the window where Maddy had almost crawled through while Jolie was downstairs preparing dinner. "Oh, it's a mess up there," she'd said. "I can't possibly show it to you now."

Her insistence on his not going up—he'd been trying to persuade her to let him run a photo of Clement and the baby in front of the ominous window—convinced him the whole thing had been a total fabrication. Even from the street, the window looked too high for Maddy to surmount, let alone at two and a half remove the screen on her way out. As if sensing his suspicion, Jolie went back to writing less heart-stopping columns about the family's character breakfast at Disneyworld or Maddy's encounter with a harmless bull snake during a picnic in a nearby park.

Now Reuben heard her telling a caller, "I'd *love* to talk to you about your recipe contest." Her major drawback as a reporter—she couldn't say no to anyone. They had a three-month backlog of her stories. "How about if we set up an appointment for next week?" she offered.

After hanging up, she announced, "That was *very* promising. The lady holds an annual recipe contest for the best desserts of Northern Colorado. And she just moved to Welton! We're going to be the center."

"Center of what?"

"Of a national contest!"

"I thought you said it was for Northern Colorado."

Jolie overlooked his observation. "By the way, I have some happy news. Bobby Lucas Mattson is on his way here!"

Reuben blinked at her. "Is he a relative?"

"You bet. He's our son."

"You have a son?"

"I'm pregnant!"

Again? he almost blurted out. The column would go on

forever now, with new blood. "Congratulations," he forced himself to say.

"Mazel tov to you too," she said.

"Why?" he asked.

"Why what?"

"Why did you say mazel tov?"

Jolie flushed. "Isn't that what you wish people in your faith? Kind of like, right back at you!"

"Kind of right back at you?"

"You know, like when someone says have a great day. You say, you too!"

"But I'm not having a baby."

Jolie giggled. "I sure hope not!"

"Okaaay," Reuben said, and let it go.

At six p.m., he left the paper and drove the six blocks home, parking in the driveway. The garage wasn't usable yet. The yard was overgrown with thickets of juniper, woody lilacs, and aging unpruned apple trees. A depleted garden choked with dandelion and thistle took up the northwest quadrant of the yard. Reuben had torn up both porches, front and back, but had never gotten around to replacing the wood. To get in or out of the house, they had to use a mudroom side door that dropped precipitously down to makeshift cinderblock steps. Ardith had been begging him for weeks to get someone over to finish the job he'd started.

He turned the key in the door and went inside.

"He's upstairs," Ardith said, when she saw Reuben. "He won't tell me anything."

"Should we call him down?"

"Leave him be," said Ardith. "He told me you questioned him as if he were a terrorist."

"That was his word for it?"

Ardith nodded. Her hair was pulled back and she had on jeans and an olive green silk blouse on this spring day and he remembered once putting his Cubs cap on her head and pulling her ponytail through the opening in back and how pretty she had looked with her hazel eyes shaded under the brim.

"Is the tooth still holding up?" Miraculously, the dentist had been able to reinsert the tooth. He'd splinted it to the adjacent teeth with plastic resin and wire. Now they just had to wait and see if the supporting tissues would reattach and hold it in place.

"So far," said Ardith. "But we have to wait and see and hope it won't turn black."

He resisted the urge to ask her how much it had cost. "What happened this morning?"

"He woke up sick, coughing, and he felt hot, so I let him stay home. I went running and when I came back, he was gone. Next thing I know you're calling from the emergency room."

"He said he felt better, so he went for a walk."

Ardith scoffed. "Right. As if he ever does that."

"So, what the hell is going on?"

"You tell me."

"I tried to find that out."

"Getting angry at him won't help."

"Then what should we do? Pat him on the back?"

Ardith crossed her arms over her chest, a fortress of resistance to his methods. "The dentist took me aside and said he didn't think this happened from Harry falling. The injury was too localized, as if someone poked the tooth out with a chisel, a direct hit."

"You think someone hit him?"

"I have no clue," said Ardith. "But I'm pretty sure he didn't trip on a rock. I'm going to check on both of them."

After Harry and Jamie were in bed, he and Ardith sat at the kitchen table downstairs. Reuben with a cup of decaf, Ardith with her hands folded around a mug of chamomile tea. Jamie was in his bunk bed, Harry in his room, sleeping on a sheetless futon. Their last therapist in Chicago had advised them to let Harry take responsibility for his decisions. If that amounted to a disgusting room, no friends, and failing grades that was better than always bailing him out and saving him from the consequences of his actions.

Easy for you to say, Reuben had thought, knowing the man had two grown sons, both successful doctors.

"Should we have him evaluated again?" Ardith asked in a low voice.

Reuben heard Jamie cough. Eleven years old, he suffered from allergies and asthma. All the fresh air, open space, and healthy recreation hadn't helped his asthma—one of the reasons they'd moved to Colorado. "Did you have Jamie use his inhaler?"

Ardith nodded.

They sat in silence, waiting tensely for him to cough again. Not long after they'd moved here, they'd rushed him to the hospital in Greeley for an asthma attack. Nobody could tell them what exactly set the attacks off. Sometimes a cold would lead to it. Sometimes just being outside and playing all day.

The gravity of Harry's behavior drew his thoughts away from Jamie. "I don't know who Harry would see here."

"We could get a recommendation from Tom."

Tom Watkins was their family doctor. He'd seen Harry a few times during the winter for a sinus infection and for strep throat. Harry had been laconic, as he was around most adults, until Tom let slip, having tried unsuccessfully with jokes and with talk about sports to warm Harry to him, that he'd collected comics when he'd been Harry's age. It was one of Harry's only interests, collecting comics, mostly sci-fi and fantasy, not the Superman, Batman, and Archie comics of Reuben's youth. And he liked to draw. Portraits. Faces of all kinds. He was especially skilled at precise renderings of large mechanical objects with hundreds of moving parts. He'd done a finely observed pen-and-ink replication once of a steam locomotive, exacting to the smallest sprocket. They'd praised him to the skies. "You have so much talent!" Reuben told him. "You're really gifted, Harry." They offered to have it framed, encouraged him to enter it in contests, promised to find out about art classes and summer programs for him.

Harry shredded the picture the next day. "I'm not interested in it anymore," he informed them. What had they done wrong? They never knew when they were going to say the wrong thing and push him away. He hated false praise, but as far as he was concerned any approval coming his way was false. For years they had told him he was too hard on himself. "Parents always say that," he'd respond, "just to make kids feel better." Nothing—most of all nothing he did himself—pleased or satisfied him. There was something darkly unknowable about his son, an opaque temperament with a short fuse that made life with Harry so difficult.

Jamie coughed in an unsettling spasm.

"I'll have him use his inhaler again. Why don't you turn out the lights and come to bed? We'll talk about this in the morning, okay?"

Reuben nodded as she went up. In Chicago, Harry had seen three therapists over the course of his childhood there. The last therapist, a woman specializing in hard-to-diagnose adolescent disorders, had tested Harry for everything from autism to ADHD, from dyslexia to oppositional defiant disorder. None had been conclusive. "At some point," the woman counseled, "we have to put him in that big pool of children with general behavior problems." She had referred them to a psychiatrist who prescribed antidepressants.

"At eleven?" Ardith had protested. "You're going to give an eleven-year-old Prozac?"

"It's more common than you think," claimed the psychiatrist, a man who had taken a comprehensive history of Harry and the family, making careful notes directly into his laptop while they talked. It was all so strictly diagnostic that Reuben wasn't surprised when after only one visit the psychiatrist recommended Harry needed medication for depression and/or anxiety. "Often the line between the two is hard to distinguish," the doctor said. He had closed his laptop, Reuben was glad to see. "I wish it were a more exact science, but it isn't. We have to work with what we see symptomatically in an area where symptoms can be misinterpreted more easily than blood cell counts and rashes. I'm trying to be candid. But Harry is struggling, that much is clear. He's unhappy and he deserves some relief to see that he doesn't have to feel this way. Maybe once he gets that he'll fight everything less."

After much cajoling, pressuring, and bribing ("Thirty minutes extra on Minecraft if you take your pill!"), they got him to swallow the medication. Then, just when he seemed to show a little change—he'd talked about inviting some kids over for a sleepover—he wanted to quit.

"Why do I have to?" he complained. "It makes me feel stupid. Can't you just accept that I'm different? Does everybody have to be normal in the same way? I like myself the way I am. I don't want to take a pill the rest of my life to make me acceptable to everyone else." It was chilling how persuasive his son's insights could be sometimes. Reuben had wondered the same thing, irked by the insistence on conformity. Variant behavior that once would have been acceptable as personality shadings now was seen as necessitating medical intervention. The culture was full of behavioral and emotional disorders that hadn't been around in his time, or more precisely had always been around but had a place in the differentiating of character.

But even as he was making the argument to himself, he knew he was getting carried away with his own expired rebellion: a longing for the old passions, the fight against those who would crush the individual spirit. Now, at forty-five, he simply feared what Harry might do to himself or others. No longer worrying about the soulless oligarchy of corporate depersonalization or whatever the hell he once envisioned as the death of humanity, he had only the desperate wish of a parent for his son to survive, and—if it wasn't too much to ask—with a measure of happiness.

Harry stopped taking the pills after three months. "I'm through," he said. "You can force the pill down my throat, but you know in the end it's my decision."

In the end. He was right. The finality and threat of the phrase: *In the end.* Harry would occasionally burst out with these trenchant utterings, something meant to put it all in perspective and everyone, his parents namely, in their place. And he was right. They needed his cooperation. It *was* finally his decision whether to accept responsibility for his behavior. He knew that, even if he couldn't act on it. He was asserting himself at the expense of that measure of happiness for them all. He wanted something different from what they wanted for him, and it wasn't happiness. It may have been joy, with its associations of the ecstatic, but it certainly wasn't the more antiseptic happiness. He'd forgo happiness to live "as is," unconnected to a pharmaceutical towline tugging his mind with no wake through life's harbor. He was their son, and they'd either love him for it or not. He'd made that clear, and Reuben had felt defeated.

Back then, Ardith had said, "We don't know why." They'd been over this before. The Why of Harry. In the beginning, as far back as when Harry was two years old, Ardith had been defensive at any mention of abnormality; he was just a spirited kid. Wasn't that the term? Or was it, as in the most optimistic books, "twice exceptional"? High needs maybe, but gifted and sensitive.

Except, they had to admit, that description didn't entirely fit Harry: he wasn't especially sensitive when they lived in Evanston and told kids at the pricey private school they'd enrolled him in with its small classes to "shut up," or yelled "I'M GOING TO KILL YOU!" to the neighbor's three-year-old twins standing baffled in their front yard after their ball accidentally rolled in front of Harry's bike on his ride home from school, Harry riding alone. Alone. Always alone. Never with any other friends. When he'd been small, Ardith had tried to arrange play dates for him, but he'd put up such a fuss that she didn't bother after a while. No, that wasn't quite it. She did try. The other mothers resisted. Or outright told her that they didn't want their children to play with Harry. Harry showed them knives, told them guns were in the bushes, lied to them ("I have snakes in the basement"), then terrorized them by leading them down there and dashing up the stairs and holding the door shut from the other side, the light bulbs unscrewed.

Somewhere along the line, Reuben wasn't sure when, before

they'd moved to Welton, sixty miles northeast of Denver on the Front Range, looking for a small-town cure and a fresh start, Ardith had withdrawn. Not given up exactly, just surrendered. She no longer struggled to make sense of Harry's behavior, to help him fit in. A little life had gone out of her, a little hope died. Maybe she'd displaced it on to Jamie, their gentle, sweet, second child, but Reuben didn't think so. He thought she'd just resigned herself, gotten sick of crying and beating herself up about Harry, "tearing my hair out strand by guilty strand."

Often in the aftermath of sex, when she'd felt at once most vulnerable and emboldened, she vowed a renewed commitment to finding out what was wrong—getting to the Why of Harry. But he hadn't seen that side for quite some time now. She was more likely to be efficient with Harry, responsive to his needs but not enthusiastic anymore, a way to survive, he supposed.

And perhaps he was afraid of what this meant. If she was giving up, where did that leave him? Ardith was the one whose love for Harry had guided him. He loved the boy through her, as fathers often did learn to love their truculent children through their wives' unbounded solicitations, their forgiveness, tenderness, and patience that reclaimed their husbands' lost youths with stern fathers. He'd thought this was what was slipping: this filial affection that upon seeing his son's head crowning from his mother's womb he believed would survive any assault. It filled him with a leaden remorse.

He moved aside a stack of old homework on the kitchen chair. The other three chairs had laundry, a pink geranium waiting to be repotted, and overdue library books. A cat clock left by the former owner, its tail swishing off seconds, ticked on the wall.

Reuben went upstairs and found Ardith sitting on the end of the bed in her nightgown. "Is Jamie doing better?" he asked.

"I put a humidifier in there for him," Ardith said. It was April already, spring, but the air was still so dry out here compared to the humidity of the Midwest.

"You look tired," Reuben said. "Want me to rub your shoulders?"

"Please."

As soon as he put his hands on her shoulders, she yelped.

"I hardly touched you."

"I'm just so sore. I'm afraid of your digging in."

"I'll be gentle."

He kneaded her shoulders lightly. It felt strange to be touching her. They'd gone months now without having sex. Not that he was counting, but he was of course. They could fall into a rut like this, and once there it was nearly impossible to climb the steep banks of their avoidance. The routine of working, taking care of the kids, and of beating back the demands of the house took their toll and left them wanting only sleep as a reward at the end of the day. Neither of them—he was just as guilty—initiated anything. The abstinence did no one any good. They snapped at one another. They grew tense at bedtime. They pretended nothing was wrong. They lay awake on their respective sides of the bed. They ignored the problem the next day and suffered through the impasse the next evening all over again.

At least he saw it that way. He didn't know what Ardith thought. Maybe it had to do with coming to Colorado. She had expected so much more out of the place. Instead, she was unemployed, virtually friendless, and frustrated with the house.

"That feel better?" he asked.

She nodded slightly. She'd dropped her head so he could work on her neck, giving herself over to him, murmuring encouragement so he'd continue. So why didn't she want to have sex?

He stopped massaging.

"Ohh," murmured Ardith, her head still bent obediently, waiting for more.

"How about I get some wine?"

"Okay." She gave him a shy smile. "I'll come with you. I have to look for Jamie's other inhaler anyway."

Downstairs, he opened the kitchen cabinet above the stove. Three Big-Gulp cups tumbled out on his head.

"*Jesus*," he said.

"Sorry," Ardith told him. "We've been running out of room. I don't think the wine glasses are up there anyway."

"Where are they?"

She shrugged. "I'm tired, Reuben. I think the wine will just put me to sleep. Is that okay?"

He didn't want to appear disappointed. It was part of the game to preserve your pride. See who could go the longest suffering a major sexual deficit before one or the other of them exploded over some silly argument about how long the refrigerator light had been out.

"That's fine," he said. "I think I'll have a little myself."

He got out the only clean glass in the cabinet—a Pooh jelly jar.

"I'm going to bed," Ardith said. "You?"

"I'll sit here a while longer. Just unwind." He was trying to seem pleasant, not sulky.

"Okay," she said and stood a moment. He spread out the *Denver Post* in front of him. He half expected to see instant news of Harry's missing tooth in it.

"You'll close up?"

"I'll take care of everything." His shoe crushed some burnt grilled cheese crumbs. "Get some rest." He turned a page of the newspaper, not looking up.

"I…"

"What?"

"I'm sorry," Ardith told him, and went upstairs. She had looked tired. There were dark circles under her eyes, and at forty-two, three years younger than he, her mouth had distinct frown lines.

After a half hour of staring into space, he went upstairs too.

Jamie slept peacefully with all his stuffed animals at the foot of his bed. He looked in on Harry too. Harry's room actually fit in perfectly with the house's overall distress. Clothes draped like sick ghosts hung from everything except hangers. Somewhere on his cluttered desk could be found his homework. The room did give him a certain comfort in that it appeared as normal and messy as any fourteen-year-old's room. Sleeping, Harry looked sweet as could be. What a beautiful face. Such a gentle sloping forehead and long fluttering lashes. His lips, pursed in sleep, sheltered the fragile tooth. He wasn't studious looking, less the picture of a Yeshiva student than a teen sitcom star.

In his own bedroom, Reuben sat on his side of the bed and quietly removed his shoes. Ardith was asleep, or maybe just pretending to be, curled up on her side. He thought of his poor father, a butcher, dead fifteen years now, five more than his mother. His father would come home and make this exact same gesture: pulling off his shoes and grunting, right foot, left foot. Reuben could feel the movement in his bones, he knew it so well. The whole uniform, starched white shirt and gray dress slacks under his splattered butcher's apron, bore the sign of his generation's belief in good grooming. Whacking at carcasses and hacking up chickens all day didn't change the fact that you were a gentleman underneath. How you presented yourself, how you honored your family through hard work provided enough dignity for his father to remind himself of the important man he was as he approached the nakedness of bedtime.

Reuben caught sight of himself in the dresser mirror, sitting weightily with his hands gripping the inside of his thighs, just like Pop. The same belly too. The old man would sit in his boxers and sleeveless T-shirt and black socks with their garters. He'd sigh heavily while his own wife slept.

When his brother Harry died, his mother took Reuben and Stan, the youngest at seven, to the doctor every week, convinced that they too were going to develop a sudden heart ailment and keel over dead playing football like Harry had in his third week of eighth grade. Finally, after dragging them around to doctors throughout the suburbs of Chicago—no one would agree with her that Stan and Reuben were doomed—their father had sent her away. Reuben's Aunt Mildred came to stay with them. He had just turned eleven. When their mother returned, she was quieter. She never spoke Harry's name again. Later he learned that she'd had shock treatments for depression. "We live in a house of salt," she'd say, and would start to cry, and then Reuben's father would come over and pat her shoulder, and she'd become mute. In the midst of everything, Reuben had made two decisions. He would name his firstborn son Harry. And he'd always take care of his brother Stan, who was short, fat, and not likely to win any popularity contests or break any academic records with his slow performance in second grade, the only kid unable to read. As it turned out, Stan became a successful businessman with a chain of Caribbean-style restaurants. With a two-million-dollar home in Winnetka and twin girls who doted on him as much as his lissome wife did, a former teenage model with feverish blue eyes and flawless skin and, best of all, an amazing capacity for Stan's endless puns, he needed no taking care of. As for naming his son Harry, well, despite the Jewish tradition, maybe it hadn't been such a great idea. You give a kid too much of an expectation, unconscious as it might be, to live out the life that never was, to grow up and redeem the family that might have been before it fell apart, and how can you expect him to do anything but squirm out from under the burden?

"You okay?" Ardith's hand was on his back. It felt warm and familiar there, a small palm of succoring flesh over his nakedness.

"I've been thinking about Harry. I get scared sometimes." Tears welled up for his brother, and for his son, one in the same, both thwarted by some inexplicable injustice that left him mixed up about losing a brother and having a son who didn't— the possibility crossed his mind every day—love him.

"Hey," said Ardith, "lie down."

He lay back stiffly on the bed. After all these years he was still embarrassed to cry in front of her.

"Come here," she said, and pressed herself against him, kissing his wet eyes.

4

Luisa watched the boy eat his lunch in the junior high cafeteria. He was peculiar, and her friends had said he was somewhere on the spectrum. They didn't say he *might* be on the spectrum or even that they wondered if he *was* on the spectrum or what made them so sure in the first place, just that the guy was, you know, one of those, like their classmate Peter Ackers, who walked around calculating train schedules all day long even though there were no trains in Welton. But to Luisa, there was something different about this boy than Peter Ackers. Peter's parents had some kind of deal with the cafeteria servers that Peter could have separate plates for his salad, fries, and P&J sandwich. Peter, everybody knew, was special, and you were supposed to treat him as special and not make fun of him, and come to think of it he *was* pretty special because there wasn't anybody else at school who could explain cryptocurrency, and would, in excruciating detail, if you let him, and then want to tell you the same information all over again the next day. Luisa was quite sure Peter, who could recite every battle of the Sino-American War in the post-apocalyptic Fallout video game, would be snapped up by Silicon Valley before he finished his freshman year of college, at Stanford, no doubt.

But this other boy, unlike Peter, who was actually reasonably interactive in his data-free moods, went around with a deep scowl on his face and talked to no one. He may have been the most unpleasant boy Luisa had ever seen, and she certainly had seen her share of them, including a group who shouted at her last Friday on her walk home from school. "*Chica*, over here! Come talk to us!" When she ignored them, because the tone in their voices was anything but friendly, they told her to make sure she didn't miss her burro ride back to Juarez and laughed themselves sick.

The funniest thing in the world.

She'd felt humiliated. Coming out their mouths, a bunch of white boys, *chica* might as well have been *slut*. She had gotten home and taken a bath until her skin felt parboiled. When her mother came back from cleaning the Moritzes' house, one of the biggest homes in Welton, and one that even when Luisa helped her during the summer took them five hours to clean, she told her what had happened. Her mother's face turned grim. *"¡Te dije que no caminaras a casa! Basta!"*

"Why are you mad at *me?*" she asked. "I didn't do anything wrong."

"No walk. Bus."

But she liked to walk and didn't want to take the school bus home, and all she wanted from her mother was for her to hug her and certainly not blame her for some asshole boys telling her to go back to Mexico. But it was always this way in her family. If you had any problem, it was somehow your fault for being in the wrong place at the wrong time. Her father, who worked at a dairy, was even worse. Their worry about getting in trouble made them all cowards in Luisa's eyes. For all his pride, her father turned into a different man when anyone had authority over him, which was pretty much any white person. What was the point of all that assertiveness training in her enrichment class at school if she couldn't use it? She was supposed to stand up for her own interests, deal with her anxiety over confronting people, know her human rights, and learn the line between aggression and assertiveness. But the only line in her family was staying behind any line, and she was sick of it.

There was something about this boy, with his moppy hair and eerie green eyes that spoke to her about all this even without having said a single word to him. She had seen him around the neighborhood. He lived in Old Town near her, a block over on Walnut Street, in that crumbling mansion everybody thought had been condemned until his family moved into it. He looked like he hated the world, and although she had never been anything but polite to her teachers and smiled so much that her face ached, his unhappiness fascinated her.

"Why do you keep staring at that weird dude?" her friend Carla asked. They had left lunch and were walking toward their lockers. "You have a crush on him?"

She didn't have a crush on him. She didn't even know him, and he'd never noticed her anyway.

"Well, if you don't have a crush on him, which I believe you *do*," said Carla, "I think you must just want to save him."

Carla read a lot of pop psychology articles and had all sorts of theories about boys and boyfriends they didn't have yet. And, no, Luisa didn't want to save him. What she really wanted to do was push him down the stairs and then calmly ask, "Does that make it any better?"

5

"I'll see you," Reuben said, kissing Ardith goodbye on his way out the door. He had to drop Jamie off at school before going into work. "Call me."

Ardith kissed him back and tried to put her heart into it, her old heart. She'd felt so bad for him last night, so guilty and miserable about what she was doing, and then when she had been on the verge of telling him, because she couldn't stand it anymore, he had started crying about Harry. Tenderness washed over her, and she became supple beside him, pulling him toward her and wanting him. They made love, but she couldn't come, her body too confused by guilt, and she did something she had considered a discarded part of her youth: faked it. That out of guilt too, she supposed. She owed it to Reuben, the pleasure of her pleasure.

They'd held each other afterward. This morning he was so happy, so full of cheer the way he moved briskly around the kitchen that it made her feel worse, more disgusted than ever with herself. When he kissed her, he gave her a long hug. She patted his back. They were themselves again, in a single night of lovemaking. That's all it took. At least for him.

Unable to think clearly after Reuben left, she wandered around the house and delayed calling Tom. She didn't tell him Harry was sick again, complaining of a sore throat and headache, and that she had to stay home with him. Instead she sat and watched the clock until Tom knocked at eight a.m. Harry looked up and briefly stopped eating his eggs. According to the dentist's instructions, she was to give him only soft foods until his tooth became stable. "Somebody at the door," he said, blandly. Who was he fooling? His appetite, which had been absent before Reuben left, had come roaring back, now that he knew he was staying home. She'd felt too guilty—and worried—about yesterday to force him to go to school. Secretly she hoped to get more information from him, her own way. She'd played good cop to Reuben's bad cop for so long that Harry just waited out the bad to get the good. "Better see who it is," he said, chomping on more eggs. She tried not to glare at him as she got up to answer the door.

"Hi," said Ardith, and stepped back when Tom leaned in to kiss her. She shook her head, whispering, "Harry's here."

He looked puzzled, disappointed, and wary all at once. They ran early every weekday morning, but it was on Wednesdays, when he went into work late, that they made love at his house, as they had yesterday. "I was going to call you," she said, and shrugged as if to explain all the swirling punchy feelings that had incapacitated her from picking up the phone. "Come in and have some coffee anyway," she offered.

He followed her into the kitchen. She could feel his tentative steps behind her. Dèjá vu. They'd gone through this yesterday, with the difference being she'd left Harry alone while she went with Tom. And look what had happened then. Harry had bolted from the house as soon as she'd gone. At the very moment Harry was losing his tooth, she was in Tom's bed, making love. Guilt was a merciless rider. It whipped her at the slightest whim. It forced her to think about anything that happened as her fault. It reduced all her actions, good or bad, to cheating. It didn't, however, do a damn thing to help her stop.

"Well, hello again," Tom said, boosting his voice in a cheerful greeting to Harry. Kids loved him. He knew how to talk to them. In the supermarket they'd always come up because he had his pockets weighted down with rubber thumb creatures, key chains with tiny plastic hearts, friendship rings, miniature Transformers. "Hey, I'm sagging," he'd say. "Help me out with some of this stuff!" The kids would giggle, he'd hand out the goods, and they'd skip away happily. Once, she'd been shopping, before they'd started seeing each other, and watched him, amazed at his warmth, openness, and relaxed generosity. Compared to the darker, tenser, glowering presence of Reuben, who would tap his foot impatiently in a grocery line, groaning audibly when the elderly person in front of him unraveled an accordion of coupons, Tom emanated the saintly vibes of the town healer.

"Hi, Dr. Tom," Harry said. Ardith heard a peculiar hitch in his voice.

"Feeling sick today?"

"I have a sore throat."

"Mind if I look?"

Harry turned his face away from Tom. "I'd rather you not."

Ardith stared at Harry, his rudeness stunning them both into silence. She recovered enough to explain, "Harry lost a tooth yesterday. An accident. But we got it back in. I'm sure he's just tired of people looking in his mouth."

"I can understand that and I'm sorry to hear about your tooth, Harry. Anything I can do to help?"

"I'm fine," Harry said, to Ardith more than Tom.

Tom turned to her. "I guess you won't be running today then." She heard the disappointment in his voice, the wanting. And she could feel Harry watching her, his demands, both of them needing something.

"I can't. I'm sorry. I should have called you."

"No problem," he said. He gave her a quick, tight smile that she read as reproach and left her alone with Harry.

Tom lived on an acre lot, in a newly annexed section of Welton. He had moved into one of the first houses built up here when he came to Welton five years ago. On a scouting trip from Chicago, Reuben and Ardith had been driven up by an enthusiastic realtor named Cassie for a look at the final phase of the same development. A few of the lots were still available and backed up to greenbelt with a view of the snow-capped Rockies. "Eagle Crest is a planned community with its own golf course and country club, tennis courts, swimming pool, and sensible covenants to preserve property values," Cassie recited, barely pausing between words.

"Is that stream going to be there?" Ardith had asked about the water flowing in a high-sided channel at the base of the hill.

"That's an irrigation ditch," Cassie said. The irrigation ditch would be filled in eventually. "Most of the farms in the immediate area are being developed anyway, so it won't be needed. Believe me, you don't want your kids falling in one of those. They can't climb out. And the mosquitoes will eat you alive if it's there."

Ardith had gazed at the slippery trickle of water running through the grass gully. The stream kept her from feeling completely parched as they stood on the windswept half-acre of prairie with the baking sun overhead.

That same morning they looked at a narrow three-story Victorian house in the old section of Welton, on a tree-lined block with a corner grocery that had been operating since the Second World War.

Jumping with the nimbleness of a tap dancer onto a different stage, Cassie poured on the bliss. "You won't, in all your looking, find a home with this much character and charm. Build all the new homes you want, but *this* kind of workmanship doesn't exist anymore."

She pulled out a kitchen drawer that fell to the floor. "A little short," she apologized. Ardith chose to overlook the frayed carpeting, the water stains on the dining room ceiling, the "slightly" tilted kitchen floor, the master bathroom door so warped closing it left a two-inch gap. Cassie caught her worried look as she examined the missing knobs on the stove. "Of course, the place needs some TLC."

A week later they phoned from Chicago to make a low offer, which (to Ardith's dismay) was immediately accepted. "I guess this means it's meant to be," Reuben said, looking as worried as she. They'd spent all week discussing the pros and cons. It was in the older section of town, walking distance to the newspaper office, on a shady, quiet street with tall oaks and maples, and just around the corner from Welton's first firehouse built in 1890. How much safer and homier could you get? The kids could walk to school. The house had a large, fenced yard for a dog someday and, for the money, lots of creative space—nooks and turrets and bay windows and a roomy unfinished attic with a ceiling stairway that pulled down. "We could make that quite a nice study or guest bedroom," Reuben said.

Ardith kept hearing the word *we*, wondering what it meant exactly. The two of them alone? A contractor? "I can do most of it myself," Reuben insisted. "I'll sub out all the electrical and plumbing. What do you think?" She didn't know what to think. Except for building some shelves once in their basement rec room, he had never fixed more than a leaky faucet in all the time she'd known him. "I'm ready for the challenge," he assured her. "After all, my father worked with his hands."

"He sawed meat," Ardith said.

"It's all about cutting at the right angles." He held up his hands for inspection as if posing with invisible cleavers.

When she went to Tom's on Wednesdays, she always took a bath in a copper slipper tub that looked out a bay window toward Longs Peak, the highest mountain in Rocky Mountain National Park. The planned community wasn't as bad as she'd feared. The golf course consisted of only nine holes and a putting green. The clubhouse proved a relaxing place to have lunch, the staff unassuming—and discreet: they greeted Tom as Dr. Watkins and politely nodded at her. And she had to admit it was satisfying to push a button and drive into a useable garage and not have to leave your car outside baking in the sun or buried in a snowdrift.

Reuben could never have enjoyed a home like Tom's. Its updated amenities—heated floors, crisp bathroom lighting, solar shades, a programmable thermostat and smart doorbell— didn't interest him. He wanted to go backward: remodel their home to look like 1908 when it had first been built: a ball-and-claw tub in the bathroom and a stand-alone ceramic basin; bedrooms with floor-length drapes; chandeliers that thumbed their noses at LED fixtures; and a walnut-paneled "library" (a mud room filled with junk at the moment). Everything but a coat of arms. He'd intended to replace the one-hundred-year-old single-pane windows that rattled in the slightest breeze. But the custom-made, double-hung mullioned windows he wanted would take at least three months. "Can't we just get factory windows?" Ardith had pleaded. Reuben was adamant that if they were going to restore an older home, they should do it right. "I hate those patched-together jobs that are neither here nor there." He'd shaved his beard, cut his hair, and spent nearly three hundred dollars at Home Depot on a tool belt, saws, a planer, a cordless drill, and a twenty-four-piece set of screwdrivers. He'd ordered a "hundred-year" tile roof, but the roofers couldn't put it on until he first decided whether to cut skylights for the large attic they wanted to finish as a fourth bedroom. Columns of stacked slate-blue roof tiles waited near a rusty wheelbarrow in the backyard.

"Do you see anything wrong here?" Ardith had asked him one evening. In Chicago, at least, he'd spent his time at home cutting the grass and changing light bulbs. He'd had bigger expectations, he admitted, about living in Colorado. He'd run the town paper, he'd remodel their home, he'd start working out, he'd eat better, he'd write a book.

"You lost the beard," said Ardith. "You did get that done."

She suspected the real reason he would never move into a house like Tom's, in a neighborhood like his, was because chaos didn't rule. Despite his cries of wanting the simple life, he thrived on keeping matters unresolved, all of which offered him the familiarity of his angst and the comfort of entropy. Things had to get worse before they could…get worse. Completion was the enemy. Meanwhile, when she floated in Tom's tub, she forgot about everything and everyone. It was just so quiet up there.

She would regularly go through shopping catalogs and, with Tom's credit card, order furnishings. He had moved to Welton with virtually nothing, leaving his ex-wife with the house and most of their possessions. It was something Ardith neither had the money nor the inclination to do with her own house. So

much needed to be done that it was discouraging to buy anything new that would only show up the house's ugliness and dis-
repair. She really didn't know what she could have been thinking when they bought it. They were in way over their heads. She
had secretly called a contractor who specialized in remodeling
older homes. When he saw the place, he just whistled. "About
one five," he said, "to do it right." "One five?" "One hundred
fifty thousand." They'd only paid two hundred and twenty
thousand, a real bargain, they thought. The plan had been
they'd bank the equity from selling their home in Chicago and
use the extra money to contract out the jobs Reuben couldn't
do himself. That had been plan A. Plan B…well, there *hadn't*
been a plan B because they never got that far, and they needed
to do plan A because they didn't get as much equity out of the
house as they'd hoped. The equity turned out to be less than a
hundred thousand, and she believed Reuben when he told her
he could remodel the house himself. It was no coincidence that
he was a copyeditor, a checker of other people's work. The
truth was he couldn't finish anything of his own, couldn't set
the same deadlines and standards for himself he enforced as
an editor for others. When Ardith went to the *Sentinel* and saw
the fractured disarray of his desk, the only area Rosa couldn't
keep orderly, it looked exactly like the house's torn-up front and
back porches with their splintered boards so spongy and rotted
from the hot sun and cold winters that they sagged like foam
rubber when you walked on them. Bags of nails, lumber, rolls
of insulation, drop cloths, cans of paint had all been delivered
and stationed around the yard among the pried-up boards, the
duct-taped mailbox, the rusted pipes, the ripped-out shingles.
Inside, displayed along the perimeter of the living room like a
showroom for interior design, waited product samples: kitchen
tile, cabinet doors, carpet folios, bathroom fixtures, and paint
strips with exotic and inspirational sounding names like vanil-
la mirage, tangerine surf, and (simply) hope. She had no idea
where to begin. They couldn't pay one hundred and fifty thousand to "do it right," or seventy-five to do it half-right. So it

would all remain in preparatory chaos. Nothing would change.

She enjoyed so much playing at this other life with Tom, the one she'd imagined Reuben and she and the boys would have in Colorado. His spacious closet, with everything organized, his dress shirts sorted from his knit shirts, his hung-up ties, his soft sweaters in their delicious colors of forest and plum folded away in dust-protecting plastic drawers, his shoes aligned on slanting shelves like disciplined soldiers—it was so different from their tiny shared closet with its soiled laundry commingling with fresh clothes that kept falling off their slippery wire hangers. She gladly cleaned Tom's kitchen, just because it was gratifying to wash the quartz counters and cast-iron sink that didn't have implacable stains that defied scouring. The blinds opened without incident (theirs, old venetians, had collapsed on her head once when she yanked on the cord too hard). And she could pad across the gleaming maple floors without sneezing from dust and mold in the purple carpeting Reuben had sworn he'd rip up six months ago because of Jamie's asthma.

She wondered at times if she was more in love with his house than with Tom, if it represented everything—with its newness, openness, and effulgence—that was wrong about her life and marriage. Or, if at some point, she didn't need to be ashamed of believing that materialism counted in love and that she'd grown up, or just grown tired of doing everything the hard way. All those years of taking care of her mother. Finding her standing in the living room folding her soiled pants. Lucid enough to know that she'd had an accident and needed to find something else to wear, she would take them off. But by the time she stepped out of her pants, she'd already forgotten what was wrong and had wandered naked into the living room and stood there in front of Harry and Jamie folding her pants to hang them up. A neat housekeeper for years, her mother tried to help around the house, but her "help" was exasperating. Give her forks and knives to set the table and she'd bring them back two minutes later and put them away in the silverware drawer. Tell her to bring Jamie his stuffed rabbit for his nap, and she'd pick up the animal from the sofa in the living room and wander outside with it and hand it to the neighbor boy playing on his trampoline.

They'd installed a bell on both doors and an electric eye for her bedroom. The buzzing, which went off several times a night, as her mother got up to use the bathroom and was more likely to go downstairs and wander, would wake Ardith out of a deep sleep, just as Harry's or Jamie's crying had when they were babies. They briefly tried putting her in a home, but when, after the first day Ardith came to visit her, her mother sat in a corner and told her, "I feel like an iceberg surrounds my heart. Why won't you take me home, darling?" "She'll adjust," the nurse, a hefty woman with a brightly lipsticked mouth, assured her. "When you're not here, she's better off. She doesn't remember from one moment to the next what's happened, so it's more painful to watch than it is for her." The nurse spoke in a loud voice: "ARE YOU READY TO EAT, MRS. LEY?" Her mother, not deaf, had the panicked look of a trapped animal about to gnaw off its foot. Ardith took her home. Reuben had been disappointed, she knew that, but she couldn't have done anything different. She was her parents' only child. For so long after her father died when she was fifteen it had been just her and her mother. She would rather get woken up twenty times a night than have to think of her mother so alone with that terrified look on her face.

Add to that the years of being a mother and a wife and it had just drained her down to nothing. They all needed so much, emotionally and *bodily*. She shopped and cooked, kept them clothed, and occasionally shopped for Reuben because he'd wear the same thing all the time unless she intervened. She made sure the children washed and had all their lunches for school, their various registration and field-trip forms signed, their dental visits and haircuts and presents for birthday parties, their Halloween costumes ready and "star of the week" posters done. Reuben and Harry were such loners too. Their social needs fell mostly on her. So often she felt the overwhelming burden of not only being her mother's sole keeper but theirs, their only and best friend; they all looked to her as the wife/mother/companion/attendant who would take care of them without thinking of herself first. Her life, she thought, had turned out to be an endless game of tag, with her being chased by a family of Its. Tom's house had become home base.

After a visit to Tom's office for Jamie to have a school physical, when Tom had asked Jamie what his favorite sport was and then asked Ardith the same question, and she mentioned she had played on the tennis team in high school, he invited her to the local country club for a match. She'd demurred. It had been too long. She was out of shape. She worried mostly about what she'd look like jumping around in shorts on the court, which should have been the first sign something in her was overly concerned about his opinion but that she passed off as just shyness. But he'd insisted through all her protests. Exercise was important—for the whole family. During Jamie's checkup, he'd appealed to her youngest child. "It's a good model for you to have your parents getting exercise, right, Jamie?" Never mind that Jamie needed no role models in that direction; he was sports crazy, unlike Harry.

She gave in, bought herself a sleeveless tennis dress online and joined him on the court, surprising herself at still being able to prolong a strong volley. His compliments and yet lack of any pressure to start a competitive game—she felt winded enough as it was—struck her as attentive, a chivalrous gesture that made her feel noticed and considered in a way she had only felt overlooked by the family. Four tennis dates later, again with the same solicitude, slowing down their games when he sensed her tiring while never showing a hint of bravado, she accepted his invitation to go back to his house for lunch. That she didn't hesitate, that she didn't avoid his eyes, that she didn't care if she was sweaty (or he was), that she had already ordered two more tennis dresses with him in mind, that she said, "I would like that," sealed her willing fate. She'd known she would wind up here. She'd given no signals otherwise. She had rediscovered herself through a game that had once made her feel desirous as an otherwise gawky adolescent. Tom had brought her back to that self, not with suggestive comments or so much as a touch on her arm but as a free body in motion. He had let her seduce herself from within by her own fiat.

He'd opened a bottle of Dom Perignon, 1988. Not exactly a cheap year, she had guessed. "What should we toast to?" Ardith asked. "To the long view," he answered. He stood behind her, his hands lightly on her shoulders, as they looked out the two-story window at Longs Peak. He led her upstairs.

In bed she had felt unsure enough that she'd asked him to stop and just hold her.

"Nothing has happened," he said. "I can still take you home if that's what you want."

She shook her head. She felt a strange flip of her soul when he entered her. She had once read that the soul encompassed all the complicated shadings of a person's history whereas the spirit remained inviolable and perfect. She had certainly darkened her soul and she felt a thickly moving pleasure course through her as he thrust into her, a roiling, exalted madness at what she'd just done.

Sometimes, after they made love, she'd just sit on the bed behind him and listen to his breathing. He'd take care of the calls from patients who needed immediate answers and couldn't give him his Wednesday mornings off. He did it without resentment. She liked to listen to his soothing voice, the simplicity of his advice. She enjoyed a girlish, secret excitement over his nakedness, hidden from the callers by his professional demeanor over the phone. This part of him she possessed. It had been so long since she'd held on to anything rare about someone, felt the thrill of a finder, the delight of *mine*. His legs were long and muscular, his back solid, his right shoulder scarred from a rotator cuff operation. She'd trace the thin scar with her finger while he talked, and then move her hand around to his chest and down to brush the spout of hair below his navel, trailing her fingers to his groin, stroking him until she could hear him, in spite of himself, his cool demeanor that she so liked to rattle, talking faster, rushing his last patient off the phone, ready to make love to her again after conversations about fevers, rashes, vomiting, and diarrhea. His wife had always minded the time his patients took from him. She'd resented it more as their daughters grew up and they spent too little time together as a family.

"We married early," Tom had explained. "I was a different and, frankly, at times difficult person back then, an absent father with a doctor's unquestionable excuse for his time away from the family. I got into a big practice to get some leverage with the insurance companies and cope with the whole managed care business in California, and things just went from bad to worst. I had less time than ever, and more headaches with the business side of things. I can't go back and undo that, but I've always tried to stay close to my daughters." He had two grown daughters who both lived in California. "Early on Carol and I had things we wanted, a family, a splendid house, weekends entertaining by the pool. Beyond that—and that's a lot to get beyond—we weren't compatible."

By which he meant he liked to *talk*—with Ardith, about small matters (houseplants to wines) and intellectual ones: politics, child-rearing, education, movies, books and beliefs, while Ardith delighted at the way everything came so easy for him, from running his office to overhauling the outboard engine of his boat to cooking homemade ratatouille to being in bed and demonstrating how to tie a double fisherman's knot with the sleeves of his white dress shirt. A shirt she happened to be wearing. Her arms and hands bound in the improvised strait jacket. An excruciating, helpless, delirious pleasure. He would slowly unbutton the shirt and plant a column of kisses down her bare midriff, moving his lips south—the hungered for easiness she wanted and believed she had deserved for a long time.

6

Reuben didn't deserve her.

Rosa had just finished billing their ad accounts, bless her heart, when he came in Thursday morning. He was embarrassed to ask her how long she'd been here already. She worked without complaint, offered him nothing but pleasant greetings, kept everything organized except the anti-oasis of his desk, and still had time to be the matriarch of her big family of four kids, nine grandchildren, countless sisters and brothers, nephews and nieces. She and her husband, a retired CenturyLink field technician, lived in a small ranch home on the north end of town where her four children had all been raised.

Reuben had dropped her off from work one cold winter evening when her car was in for repairs. He'd peeked in the converted garage of her husband Lee's shop—clean and organized as a NASA laboratory. A table saw with teeth so long it might as well have been growling stood beside the workbench, ready with a pair of clear goggles on top. Next to it was a hefty belt sander and an industrial-looking drill press. A red tool chest, nine drawers high, its hinged cover folded back to expose gleaming forged wrenches, loomed up like a small refrigerator. Screwdrivers so long they could have been drawn from scabbards, their plastic handles the bright colors of rock candy, waited on the peg board to be of service. In the back corner, a spiffy red and black compressor was plugged into a heavy-duty extension cord. While snow fell outside, a space heater provided warmth, its hot smell mixing with that of sawdust and polyurethane and grease. This was a man's shop. He had backed out of it, embarrassed by his own boast of ever being able to remodel their home. He couldn't even get *into* his garage. The door had been blocked for months now by a pile of gravel he was supposed to use for their driveway.

Rosa smiled at him. She was presently downloading the third quarter's attendance list for the local elementary school. Those who had a 95 percent attendance rate got their names in tiny seven-point type that parents would then clip out and put proudly on their refrigerator doors.

"Know a lot of people on the list?" Reuben asked.

"Three of my grandkids, Anna, Raymond, and Margaret."

"That's terrific." He looked at the block of names, hoping to see Harry's. Of course, he knew it wasn't there. Harry was lucky if he'd hit the 75 percent mark.

"What else is happening?"

"We've got some good pissing wars going on," Rosa said.

He was always a little taken aback at how Rosa, sweet grandmother that she was, could suddenly switch to a more colorful vernacular.

"Who is it?"

"The banks. First Western saw Bank of Colorado's ad and wants to make theirs as large this week."

"That's great. You didn't tell them First Western's was only a one-week deal."

"They'll know soon enough," said Rosa.

"Good girl."

"Three hundred dollars extra."

"That will pay the lights."

"One more thing," said Rosa. "We didn't get our mail yesterday."

"Why not?"

"I have no idea. It's the second time this has happened in the last month. A few advertisers called me after they got a delinquent notice about billing and complained they'd sent in their check weeks ago. Their checks must have been in the first mail we didn't get."

"And you called Dennis?"

"He says it was delivered, period. I think it's time for you to talk with him."

"Do I have to?"

"You're the boss."

"I guess."

"Enjoy the morning," Rosa said. She went back to the attendance list, and Reuben walked slowly toward his office.

Jolie was at her desk working on something. He thought he should ask. "How's it going?"

"I'm writing the most amazing story."

"Really," said Reuben, moving piles around on his desk.

"These two little girls were at their grandmother's house and they leaned back against the basement wall and it gave way."

"And?" he said.

"Treasure."

"Treasure?"

"You bet," said Jolie. "They found items behind the wall from ninety years before they were born. A copy of the *Christian Evangelist* from 1921, an RCA music catalog full of orchestra music, and—get this—some hand-carved wooden dominoes! The girls are going to turn it all over to the Welton Historical Society to see if they're interested in displaying any of the items at the museum. I want to go out and take some pictures of our treasure finders holding their discovery."

"Quite a story," Reuben said, moving the same piles on his desk back to where he'd had them originally.

"It's Thursday, Mr. Rosenfeld," Jolie pointed out. "Are you looking forward to the weekend?"

"I suppose." He forced himself out of his morose donkey indifference to ask back, "Are you?"

"You bet. We're going boating at Lake Finnegan—our first time this season! The whole clan."

"You have a big family?"

"My two brothers and three sisters, my mom, dad, our grandparents, and great grandparents. And all my husband's family. Joe and I were high school sweethearts. Jolie and Joe!"

"Must be nice to have your whole family in town."

"Family is wunnnderful," Jolie said dreamily. "And you, Mr. Rosenfeld?"

"Me?"

"Where is your family?"

"I have a brother Stan. My parents are dead."

"I'm *so sorry*."

Reuben waved away her concern. "It was years ago now."

"You must be very close with your brother."

"Not particularly," Reuben said. She looked stricken. Not close to family! "We're just very different."

"Oh," said Jolie. He pictured her whole clan at a tailgate party, cooking up ribs and barbecued chicken, hooting greetings to the many relatives and friends they knew in the stadium parking lot. It filled him with a kind of sickening remorse. His own family's roots were so shallow that an ant could uproot them. Shortly after they'd moved here, feeling the loneliness of having left what little family he did have, he'd invited his mother's only other surviving sister, Aunt Mildred, out from Chicago. It was the first time she'd been to the "Vild Vild Vest." They took her to a rodeo in Cheyenne, fifty miles north. Wearing a just-purchased red-felt cowboy hat, its black leather chinstrap snug under the loose flesh of her throat, she watched the steer wrestling competition. Impressed by the first contestant, she gave her seal of approval: "Very nice. He did that very well." A minute later another cowboy came out of the chute and wrestled down a steer. Aunt Mildred shook her head in dismay. "They're doing the same thing all over again?" she said. "They can't think of anything new?"

"Mr. Rosenfeld," said Jolie, snapping him out of his reverie. "I was wondering if I could speak with you about something."

Uh-oh. Here it is. She wanted a raise. She was going to hit him up, and he was going to have to say no and she'd quit and then he'd have to go out himself and do the theater review of *Blazing Guns of Roaring Gulch* at the Welton Community Playhouse. He glanced over at his desk. He eyed a message reminding him that he had promised to write up Bank Western's teller Eli "Bugs" Jackson as the Employee of the Week and needed to get a photograph of Bugs at work.

"About my column. Well...I don't know how to ask you this. I want to do something a little, you know, controversial, and I guess I need to find out if it's okay first."

"What could be controversial?" he said, a little too sharply.

"Here's the scoop. I was at play group with Maddy last Friday and there's this one little boy who loves tools, and he had gotten this *really* long screwdriver—it must have been a good sixteen inches—out of his dad's toolbox—it was the boy's house we were at—and he brought it up to his dad who was home that day and said, "Screw something, Daddy!" Jolie flushed. "So, all us moms started laughing. We thought it was *so* funny. You know, the things kids say. And then Sondra, another mom in the group, told us about this time her first grader raised his hand in class and asked the teacher how you spell the word *penis*! They were doing this lesson on writing about feelings. And his teacher took him aside and said, 'Robby, I don't think you understand the assignment.' And then Robby told her, 'I *do*. I know how to spell the *hap* part of happiness, I just don't how to spell the last part.'"

Jolie smiled shyly at him. All the talk of giant screwdrivers and penises was having the unexpected effect of rushing blood to his own organ as he watched Jolie's cupid-sized mouth and pictured her lips forming an *O* of pleasure around her husband Joe's tool. He wanted to call Ardith and have her meet him for lunch and then they could go home for a quickie—follow up on last night.

He remembered Harry was home sick.

"So anyway—" She was batting her eyelashes at him. He pushed his chair further under his desk, because his erection was fast ascending into "Jack and the Beanstalk" territory. Was this all from last evening? The release had turned him into a satyr, for anyone, even Jolie. "I'd like to write about the cute and embarrassing things—embarrassing to us grown-ups!—that kids say."

"Pardon?"

"For my column."

"Yes," he said. "Your column."

"So, it's okay?"

"Fine," he agreed, hoping his erection would settle down. He thought of the soft white curve of Ardith's smooth belly. The lazy tremor of her hips when she arched her back on top of him and came. The lacy fringe of the black lacy panties she'd slid down her long legs. When had she gotten them? They were a wonderful surprise when she'd pulled the nightgown over her head last night. He remembered when they'd met at Northwestern. A graduate of the journalism department and now a new reporter with the *Tribune*, he'd returned to give a talk to an introductory class about what it was like "out there." He'd crowed a little bit, talked about developing disciplined habits (though he had none to speak of himself) and taking accurate notes (which he was good at). In the front row, a girl with murderously long chestnut hair had raised her hand and asked if he liked himself as a reporter. "Like myself? I suppose so," he said, "but I don't really know because I just started. Maybe I'll think differently after I've flubbed a few stories." Polite laughter. Someone else asked a more appropriate question about protecting sources. But the girl's question stuck in his craw; what did she mean asking him if he *liked* himself? Of course he didn't like himself! As the class filed out, he asked his former professor who she was. Ardith Ley: a name that at once sounded exotic and intimidating, suggesting anything from a French torch singer to a financier's daughter.

Three months later they were at his apartment showering and talking about marriage. She didn't want to live together. She never had with anybody. No (anticipating his question), she wasn't a virgin. No, she wasn't old fashioned. No, it wasn't that she gave a damn about whether he got the milk free without buying the cow. She just wanted to marry him, plain and simple. A lifelong smoker, her father had died at forty-two of cancer when she was just entering high school. She didn't take time for granted like other people her age.

They were arranging their marriage in the shower.

Reuben stood there, dumbstruck by her lithe beauty, watching her work up a lather of shampoo suds. Her self-possession. The lovely intentionality of her long fingers wringing her darkly soaked hair free of water. Her bare knee bent in a precious symmetry of effort and grace. The shelf of her pubic hair diverting water across to the junction where her hips curved and met her sleek thighs. Her breasts slick with rivulets of pear-scented shampoo and her nipples erect under the warm water.

She'd looked up from her work and gave him a fetching smile. Her hair took a good ten minutes to wash. The hot water would run out soon. Standing with a kind of happy paralysis, his chest hair matted, hot water pouring over his steamed skin—his blotchy red, hers pink—he felt too overwhelmed to touch her, too beholden to stare at her without the gratitude of the big dumb cluck he believed himself to be. "I love you," he said. He said it again. She listened carefully, not looking at him, going on with her washing. And then she said: "For our garden," and squeezed a stream of soapy liquid from her long-corded hair over the inflamed head of his penis, watering it into a frenzy.

"Thanks, Mr. Rosenfeld," Jolie said about her column. "I knew you believed in freedom of the press."

"Always." He went into the vault with its two-foot-thick cool iron walls so he could decompress.

Ardith called him an hour later. "We have to talk," she said.

"What's up?"

"I just overheard him talking on the phone to Ricky Ryan about his brother."

"Him? Harry? Wait—who's Ricky Ryan's brother?"

"Vic."

"*Vic?*"

"Harry told Ricky he wasn't going to say anything and to leave him alone. Then he must have heard me listening because he hung up quickly."

"Okay, let me get this straight. Harry was with Ricky Ryan's *brother?*"

"I don't know," said Ardith. "I just know this Vic is somehow involved in what happened. I asked Harry about it after he got off, and he said he didn't know what I was talking about. Yeah, right. Supposedly, he hasn't seen Ricky since school two days ago."

He was trying to comprehend how any of this fit together: his son's knocked-out tooth; Ricky Ryan—Harry's only friend and a budding juvenile delinquent at that; and some character named Vic…and what the hell he was supposed to do about it anyway!

"You need to talk to him," Ardith said.

"Harry?"

"*No*, this Vic person, Ricky's brother."

"Who is he, Ardith? I've never heard of him before!"

"Call Wade," she said. "He knows everybody in town. Maybe he should go with you. I mean it, Reuben, we can't just let this go by. Do you want me to do it?"

"No." Though he couldn't think of a good reason why she shouldn't, except some father-son blood rite that required him in the great chain of manhood to defend his cave. "How's he doing otherwise?"

"He does have a slight fever. Listen, you have to tell this person Vic to stay away from Harry. Make it clear. Can you do that please?"

"Shouldn't we find out what exactly happened first?" Reuben said.

"That's what you're going to do. And you know Harry won't tell us anything, and then it will be too late."

"Too late for what?"

"I'll be right there!" Ardith called. When she came back on, her voice was lower. "Other than this mind-boggling news, we've had a good time playing Scrabble. Harry made the word *xenon* for thirty-six points on a triple word score."

"Is that a planet?"

"It's a gas used in laser-pumping lamps."

"How did he know that?"

"I wish I knew. And I wish he'd use his brain more for school. So you won't put this off, Reuben? I was furious when I overhead him. I've got to get off."

"Wait—"

"What?"

"I had a good time last night."

"Me too," Ardith said, and hung up.

"I'm going out for a bite," Reuben said to Rosa just before one.

Though he hadn't planned to do so, he found himself taking a detour toward the park, empty now. He sat on a bench and rubbed his temples in the April sunshine.

"Reuben Rosenfeld!"

He jumped up.

It was Dennis Olberg standing behind him. "I heard you want to see me."

"Here?" asked Reuben.

"I didn't plan to be here," Dennis said. "I'm on my way back to the post office from lunch at home."

"Did you enjoy your lunch?" Reuben said, trying to make nice with the man.

"What do you mean?"

"I mean…your lunch. What'd you have?"

"I have the same lunch every day. Chicken raisin salad on home-baked oat bread, with lettuce leaf and a ripe tomato, preferably from our garden in season. A glass of skim milk and an apple cobbler. Mary has it ready for me at noon. Followed by my walk."

"Terrific," said Reuben. Everybody was so damn healthy out here. Hadn't Colorado been voted the "skinniest" state in the country? People watched their weight. They ate egg-beaters for fun. They detested smoking. They drank healthful micro-brewed beer that had vitamins. They mountain biked in preposterous Hannibal-like century rides across the Rockies with CamelBaks strapped on for nonstop water injection. They cross-country skied into the wilderness in subzero weather to stay in remote yurts. Even Ardith had embraced the lifestyle, playing tennis with Tom, their family doctor, and then, when the weather turned colder, both of them jogging every week-day morning. Tom suggested Reuben join them—Tom was a nationally ranked runner for his age group, fifty plus—but Reuben would have nothing to do with it. "I just wanted to mention about our mail getting lost—"

Dennis cut him off. "Let me stop you right there." Obviously, Reuben had uttered the dreaded word: *lost. J'accuse.* "We have never lost, without subsequently recovering, a patron's mail in my thirty years as postmaster." Dennis had a long Nordic face, white second-story hair, and eyes calibrated to the exact pinpoints of dental lasers. He was one of these men that examined you like a bug while having no idea you were observing him too.

"I just thought you could look into the matter and possibly see if you could trace the two days in question."

"I've already done so. Nothing was reported amiss."

Reuben wanted only lunch, and to turn his face up to the warm sun before he had to confront the demonic-sounding Vic. He'd called Wade who had said, "Yeah, that character. He works over at Mel's Tires. He's a tough ass and whiner, an ugly combination. I got him on a domestic assault charge, but the gal he clocked with his fist wouldn't testify, and we had to close the case when she split town. Probably to get away from him. I'm just waiting for him to step one toe over the line. What's he have to do with you? Did he come around the paper?" Reuben told him no, Harry was friends with Ricky, the little brother, and, well, he just wanted to check out the family. "Get Harry away from them ASAP," Wade warned.

"I'll be in the office until five if you wish to file a complaint," Dennis said, with great sufferance.

"How about we just forget about the whole thing?" Reuben offered. Overhead a cloud floated by, a big, fat, fluffy Jehovah-looking thing. The lips of God, blowing a breeze his way. He suspected having Wade involved would only get Harry into deeper trouble. No, it was up to him. Wasn't he supposed to unfurl his cape and dash off on his mission to save his son?

Dennis, his heavy brows seeming to pitch like wet logs rolling furiously on a river, eyed him. "I never forget *anything* about my job."

"Oh, come on, Dennis," said Reuben, and giggled, a social non sequitur under the circumstances. "Is it really such a big deal?" But Dennis had already started off across the park to reach his fiefdom by five minutes to one.

In the afternoon he drove by Mel's Tires and tried to see who might look like Vic, based on his brother Ricky. All the employees were inside working in the pits.

"Can I help you?" The salesman was compact and clean-shaven, with close-cropped black hair and a tire pressure gauge clipped into his front pocket—*Mitch* stitched in red thread above. And an earring.

"I was wondering if I could speak to Vic."

Mitch glanced out the service window to the bays. Reuben tried to figure out from his gaze whom he was looking at. "He's in the middle of a job right at the moment. Anything I can help you with?"

"Just need to talk to him."

"Who should I say is here?"

"Reuben Rosenfeld."

He waited and looked up at the TV, with its sound off. A game show. A woman in a two-toned leather body suit the color of red and black jellybeans was putting strawberry wigs on contestants' heads.

"You want to see me?"

"I'm Reuben Rosenfeld." He extended his hand. Vic wiped his hand on a rag from his back pocket, then shook Reuben's loosely. His forehead was smooth, his eyes sunken, his mouth smiling without being happy, his lips rubbery and flappable. He looked like a primate. His fingers were short, stubby, and cold. "Harry's dad."

No reaction.

"I think you know my son."

"He's my brother's friend." It sounded sweet—Harry had a friend. How he longed for Harry to have friends. And then Vic said, "So what?" and Reuben's fantasy of loyalty and companionship and childhood closeness for Harry vanished in the tone of Vic's terse get-to-the-point words.

"Harry lost a tooth yesterday."

"Yeah?" said Vic. "Sorry to hear that."

"Know anything about it?"

"About what?"

"How my son lost his tooth."

Vic made a sound like an air gun going off. "How the hell would I know anything about it?"

"I think you do," said Reuben.

"You do, huh. Why's that, friend?"

"Because your name came up."

"Came up where?"

"It just came up. It's not important where."

Vic stuck his oily rag back in his pocket. His stitched-on name said *Kevin*, not *Vic*. Maybe he had the wrong guy. Or maybe Vic was just low on shirts. "Man, I think…you want to know what I think?" Reuben kept silent. "I think you're having some problems on the home front. You know, like, get your house in order, man. That's just some free advice." Vic winked, along with his smirk. "Meanwhile"—Vic leaned toward him—"get the fuck out of my face."

The salesmen looked up from their registers.

"Hey," Vic said. He poked his chin toward the men behind the counter. "I was working all day yesterday. I was here, right?"

"Far as I know," said Mitch, as if this were all just a customer satisfaction problem.

"I don't believe you."

"Look, *Harry's dad*, I got to get back to work. If your boy is freaked out about something I done to him, he should get his days straight. I'm too busy working to play make-believe."

"Maybe we should talk about this elsewhere. Say, the police station?"

Vic leaned his torso back, his hands balled up at his sides, a boxer's dare. He smiled with astonishing elasticity, those rubbery lips. "I'm finished talking with you. You got some problem, you go to the police. You come bothering me again, and *I'm* calling the police."

Reuben looked up at the guys behind the counter. They had their neutral salesmen smiles on that meant he was an asshole and the minute he left they'd dis him.

"Stay away from my son," Reuben said, which is what he had wanted to say in the first place, his anger rising in furious disregard of any danger. "Stay the hell away from Harry."

7

"I can't find my dry cleaning." She'd spent an hour looking for the jacket and skirt that needed to go to the cleaners before ten this morning, so she'd have them for tonight. "Have you seen it, Reuben?"

"Where'd you leave it?"

"By the back door. If I get it in now, they can rush it for me by four."

They'd been invited to Lyle and Ellen's for Ellen's fiftieth birthday party. Ardith had bought the outfit from Neiman Marcus as a going away present to herself before leaving Chicago. She'd worn it twice since coming to Welton and had put it in a bag with some other articles that needed to be dry-cleaned.

Tom had been invited to the party too. He was Ellen and Lyle's family doctor as well. A brief phone conversation while he was at work had been all she'd spoken with him since last week when he'd come to the house and Harry had been sick. No, he wasn't mad at her. Absolutely he understood she needed to stay home with Harry. Certainly, he wanted to run again, but he couldn't get away this week, even in the mornings. "So, are you punishing me?" she'd asked him. "I wouldn't dare," he said, "unless you want me to." She giggled foolishly. That was the problem with having an affair; it made her insecure all over again about pleasing a man. What did he have in mind exactly? Was he hinting at something? Should she be more adventurous with him? Reuben and she had settled into the same trustworthy and efficient configurations over twenty years of marriage; comfortable, they each got what they wanted, when they bothered (and that had become the word) to have sex. It never occurred to her to think beyond the normal parameters of their four-poster bed.

"What did it have in it?"

"A pair of silk pants, two blouses, my long black skirt, a suede jacket... Where'd you put it?"

"I think I may have goofed," Reuben said. "I might have thrown it out."

"You *what?*"

"When I was cleaning out the garage last night, I saw a full trash bag sitting next to the back door and I just assumed it was garbage."

"You put it in the *trash?*" He nodded. "So, it's out there now?"

"They already picked up the trash."

She was stunned. "You've got to be kidding, Reuben."

"I didn't know, Ardith. It looked like trash. It was by the back door. What else am I supposed to think?"

"You couldn't see there were clothes inside?"

"How would I know?"

"You *look.*"

"You shouldn't have disguised the clothes in a trash bag if you didn't want them thrown out."

"I didn't disguise anything! Those were my best clothes, Reuben! Did you think about what you were doing? The bag wasn't even closed up."

"Look at this place! Cereal boxes on the television, dirty dishes in the bathroom, a basket of laundry in the fireplace. Is anything where it belongs? How should I know that it's dry cleaning and not trash ready to go out?"

Ardith wiped the tears from her face. She started upstairs but tripped on Jamie's baseball bat and hurt her foot. She screamed silently and rocked forward on the step, holding her big toe, the pain unbearable.

Reuben came over and stood at the bottom of the stairs. "You okay?"

"No," she said.

"I'm sorry." He put his hands on his hips. "I'm sorry I threw away your clothes."

"I'm a terrible housekeeper. I stink at it." She rocked back and forth from the pain of smashing her toe against Jamie's aluminum bat, which should be…that was the problem, nobody knew where to put anything! It was all so overwhelming, everything. Just having her mother around had forced her to keep a nicer place in Chicago.

"We could hire one of those people who come in and organize everything," Reuben said.

"You want to be the person to spend hours discussing with them the possible relocations for the contents of our closets? I don't."

"Then we should do it ourselves. Just start with one room at a time. Get our priorities straight."

Ardith shivered.

"It's part of the adjustment," Reuben said. "It takes a while after you move somewhere."

She thought about her two-hundred-dollar silk pants all twisted around in rotten food and old coffee grounds at the dump.

"Unless we just don't want to make the adjustment," Reuben said.

She stopped rubbing her toe. "What do you mean?"

"If we wanted to—and this is just something to think about—we could move."

"Move?"

"From here."

"You mean another house?"

"I mean back to Chicago."

She stared at him. "I couldn't—"

Reuben put up his hand. "Just think about it. We've given it almost two years here. Things haven't worked out as we'd hoped. We can either stay and see if they do, or we can cash in our chips and go back. There's nothing to be ashamed of in going home. Chicago might just *be* our home. I'd hate to spend the rest of our lives here learning that lesson just out of principle."

"I don't want to leave!" She felt a panic rising that he would make her, and an uncontrollable urge to rush to the phone and call Tom.

"Well, we're not going to do anything right away. It's just something we need to keep talking about."

All she could find to wear was a tight red dress that she should have gotten rid of years ago. Her favorite outfit was gone, all her best clothes. The long black skirt with its lacy hem, her suede olive jacket, and—she wanted to cry whenever she thought about it—the silk-screened scarf of silhouetted birds, trimmed in silver beads...gone. All of it thrown away. How fucking maddening!

She had only this stretchy rayon dress that came down mid-thigh and advertised every curve and bump of her body. Five years ago, in a reckless moment, she'd worn it on a rare night out when she and Reuben had gone to see a revival of *Cabaret* in Chicago. All evening she'd been aware of her nipples prickling under the fabric and men staring at her during the intermission.

She took it off the hanger and tried it on, examining herself in the full-length closet mirror. It wasn't a disaster or a hoot, as she feared, even with the addition of five years and a few (or more) pounds. As she walked away, she glanced over her shoulder trying to see her butt. Good. It didn't look as if a cement mixer were following her. Still, she wouldn't want one of those rock video shots of her from below and behind. Some sensible jewelry would help, her small silver earrings set with onyx stones, and keeping her makeup light.

Shutting the bathroom door, she took off the dress, and with her hair still tied up, she scrubbed her face again, looking at herself sideways in the bathroom mirror. She inhaled the slight pooch of her stomach and convinced herself she was up to the dress. It was a blushing color of come-hither red, and she remembered buying it one snowy Saturday afternoon in Chicago when a neighbor had babysat the kids and her mother. She'd run out to Saks and, in a fit of impulse buying, imagining herself a freer woman than she was as the full-time caretaker of her mother and three males, she'd thrown her credit card down and bought the dress without even trying it on, too afraid to see that it might show every frumpish droop of her body and look laughable.

She shook her head and hurried downstairs. She couldn't afford to stand in front of the mirror like a teenager picturing the perfect her. The fruit salad she'd promised to bring to the party was still waiting to be made, and she had to get Harry away from the computer and Jamie up from lying on his belly, poring over baseball stats on Reuben's iPad, and chase them both into the shower, their first in days—how many exactly she couldn't bear to think about. They'd just come home from school. Meanwhile she was a nervous wreck. Maybe because she knew Tom was going to be at the party. Maybe because she was wearing a scarlet dress that made Harry say, "You look like the devil," after she poked his shoulder and told him to get in the shower. Everything was making her frantic. The domestic life. The secret life. The new life they were supposed to be enjoying in Colorado.

"You need to hurry," she said.

"Where's Dad?"

Ardith glanced at the clock. They were going to be late. "He's washing the car. You still have ice cream sandwich from lunch around your mouth."

"Can't I stay home? I just got here."

"No."

"Please."

"Harry, *go*. Jamie, you use our bathroom."

They grudgingly went upstairs. Yesterday she'd taken Harry to the local barbershop—an old-fashioned one on Main Street with the blue and red ribbon pole out front. They didn't have any kids' places in town. Sam, the barber, had asked how he wanted it. "Buzzed," Harry said.

"He just needs a trim," Ardith countered.

"Shave it off. It's my hair. I want a baldie." Sam, a broad man with a stubby mustache and wearing a barber's mint-colored

smock, waited with his scissors and comb. He'd obviously witnessed hundreds of these battles. "Everybody's getting them,"
said Harry. She only knew one kid, his friend Ricky Ryan, who
Harry had now been forbidden to see. As far as Ardith could
tell, Harry was staying away from him—and his brother, Vic.
Reuben had confronted him to no avail. He'd made it sound as
if they were about to go *mano a mano*. And she'd had a moment
of feeling guilty for putting him at risk. Her assumption had
been, compared to Chicago, how dangerous could things get
in Welton? He'd talked her out of his bringing Wade along,
though Ardith had called him herself and explained what she'd
overheard. Wade had listened, sympathized, said he'd love to
nail that degenerate and then admitted there was little he could
do unless Harry cooperated. Which he wouldn't. He'd turned
pale when he found out Reuben had gone to Vic and screamed
to leave him alone about it. It was nobody's business but his
own. And theirs, of course, given the four-hundred-dollar dental bill. At least the procedure seemed to be working, the tooth
hadn't turned color.

"Whatever," Ardith had agreed reluctantly at the barber. Five
minutes later her son's head was that of a bristly hedgehog, his
gorgeous, wavy golden hair in little armed-services clumps on
the floor. Somehow it didn't look like the other "baldies" she'd
seen, less a tough celebrity like Vin Diesel and more a victim of
lice. "It's fine," she lied.

"Yeah," Harry said, looking at himself in the hand mirror
that Sam gave him. "Cool."

On the way home she asked him again about Ricky Ryan.

"I told you, nothing happened."

"Right. You tripped. On a highway, miles from here. That
really adds up."

"I just want to stop talking about it, all right?" He ran his
hand across the top of his head and looked at himself in the
visor mirror. "I like this," he said.

She brought him the shampoo he asked for—not that he
needed any now—and caught a glimpse of a faint shadow of

hair around his groin through the shower door smoked glass. He turned his front away from her and reached out blindly for the shampoo. An hour later, after both boys had showered—it gave her such satisfaction to have them both clean at once— she finished making the fruit salad just as Reuben pulled up. He jumped out of the washed van, all smiles.

"*Va-va-voom*," he said, seeing her.

She wanted to bite his head off. "Let's just go, all right? We'll never get there if we don't."

"You look really great. I haven't seen that dress before."

"You have too. Carry this wine, please." She was trying to hold the fruit salad, her purse, and her makeup to be put on in the car.

"Let's go, everybody," said Reuben. "Into the high-flying, immaculate van."

Harry shuffled like a prisoner in shackles, his every step an outcry at the injustice of making him come along. He wore baggy shorts and a T-shirt that said: *Just Undo It.*

"All buckled?" Reuben asked.

Ardith didn't know whether she felt relieved or worried that Tom wasn't at Lyle and Ellen's when they got there.

"How's the house?" Lyle asked her. He was fixing hamburgers and barbecued chicken on the grill. Lyle had moved to Colorado after college, lived on a commune, and then borrowed money from his parents to start a dairy farm, which he ran to this day, along with Ellen, his partner of twenty-five years. They had never married, though later in life they had a near genius daughter of twelve, Isadora, whom they'd named after Lyle's Russian grandmother.

"We're working on it," she said vaguely.

"You live in the old Sherman place?" a man asked her. He'd been introduced with his wife as neighbors of Ellen and Lyle's, the both of them potters.

"The very one," said Ardith.

"We looked at your house once," his wife said, "when we

thought about moving closer to town for the schools." They were both trim, wearing cowboy boots and creased jeans. In her tight red dress, Ardith felt like the saloon girl standing next to them. "Too much work for us."

"Ditto," said Ardith, "except we went for it."

Reuben came outside about the same time that Ellen did. Ardith was relieved. It was always easier to make conversation with him around. In the right mood, he was a good talker, careful to ask questions, full of anecdotes. She often let him do all the talking at dinner parties, content to listen, especially with strangers.

He'd been getting the fruit salad from the van and the flowers for Ellen, though she had said no presents. Ellen, limber and skinny, was several inches taller than Lyle. She wore sneakers and no socks and had dressed down for her own party, which made Ardith feel even more out of place. No makeup, her gray hair cut short, a simple sundress on. You had the impression her arms could go around you twice when she gave you a hug. She told Ardith how stunning she looked, read: *hooker*. But she knew Ellen wasn't thinking that, only herself, because her mature, grown-up clothes were festering in the dump right now.

More people came out back, a midwife, a husband and wife co-therapists, a couple who ran a landscaping business—lots of working teams here tonight. She'd once considered going to work at the newspaper with Reuben. It was partly her money, after all, sunk into the paper. An inheritance from her mother after she died, along with a small business loan, had given them the cash they needed to buy the local paper, crazy as that was when newspapers were folding all over the country. The reality of working with Reuben was troubling. His habits drove her crazy enough at home. And while she admired his doggedness, that same insistence often made him impervious to even the mildest suggestions from others.

Yet more people arrived—she didn't catch their names. A music teacher, a veterinarian, a Spanish tutor. The midwife came over and introduced herself as Colleen. She'd wanted to meet Ardith for a while. She and her son Ben had only moved to the area a year ago themselves. "I've heard a lot about you from Ellen."

Like what? Ardith had wondered. What was there to possibly say about her other than gossip?

She kept waiting for Tom, expecting him to walk through the door at any moment. It prevented her from being able to concentrate on the conversations.

"Watch this," Lyle said. Standing ten paces away from the grill with his back turned and a hamburger patty extended on a spatula, he flipped the patty backwards over his shoulder. Amazingly it landed on the grill. Ellen rolled her eyes.

"He wants to try that trick sometime with a mirror and a gun and use me as the target."

"That's not true! I want you to put a flowerpot on your head. I would never shoot you, honeybunch." He leaned over to kiss her, and Ellen turned her cheek toward him with an exasperated sigh.

"Happy birthday." It was Tom. He was standing in the doorway of the patio. A bottle of red wine in hand and a big smile on his face, a public smile. She felt frozen.

"The good doctor," said Ellen. She went up to him. He gave her a kiss on the cheek, then picked her up and squeezed her in a long, warm birthday hug. They looked as if they'd known each other forever. He had this instant intimacy with everyone, able to bypass the time it took someone like her to make lasting bonds. Jealousy was whipping her left and right tonight, the latest surge at seeing how many people rushed over to greet him, while she played coy to no one's notice except her own.

Finally, he saw Ardith across the patio and smiled—perfectly normal.

Reuben suddenly appeared. He'd come up and taken her elbow, proprietarily. "Harry and Jamie went to see Isadora's horse. Are you doing okay?"

"Just feeling a little shy tonight."

"You want me to make you up a small plate of appetizers?"

"That would be sweet." She forced herself to take her eyes away from Tom and smile at Reuben.

He went off to get her some food. The vet, the two therapists, and the potters, all of whom were talking with him about something or other, surrounded Tom. He had so many hobbies and interests aside from his practice—sailing, fishing, gardening, golf, skiing—that it was no wonder he could engage so many people. And he was on the fundraising board for the library, a volunteer coach for the high school rugby team (they hadn't had one until he came and organized it), and co-director of the newly formed Bicycle Advocacy Alliance. Most intimidating of all, he could really dance and had taught her the country swing one afternoon in the privacy of his bedroom. The memory of his whipping her around in her bra and panties, giddy with delight at her body bouncing and twirling and nearly levitating with joy, assailed her now at the mindless blur of sensation she'd become with him.

She downed her wine and decided to go find Harry and Jamie. More than once at such parties her kids had bailed her out when she had little to say and was suffering from some terrible attack of insecurity. She could always look purposeful in attending to them, and they were glad to see her, even Harry, or maybe especially Harry.

She went toward the corral. To have taken the more convenient flagstone path would have meant passing by Tom. She tried to step in the harder-packed dirt and avoid the cow patties and ruts of mud. A few cows turned to look at her, their big, brown eyes dopey with disregard. Ellen had said she and Lyle needed to make some critical decisions soon about whether to expand. It was getting too hard to be a small operation anymore. They were considering buying cheaper land out in eastern Colorado and moving there, which saddened Ardith. The one friend she had in town was going to leave. Thinking about it made her feel all the more alone, and she turned around and glanced to see if Tom was still surrounded by people. He was. While she was surrounded by cow shit. There was Reuben too,

looking for her, holding a paper plate of appetizers and worrying about her not eating, loyal as could be, and she couldn't
move suddenly, her heels literally stuck in the mud.

She looked over at Tom. Up to her ankles in mud, she felt
absolutely foolish.

"Here it is," said Lyle, bringing out a canning jar of homemade
hot sauce from his refrigerator. Lyle, who was four years younger than Ellen, still had a full head of dark wavy hair, a reckless
beard, and intense black eyes—his scruffiness less the result of
poor choices in hygiene than having stayed up all night working on a manifesto for an underground newspaper. Whenever
Ardith was around him she felt as if she were on an out-of-
control escalator. Their fearless dachshund, Delilah, followed
him all day trying to herd the cows. "Anybody who swallows
a full teaspoon—no candy-ass sipping either—is automatically
admitted."

Everybody had gone into the kitchen to undergo the initiation for "Lyle's Club." Women were allowed if they had the
stuff, Lyle said. Ellen whacked him on the back and declared
they'd match the men one for one. Ardith had managed to pull
her feet free of the mud—they certainly didn't have "mud season" in Chicago!—although her shoes were so caked that she'd
had to leave them outside. Ellen had given her a pair of well-
scored Birkenstocks to wear. When Reuben asked, she found it
impossible to explain why she'd taken the muddiest way out to
the corral. She'd tried to let it go; they were in public; Tom was
doing the smart thing…but his cool detachment gnawed at her
resolve to play along, if that's what they were even doing.

"Who would want to be in your club, Lyle?" asked the potter.

"Hotte*sst hot ss*sauce in the city," Lyle hissed, ignoring the
question.

"What privileges does being in the club entitle us to?" asked
Colleen, the midwife. "I'd like to know if it's worth it."

"Ten hours of Lyle's taped lectures on milking techniques,"
said Ellen.

"I understand it puts hair on your chest," said the female therapist.

"That's the mild hot sauce. The hot *hot* sauce"—he dipped a teaspoon into chunky red mixture that to Ardith looked like congealed blood—"this scorched-earth baby gives you bull's breath."

"You have the most wonderful marketing techniques," said Colleen.

Lyle took out a stack of Dixie cups from the drawer. He lined them up and poured milk into each. "Hot sauce chased by a cup of milk," he pronounced. "Not that I'm pushing my niche products here. Who's ready?"

"I'll pass," said Colleen.

"Oh, come on. It's Ellen's birthday. You're not going to toast to her?"

Colleen raised her bottle of beer at Ellen. "I'll toast to you anytime, darling."

"Any other sissies?"

"I have allergies," said the potter.

"To hot sauce?"

"To clubs."

"Wuss."

"I'll renew my membership," said the landscaper, the man.

"Me too," said the vet.

"No so-called"—Lyle made air quotes—"women?"

Ellen hit him. "You pig. You're worse than Howard Stern."

"I'm PC!" Lyle protested. "Your personal cupid." He tried to give Ellen a kiss, but she pushed him away. "Hey, I'm just trying to motivate people."

"I see an infomercial," said Reuben.

"You in?" Lyle asked him.

"I'm out as could be, thank you."

Ardith looked at Tom, standing against the wall. So he was a chicken about something. "I'll do it," she said.

"All right, *Ardith*!" Lyle hooted.

Ellen shook her head. "Don't let him bully you into this."

"I want to," said Ardith, "for my country and for all women." She bowed toward Ellen and Colleen.

"*Hot,*" Lyle said, staring at her low-cut dress. "Muy caliente!"

"You brave girl, you," said Ellen and put her arm around her.

"Is it that bad?"

"You brave girl" was all Ellen would say.

Lyle dipped the spoons in the hot sauce and spread them out on the kitchen counter, each next to a paper cup of milk. His smile was demonic. "Inductees, please step forward."

Ardith stood in front of her teaspoon of hot sauce. She'd once eaten worms when she was a little girl to prove herself fearless to some boys in the neighborhood. How much worse could this be?

"Ready? Remember, no sipping."

She picked up her spoon, brought it up toward her mouth, and tipped it all in. At first, she felt nothing. Then a ferocious burning tore through her mouth—a scorching so penetrating her tongue felt like one large blistering abscess. She grabbed the milk and poured it down. Every swallow caused an agonizing stringency, as if rats were sinking their razor-sharp incisors into her throat. People patted her on the back. Jamie was hugging her waist. Her eyes bulged out. Never, *ever* had she tasted anything so flesh-eating in her entire life.

Lyle kept his head tipped back; his eyes were closed with the transcendent gaze of a man walking unfazed across a bed of hot coals. With the spoon still wedged between his lips, he flicked its handle like a lizard's tongue.

Ardith fanned her mouth and extended her cup, begging wordlessly for more milk.

"Welcome to the club, tough stuff," Lyle told her, finally taking his spoon out.

Colleen, Ellen, and the other women surrounded her, giving her hugs. "I can't believe I did that," she said when she was able to talk. She stuck out her tongue. "Is it singed black?"

Lyle tsk-tsked. "Roadkill."

"Ignore him," Ellen told her. "It's a little, let's say, agitated looking. We don't exactly have that color red in the crayon box."

Ardith swished some more milk around. Her tongue and throat throbbed with what felt like a massive allergic reaction to a bee sting. The vet and landscaper, who had been through this before, looked a little boggled-eyed, but calm and experienced. "Is this stuff legal?"

"It is," Lyle said, "if you're a weed." He downed another teaspoon. Ardith stared at him in sickened amazement.

The men, after a spontaneous and contentious discussion about their fitness—who had the best body mass index—disappeared into the bathroom to weigh themselves.

Ardith started to set the long tables on the patio for dinner. "You rest," Ellen told her. "You've done your part. We'll get everything ready."

She watched the women for a minute through the kitchen window, then wandered into the bathroom where the men were clustered around a scale.

"There's a girl in the kiva!" said the potter.

"I think we're going to have to sacrifice her as a virgin," said Lyle.

"That's good," Ardith countered. "I was afraid you were going to weigh me."

"Sacrifice or satisfy?" Tom said. Was he drunk?

"Look at that. Tom's the heaviest," said Reuben.

"It's all muscle," the therapist said. "Look at his legs, will you?"

"Implants," the potter said. He was tall and thin as an aspen and seemed to relish being packed into a small bathroom with a bunch of guys.

"Can you excuse us?" the therapist said to Ardith. "We have to talk about body sculpting now."

"Let me know if I can help." They laughed again, snickering adolescent laughter. She walked outside to see if Ellen needed her for anything.

"How's your mouth?" asked Ellen.

"Bearable. It's quick acting but it doesn't last too long once the milk hits."

"You did good," Ellen said, and went off to the kitchen to get another tablecloth.

Ardith turned and looked for her children. She wanted to feel restored to herself, her most familiar self that could forget about her burning mouth, her screaming red dress, and her lover receiving hosannas for his body fat percentage.

She went toward the corral where she hoped Harry and Jamie would still be. Delilah, Lyle's no-guts-no-glory dachshund, ran around the corral barking at the horses, darting suicidally among their hooves. She had this idea, Ellen had told them, that she was an Australian sheep dog trapped in a dachshund's body. Isadora led Jamie around the corral on her mare, while Harry, a rope in his hand, sat on the fence with a boy about his age—Colleen's son, Ben—and talked. It was such a perfect sight: Jamie riding, and Harry...Harry practicing how to lasso, just chatting about kid things on a split-rail fence. She'd almost be ready to bargain away her happiness, make a trade with the divine powers, if she thought they existed: Tom, her own wants—give it all up just for Harry's delivery.

A hand squeezed her shoulder. "You okay?" Tom. It was a friendly and casual touch, a doctor's calming hand, careful to avoid anything too intimate. "I've been trying to get over to you all night."

She kept herself from reaching out for him. "Tom," she said, and shook her head, unable to get anything else out.

"You're a brave girl. How's your mouth?"

"Scarred forever."

"Open up," he said. She did as she was told, her mouth compliant.

"Tonsils are still there."

"I never had them out. My wisdom teeth either."

"You're intact."

Ardith frowned. "Your sacrificial virgin. What was *that* about?"

"Sorry, I just looked at you for a moment and completely forgot myself. You looked so deliciously pretty with your hair pulled up and your—"

"My slutty dress."

"Vibrant, I'd say. Your face matched the dress when you swallowed that hot sauce."

"I wore it for you." She'd meant it to sound flippant, but it came out—as she knew it was—baldly truthful. "I'm going crazy. I have to touch you."

He frowned, a doctor's sympathetic concern. She wanted to pinch him, make him scream, bite his hand, ram his stomach, and roar.

"You really look lovely," he said.

"Reuben threw away all my best clothes. He thought the dry-cleaning bag I'd set aside was trash."

"Ouch. Poor Reuben. He's got a lot of doghouse time coming, I bet. Will you let me buy you new ones?"

"No, but thanks for asking."

The sky had wisps of crimson clouds laced in with bruised purplish-black thunderheads—a shower trying to get started across the eastern plains. On the verge of rain, everything smelled dark and fecund, dankly swooning, the ever-present odor of manure from the Greeley stock yards just another animal scent. She wanted to fall into him, place her head against his chest and breathe a long quavering sigh, lick the salt off his skin, and lay with him on scratchy straw. "I have to see you more," she said. "I can't stand it."

He nodded. His eyes looked as lonely as the cows'. Some entrenched unhappiness resided in him, despite all his show to the contrary. Though he spoke philosophically about his past troubles, his marriage and divorce and two grown daughters, one of whom wanted little to do with him now, and though Welton had embraced him as their long-awaited healer, he had struggled to start over too, just like Ardith. His sadness and failure trailed him here. It had drawn her to him—that private pain and his will to tame it.

"Suppose I leaned over and kissed you," he said. "What would you do?"

"I'd faint."

"Into my arms?"

"I'll try to fall backward into the fence. You're a terrible tease."

"I'm not teasing."

She glanced around her. Nobody was watching. "Okay." She closed her eyes in resolve, cloistered by the smell of gathering rain and fresh cut hay, the cows lowing, the horse flies buzzing, the clopping of the mare's hooves—

"Mom!" Harry called. She opened her eyes, dizzy from anticipation. Harry riding atop Isadora's horse, waving a lasso in the air. "Look at me!"

Tom whispered in her ear, "That boy has great timing." They both leaned back against the fence, at a distance apart, watching Harry trot proudly around the corral.

Two hours later, after a game of softball, and a drunken round of singing happy birthday to Ellen, they were on their way home. Ardith drove in the pouring rain. Reuben had imbibed too much. Sheets of water lashed the windshield, while Ardith hunched over the wheel to see.

During the softball game she'd looked over and discovered Reuben and Tom sitting together on the hay bales that served as the opposing team's bench, celebrating a home run the veterinarian had just hit. She couldn't believe it. Their buddying up seemed so out of place yet so natural that for a moment she thought she and Tom weren't even having an affair and that it was all a fantasy on her part. So thoroughly did he seem untroubled by his affection for Reuben—he had slung his arm around Reuben at one point—that it made her head spin. An hour before he'd been about to kiss her and risk sealing their fate in front of all the world. And dizzy with longing she'd been about to let him.

"*It's a long way to Tipperary!*"

"Dad's drunk," said Harry. "Cool."

"Over hill, over dale… How about some Gordon Lightfoot? *The legend lives on from the Chippewa on down of the big lake they call Gitchie Gumee!*"

"Shhh," said Ardith, trying to quiet him.

"Little voice please," Reuben mocked. "Have to use my teeny tiny itsy bitsy wee wee voice."

Harry laughed hard in the back seat. He evidently liked seeing his father blottoed.

"You okay, Dad?" Jamie asked. He leaned over and put his hand on Reuben's shoulder.

"Fine, son," said Reuben in a baritone.

After twenty more minutes of tuneless singing from Reuben, Ardith pulled into their driveway, or halfway in—a stack of salvaged lumber from the torn-up porch prevented them from going further. In the pouring rain, the three of them helped Reuben out of the car. They got him upstairs and sideways across the bed, pulling off his wet shoes and shirt. It was the best she could do, and she left him there, mumbling to himself. She'd never seen him so drunk.

She managed to get the boys to brush their teeth, and into their beds, piles of their laundry she intended to do amassed in the center of their rooms. Jamie said he'd had a good time playing softball and riding Isadora's horse. Harry, after some prodding, admitted he thought Ben, Colleen's son, was "okay," which was progress for him. "Maybe you can have him over sometime," Ardith said. "Yeah, maybe," Harry told her, and she felt hopeful all over again.

She kissed them both goodnight. Passing by the bedroom on the way downstairs, she saw Reuben was still in the same position, his mumbling having turned into long, timber-felling snores. In the kitchen, she got out an orange, cut it into four equal sections and put a handful of Wheat Thins on a plate. She'd been unable to eat at the party. The hot sauce on an empty stomach had pretty much eviscerated her appetite. And her nerves…that hadn't helped. Not that Tom seemed bothered by anything himself, yukking it up at the powder-room weigh-in with the boys, smacking homeruns and crowing with his teammates. She'd grown more and more irritated, believing he thought this was some kind of workable arrangement. They'd all be one happy tribe, while she took turns trading herself off between her husband and his new buddy, some extramarital stunt work.

Upstairs, she looked at herself in the bathroom mirror while listening to Reuben snore. The dress looked as if it had wilted: the front wrinkled and soaked from the rain, her hair dripping wet on her shoulders. She stripped the dress off and stood there in her underwear, the bikini panties that she could barely get away with, her lace bra and the onyx-stone earrings. What was he doing now? Staring in the mirror, wanting her too? Men didn't stare in mirrors after parties and run back the film of the whole evening through their reflections. She unsnapped her bra, peeled off the panties, and turned on the water in the tub, a combination bath and hose shower, not Tom's commodious slipper bathtub that submerged her in lavender soap suds and offered a vista out the window of snowcapped Long's Peak. But it would do. The water came out in a narrow stream and she sat on the edge of the tub and squeezed her legs tight until she could get in.

8

The next morning she called Tom. She listened to his message and waited through the beep, until she lost her nerve and hung up quickly.

She called back, took a deep breath, and whispered into the phone—a little girl's voice that she couldn't help—"Tom, it's Ardith. Call me, please. I have to speak with you." It was the first message she'd ever left on his phone, and its illicit existence felt one step closer to mayhem.

Turning around, she saw Harry. Was he spying on her? He walked off to his room.

Reuben and Jamie had gone out to practice baseball at the park. Jamie's Little League team was going to have their first game soon. She'd barely gotten him registered in time, and tomorrow she needed to go to the town's youth baseball office and pick up his uniform. They had no food in the house, nothing that wasn't sour or spoiled. They could order pizza again, but they'd done that so much it was getting embarrassing to call. She was killing her children with poor nutrition. One more thing to feel guilty about. Just as soon as she baked the two dozen cookies she'd volunteered to bring on Monday for Jamie's fifth-grade class's upcoming May Day party. She should be looking up recipes right now. Instead she stood in the middle of the living room, gazing out the front window at Oak Street, feeling as if she were in the middle of nowhere, and waiting, she knew, to try Tom again in fifteen minutes.

The phone rang, and she hurried to answer.

"This is Ben. I was calling to see if Harry could come over."

"Oh, *hi*. Let me get him for you, Ben." She went overboard if someone called to play with Harry, trying to compensate for his indifference—as if she could!—by being the super friendly mom.

She called up for him to answer the phone. He picked it up in their bedroom, and she forced herself to hang up and not listen. Still she couldn't stop herself from sneaking halfway up the stairs and eavesdropping on Harry's responses: "Hi...uh-huh...okay...kinda...nothing much...I'm just going to hang out...maybe some other time."

Her heart sank when she heard him walk back into his room.

"Harry, come down here." She tried to keep the edge out of her voice.

He appeared at the top of the stairs, with his headphones dangling from his neck.

"What did you tell Ben?"

"I told him I couldn't do anything."

"Why's that?"

"He wants to go to a roller rink or something."

"So? Wouldn't that be fun?"

Harry shrugged. "I don't have any Rollerblades."

"You can rent them there."

"I can't skate that well."

"You can too. You wore out your old skates when we were in Chicago."

"I'd just as soon stay here." He started heading back toward his room.

"Harry," she said sharply. "What more do you want? Someone calls to ask you to hang out, a simple invitation to go skating, and you can't say yes? Ben's a nice boy. You said so yourself."

"I said he was okay."

"Come on, Harry. *Please*. He's trying to make friends with you."

"His mother probably made him call. On your request."

She glared at him. Any other kid would have jumped at the chance. Any other kid...what a stupid phrase. "I'll drive you over there. Just go and see what happens."

"Sorry to be so oblong." He walked off to his room. Oblong. God, she wanted to go up there and strangle him.

"Who would you rather have pitch to you, Noah Syndergaard or Aroldis Chapman?" Jamie asked.

"I wouldn't be able to stop trembling long enough to swing the bat either way," Reuben answered.

Jamie took off his Cubs baseball cap and rubbed the back of his head.

"I'd rather have Noah Syndergaard."

"How come?" Reuben stood up to stretch. He'd been kneeling for the last twenty minutes catching Jamie's strikes. The boy, at eleven years old, was a natural.

"Because Aroldis Chapman hit Jake Cronenworth in the ribs with a fast ball that left a crater-size bruise in his ribs. Right here." Jamie pulled up his shirt and pointed to his side. The thought of his youngest son being maimed by a 100-mile-per-hour fastball made Reuben shudder. "Noah Syndergaard's fastball is actually harder to hit even if it's slower, but he has more control."

"Sounds good to me." Reuben threw the ball back to him, slowly. "You want to try hitting a few?"

"Yeah!" said Jamie. His eyes shone like polished coins. He had a soft moon-shaped face, an overall roundness that went along with his gentle disposition. His frustration threshold— even as a toddler if he fell he'd just pick himself up without crying—was as high as Harry's was low. Harry had tried Little League when he was eleven too, back in Chicago. His first time up to bat he'd swung limply for the final strike with only one hand on the bat. He'd looked directly at Reuben after the ump called him out. Reuben's face at the very least had shown irritation, at the most—it seemed Harry's quitting the next week must have indicated as much—disgust. Unable to hide his disappointment at his son's apathetic, one-handed swing, Reuben had failed the test. Afterward, patting Harry on the back, telling him he gave it a good try, did nothing. The damage was already done, the post-game encouragement belied by the truth of that initial locked-on glance between disappointed father and rejected son. You couldn't fool Harry. Other kids let you talk them out of your rashness, forgave you your stupid self-serving expectations, based on your own failed sports dreams, when you came to your senses later and sat on the edge of the bed making up with them, telling them how much you loved and believed in them and that it was all right if you strike out every game so long as you try. Hadn't he read somewhere, a Jewish proverb, that a boy becomes a man when he has children of his own? But how shortsighted! You only became a father when your son gave you his blessing, not the other way around. And Harry, unlike lighthearted Jamie, could and would hold out forever. Or maybe this was all an elaborate rationalization to explain the Why of Harry again.

"Dad!" Reuben turned around. It was Harry racing toward him.

"Join us!" Reuben said, delighted he'd shown up. He'd tried to get him to come along earlier. It was his fondest dream to have both boys out here practicing with him.

Out of breath and holding his sides, Harry bent over and huffed, "Mom. She needs you. I've been trying to call you."

"What's wrong?" He'd silenced his phone to play with Jamie.

"I don't know. Something's happened."

She wrapped her arms around her stomach and swayed forward hitting her forehead against the filthy wood floor. *Tom Watkins is dead.* She wanted to see the body. Some possibility existed it was a mistake. She went into the bathroom and vomited. Her ribs ached from the retching. She vomited again and again, her chin on the rim of the toilet, please *please* God…she had no idea to whom or what to pray for, just to help her, he was already dead, to help her die, take her life too, make her dead, make her not know.

Reuben came home. She managed to crawl over to the tub and lean back against it. He found her like this, the smell of vomit, her eyes stinging, her head drooped back.

"Ardith…what's wrong?"

"Tom's dead," she said.

"What?"

She couldn't say it again.

"How…what happened? Ardith?"

"An accident. Coming home from Ellen and Lyle's in the rain." She didn't want him to ask any more questions. *Her lover was dead*, the truth nailed her tongue wordless.

"Let me help you," Reuben said. "I'll take you upstairs." Her body went limp when she stood up. Reuben reached her before she collapsed. Jamie and Harry watched from a distance, worry in both their eyes.

"Mom's just very upset," Reuben said. "She needs rest. Don't worry, okay?" They nodded blankly at him; they'd never seen her like this, not in control.

He carried her all the way up the stairs like a child and laid her down gently on their bed, covering her with a thin plaid blanket.

"Just a second," he said, and went into the bathroom. He returned with two wash cloths, a cool one that he draped across her forehead and a warm one that he sponged her mouth and chin with, wiping the vomit off. The cleanness, in the midst of everything dirty and dead, felt like her first gulping breath after almost drowning. She started to cry—in stifled grief and guilty misery over his ministrations. He told her, "Shh, shh, just rest. Sleep a little bit if you can. You'll feel better when you get up." He removed the cold washcloth from her forehead, dabbed at her eyes, and with his hand stroked her cheek. "I'll find out what happened."

Reuben felt absolutely numb and disbelieving. Tom was only fifty-three. They'd been drinking beer and playing softball. They'd crowded into a powder room and flexed their pathetic muscles—sad wannabes all of them, except Tom, who rippled with health.

Upstairs, he could hear Ardith quietly sobbing into her pillow. She was taking it hard. He went up and sat on the edge of the bed. When he put his hand on the back of her neck, she convulsed harder. "It's okay," Reuben said. "We're all okay here. The boys are fine."

She lifted her head up and looked at him through her tears, her face a streak of misery. "Why?" she said.

"What do you mean?"

"Why did you say that about the boys?"

"I was just…I wanted to assure you we're okay."

"I know *we're* okay." She sat up against the headboard and stared wide-eyed at him for a moment. "I was too upset to ask Wade what happened when he called here. I think I dropped the phone. Have you called him back?"

"I had to leave a message." There would be questions. He'd have to do a front-page story for the paper, maybe a special edition.

Reuben handed her a box of tissues. She blew her nose in a prolonged trumpet blast ending in a sob. "I just need to be alone for a while, okay? I'll come down later. Please."

"Sure," he said. "Can I get you anything?"

She shook her head.

"I have to tell the boys what's going on. They're concerned."

She heard something—blame?—in his voice. Her behavior was worrying the boys. Pull it together. Be the mom everyone expects.

She curled up in a ball, pulling the pillow across her face to muffle her sobs. Reuben rubbed her back. She felt the pressure of his hand but nothing else, no comfort, no relief, and no sympathy for how hard he was trying. "I just need to be alone," she told him.

"Sure. I'll be downstairs if you want anything."

Even with her back turned, she could feel him standing in the doorway watching her, wanting to help or just wanting, she didn't know. Then, mercifully, he shut the door.

Two hours later, Wade drove up in his patrol car. "A hit and run," Wade said, coming in the side door because the front and back entrances still had their porches torn up. It made Reuben sick of himself, his ridiculous procrastination. How much time did he think he had anyway? You were cut down in a second, as his father would say. "I have some questions, if you don't mind. Where's Ardith?"

"Upstairs resting," Reuben said. "She's taking it hard."

Wade nodded. "I know you all were friends with him."

"It's just such a shock. We played softball last night."

"This whole thing stinks." Wade took off his hat and put it on the coffee table. He was dressed in his uniform, his armpits sweating through his khaki shirt. "The nicest guy you'd ever hope to meet."

Ardith suddenly appeared on the steps, her hand braced against the wall.

Reuben and Wade both stood up. Harry, sitting on the bottom step, looked over his shoulder at her.

"Are you feeling better?" Reuben asked.

She nodded. "A little."

"Hope I didn't upset you too much with the phone call," Wade said. "I thought to myself afterward I should have come over here in person and told you both. It knocks the wind out of you, all right, when a fellow like him—"

"What happened?" asked Ardith.

"I'm hoping you all can help me with that."

"How so?" asked Reuben.

"I understand there was a party out at Lyle and Ellen's farm? And there was some drinking going on?"

"Yes," said Reuben. "And?"

Wade raised his hand. "Nothing wrong with that. Just trying to get the picture. Everyone got in their cars afterward and drove off?"

Reuben nodded. "As far as we know."

"What time was that about?"

"Around ten."

"Did you know Tom rode his bicycle out there?"

"What?" Ardith said. She had no idea. She'd assumed Tom drove like everybody else. "Why would he do that?" But she already knew. Tom couldn't be idle for a moment, and even driving felt inactive to him. If he wasn't walking, he was running, and if he wasn't running, he was bicycling. It was nearly obsessive. He took pride in not using his car for weeks.

"I know you're all as torn up about this as I am," Wade said.

"Where did it happen?" Reuben asked.

"Out on Route 7 where the road takes a sharp turn by those radio towers. He got knocked off his bike and into a gully there. The impact broke his neck when he got run down."

Ardith let out a sharp cry. The words were horrible, coarse, and true, unbelievably true. *Run down.* She pictured Tom's mangled body by the side of the road. *His* body *hers.* She knew it as well as her own.

"I've already talked to Ellen," Wade said. "I asked her to give me a list of everyone who was at the party that night."

"You think it was somebody from the party?" Reuben asked.

"It's a busy road, even at night, so, no, not necessarily, but we have to check out every possibility. Two boys walking along the road this morning on their way to a fishing spot found him."

Ardith sat down on the stairs and pressed her head into the wall.

"Want some lemonade, Mommy?" Jamie asked. He'd made a big pitcher of lemonade to give himself something to do.

She nodded.

Reuben patted a seat next to him on the couch, shoved some books aside to make room for her. Like a somnambulist, she came over and sat beside him. She touched her face and could feel its paleness.

"What happened after the party was over?" Wade asked.

"I don't know," Reuben said. "I didn't even see Tom leave. Did you?" he asked Ardith. She shook her head slightly. She hadn't seen Tom go. She'd looked for him, fretted over his leaving without saying goodbye but could only dwell on his absence for so long before having to attend to Reuben in all his boozy stupefaction.

"Here's the lemonade, Mommy," Jamie said, looking worried.

"Was Tom intoxicated?" Wade asked.

"He looked better than any of us from what I could tell," Reuben said. "But I certainly didn't see him pedal away drunkenly on a bike. We would have stopped him."

"Why?" Ardith asked. She had sat up straight. "Why are you blaming him?"

"I'm just trying to get a clear picture of the events that led up to Tom's death. I'm not blaming him, Ardith. He's a victim."

"You should be out there looking for this driver. This *murderer* who killed him. Have you even notified Tom's family yet?"

"We have, Ardith. We're collecting information as fast as we can. I have my best traffic investigator working on this. As we speak, he's at the scene trying to reconstruct exactly what occurred. I came here to interview you all, but also because I know this is going to get into the Denver papers, and I wanted Reuben to have the facts straight for the locals. And frankly, we need help asking for information anyone might have." He turned to Reuben. "I'll get you my report by the end of the day."

She looked at Reuben. "Don't you dare write anything about his drinking. That's all people will hear. He was on a bike, for God's sake, a flimsy bike! How helpless can you be!" She burst into tears. Reuben reached for her hand, but she pulled it away.

"Well," said Wade, "this is sure delicious lemonade, Jamie."

"Thank you," Jamie said.

Harry sat motionless, listening on the bottom step. Whereas Jamie appeared distraught and nervously busy, Reuben's eldest son looked like stone. Had he no feeling for what had happened?

Wade stood up to leave. His neck, the color of reddish bark, spilled over the collar of his tan shirt. He was sixty-three years old and not in good shape—a major heart attack he'd been lucky enough to survive. Reuben was afraid he'd have another one in his house. The whole place reeked of misery at the moment.

"He was one hell of a fine individual. This whole town's going to cry its heart out." Wade put on his tan hat. "I'm sorry if I upset you, Ardith. That wasn't my intention. I just need to know everything I can to get this case solved, and I promise you it *will* get solved." He went out the side door, jumping down with a grunt.

In the morning, Reuben drove out Route 7 to the spot where Wade said Tom had been killed. In the gulley, a massive cotton-wood stood just to the north where the road curved. Reuben stepped back onto the road to look at it and wondered if the driver approaching the bend had focused on the looming tree instead of Tom riding along the side of the road. If he was indeed on the side and not impaired in the middle. He had no reason to think otherwise. Tom never struck him as careless about his welfare. If anything, he was a one-man cheer squad for getting in shape and staying healthy, including convincing Reuben to finally accept blood pressure medicine. Standing in the high grass, the wind rustling the cottonwood's leaves, a field of alfalfa stretching out to a weathered farmhouse in the distance, you'd never know there had been a death here. It was almost too peaceful, he thought.

He went back to his van for his camera and snapped a series of shots of the tree and then the ravine.

A truck pulled up.

"Hey," said Lyle. He clomped over in his rubber farm boots caked with mud and manure. He had once told Reuben each of his five hundred cows generated fourteen gallons of feces and urine a day. The sum boggled the mind and the senses. Lyle had called earlier, and Reuben said to meet him at the accident scene. He wanted the company, and he felt Lyle needed to be here with him. Drawn and sleepless, his eyes hollowed deep in their sockets, his mouth wiped clean of the usual mordant grin, he hugged Reuben, a hard embrace imparted with a hint of desperation. They'd talked on the phone Saturday night, he and Lyle, then Ellen with Ardith. Ardith had taken it the worst, staying in bed this morning and seeming to want no more dis-cussion on the subject. Reuben felt defensive around her, as if she somehow blamed him. No, she said, she just needed to be alone, refusing to eat and speaking only to Ellen, and that just for a few minutes.

Lyle nodded at Reuben's camera. "For the paper?"

"Unfortunately." He was actually hoping he wouldn't have to use any of the—as they were called—death-scene shots and could get away with a dignified photo of Tom, if he could locate one.

"I guess it sells papers."

"I'd rather be fishing."

"And you don't even fish. How's Ardith?"

"She's struggling over it. Actually…she's mad. Mostly it's coming out on me. Not sure why I'm at fault for any of this."

"Well, Ellen isn't mad, she's just sick, physically sick about the whole thing. That's the last party we ever give."

"You can't blame yourselves."

"You'd be surprised." Lyle picked up a stone and chipped at the ground, scraping a line in the dirt toward the roots of the cottonwood. "Tom hung around afterward, you know. He was the last one to leave. We had another beer together, talked about where he used to live in California and what he missed about the place. Not the traffic of course. But around Big Sur, how wild and misty and sparsely populated it is, and then the divorce tainted it all and he just wanted out. He said he was finally approaching the happiness here that he'd once had back then. And then he got on his bike, helmet on, back straight, kickstand up. I said, 'Hey, why don't you put your bike in the back of my truck and let me drive you home?' The storm had passed, but still. He gave me a good long look, obviously assessing my condition, and laughed. And then off he went, beaming down the highway with his front bike light and a blinker on the back. He looked prepared. I didn't think a thing of it. I mean, this was Tom Watkins. Who didn't trust that guy to make good decisions?"

A flatbed truck passed, taking the curve at a high speed, its brakes squealing like train wheels when the driver tried to slow down. They watched him straighten out and head on down the road. "You see that truck just now?" Lyle said. "That's on a sunny spring morning under dry conditions. We've been trying to get a flashing warning light here for years now."

"Who's been?" Reuben asked.

"People around here."

"You and Ellen?"

"Not us per se...*look*, it doesn't matter. The point is this is a dangerous curve. You can see it just sitting here. Factor in the hour, and you've got an accident waiting to happen."

"It sounds like you're trying to let this driver off the hook."

"I'm not. I'd like him to go to jail for the rest of his—or her—life. I'm just saying... I don't know what I'm saying. I'm looking for a reason where there is none. The guy's gone."

"I think I'll bring out some flowers," Reuben said. He wanted to change the subject. He felt as if Lyle were a step behind him, flipping back and forth from rationalizing to self-flagellation. Reuben had already tortured himself about it yesterday. Despite knowing he was blameless, he felt steeped in remorse. "He probably wouldn't want a cross or anything."

"Not from a couple of Jew boys, anyway."

"You want to drive into town with me and pick up some flowers?"

"I've got a friend in back who needs looking after at the vet hospital." Lyle nodded at the sloe-eyed cow watching through the metal slats of the trailer. "She's got some lesions on her udder that look mighty angry. Here—" Lyle handed Reuben a twenty-dollar bill, thought better of it and stuffed a wad of cash into his hand. "Buy the store out. Cover the damn ground out here with them."

9

The school held a memorial service for Dr. Tom. He'd been a doctor for many of the students, and the principal had wanted to do something to mark his passing. Harry, with his fellow eighth graders, had to stand outside in the drizzling rain on a damp day. He hadn't brought a jacket with him to school, and he watched the skin on his arms get wet and slick, watched the drops bead up and run in rivulets down between the channels of the tendons on the backs of his hands and stream off his fingernails into the dirt. They were planting a tree for Dr. Tom, a Colorado blue spruce that their eighth-grade English teacher Mrs. Neidecker said would grow straight and tall and provide shade and protection from the sun. In the winter its branches would be covered with white boughs of snow and in the spring verdant with new growth. Told it wasn't required to pray, they could, alternatively, partake of a moment of silence. Dr. Tom had done so much for the town and had meant so much to the families here.

Harry lowered his head and thought about lunch.

Afterward they went back to their classrooms and did DOL, Daily Oral Language. Harry was correcting a sentence that read, *Less mistakes happen when you look over your work.* He was supposed to fix the error. English was not his subject, but he knew that *Less* was not the right word. He knew that it should be *Fewer* because it was one of those usage things his father, a copyeditor, was always drilling into him. He crossed out the word *Less* but instead of putting in *Fewer* wrote *Dumb.* Then he looked at the sentence and changed it to *Dumb mistakes happen to dumb stupid people.* He sketched a large man with a stethoscope around his neck. In a bubble above his head, he wrote in very precise lettering, *Fewer people make for less trouble.* He handed it in like that, and his teacher called his parents. His father had to come in, because his mother was home in bed. She hardly left the bedroom, except to use the bathroom or make a pot of tea downstairs. Mrs. Neidecker said she found his response disturbing, but she guessed Harry had reacted this way because he was upset about what had happened to Dr. Tom. Was that it? Was being offensive a way to express his fear? His father looked at him, equally interested in an explanation. His father added, though nobody had asked, that Harry's mother was taking this very hard. He wouldn't be at all surprised if Harry was having a similar reaction, albeit an inappropriate way of expressing it.

Albeit. Harry sometimes wondered if his father used such words only around him. A special vocabulary to make him feel like an idiot.

"So, is that it?" Mrs. Neidecker asked. She was older than most of the teachers, plump, with a double chin and too much perfume. She'd always been nice to him. "Sometimes it's hard to explain why we act and feel as we do," she told Harry. "Do you think your doctor suddenly dying scared you?"

Harry said it certainly did, and he could see his teacher and his father breathe with relief.

"Let's find more constructive ways to express our feelings next time," his teacher said. She turned to his father. "We have counselors available this week to help the kids cope with what happened. Maybe Harry could—"

And here Harry stopped listening, because he was already at home, watching his mother. Lost in her misery, wearing her bathrobe in the middle of the afternoon, she barely noticed him; they passed by each other in the hallway like ghosts and moved on.

10

On Monday, four days after he died, Ardith drove to Tom's house. She parked at the club and walked up the hill to his front door. He'd given her a spare key, just in case she wanted to get away from the stress of her own home and come over when he wasn't there. Too afraid to get caught, she'd never taken advantage of the offer. Now she didn't care—or even knew that she should care. She turned the key in the lock and went inside.

She stood in the entryway, its gray marble floor and winding staircase that led up to the bedrooms. Everything was untouched and clean just as it had been two weeks ago when she was last here.

The shades were drawn, probably as he'd left them before going to the party. A few of the plants had wilted slightly, though the house stayed cool. She tried to walk and not touch anything, as much not to disturb things as to pretend she wasn't here so as not to feel his presence or hers with him. She went toward his study and stood in the doorway for a moment, looking in, half expecting to see him in his leather chair where he often sat in his boxer shorts and worked at his computer—while Ardith lay on the couch across from him reading, a T-shirt barely covering her hips. She could see herself stretched out, enjoying his admiring gaze, her legs extended for him. He would come over and touch her neck, tuck a lock of hair behind her ear, kiss her throat and the damp hollow between her breasts, caress the curve of her thighs, then leave to do something: make more coffee; put music on; check his messages on a landline that he let the answering machine take while they were together. Then he'd come back, and they'd talk or make love again, and time would both stop and fly by until she had to leave.

She knew his cell phone was with Wade and that by now he'd no doubt scanned all their exchanged calls and listened to her panicky message wondering where Tom was. She figured it was only a matter of time before Wade contacted her. The prevailing numbness of her existence—her dreams were full of immobility—dulled her to that likelihood.

Upstairs, she wandered into the master bedroom and sat on the edge of the made-up bed with the duvet cover of midnight blue half-moons she'd picked out for him. Photos of him and his two daughters as teenagers when the family used to come out to Colorado for ski trips. Marian, with long blonde hair and a pretty smile, was the younger daughter. She had recently applied to law school at the university in Boulder to be closer to him. According to Reuben, who heard it from Wade, it was Marian who had come alone from California to make the funeral arrangements. Hearing about her arrival had riveted Ardith, one of the few times she'd actually engaged with Reuben in the last days, a situation that sickened her for its obvious selective attention and yet she could not stop. She soon returned to her stupor after he'd given her this news, until she'd gotten up the courage to come here today.

In the photograph, his older daughter, the one Tom had said never forgave him for the divorce, had ski goggles on and a knit hat pulled low over her forehead and looked incognito. He loved them dearly despite their anger at him, he'd said, and hoped Ardith would meet them one day. And she had wondered what had that meant? Did he imagine them—her and Tom—married and meeting his girls? Had he pictured their relationship as an open fact? Would he have taken her to Vail, teaching Ardith to ski as he'd promised? Was he going to ask her to leave Reuben? Such questions, ones she wouldn't allow herself to consider before, were a ceaseless drone now. They exercised a selfish grip on her that hadn't been there when he was alive.

She opened the top drawer of the bureau and gathered up the change of underwear she kept here. He'd given her the whole drawer to use, and more if she wanted, but she took up very little space. This one small drawer neat and orderly with a change of underwear and a pair of wool socks to pad around in represented all she had pretended was real about playing house here. If anybody had already been here to look through his drawers, they would have assumed Tom had a lover. She stuck the items in her purse; they'd be one less clue as to their relationship, though could discovery be far away? She wondered if she should go to Wade and confess. And what would Wade say? He'd want to know how she fit into Tom's life and what that meant for his death. She wanted to know the same thing herself.

In the bathroom she found her shampoo and the bar of Aveeno soap she used to keep her skin from drying out in Colorado, stuffing those in her bag too. Checking around one more time to see that no trace of her was left, she started downstairs. The front doorknob turned.

She froze, standing with her knee bent on the stairs. Again, the doorknob was rattled, and she backed up the stairs and into the bedroom, waiting beside the mahogany armoire, her heart hammering, her mouth pasty. She could hear someone walking along the gravel bed on the side of the house. A minute passed, then two. She heard a car start up outside and edged the blind to the side to see.

A patrol car—one of Wade's officers driving. Wade must have sent him up here to check on the house. She let out a breath but instead of air, a loose cry broke from her. She went back to the bedroom, slipped one of his dress shirts off its hanger and slumped down against the wall holding the shirt in her hands. She buried her face in the clean smell—in the threads left of him.

11

Luisa found her father out in the shed when it was time for dinner. Her mother had sent her there to look for him, and when she opened the creaky metal door, barely attached at its hinges, he was sitting in the middle of the dirt floor staring at the parts of a lawn mower engine.

He sometimes made extra money repairing their neighbors' appliances—from small toasters to washing machines. It was off the books, he said, and Luisa shouldn't say anything about it. Just as she shouldn't say anything about her mother cleaning the houses Luisa sometimes helped with. They paid their fair share of taxes other ways. From his work at the dairy farm and their property and sales taxes and lottery tickets.

"Lottery tickets?" Luisa said. Her father spent too much on lottery tickets according to their mother.

"Sure, mija."

"That's gambling."

"Trails, parks, pools, recreation? Are these not where the money goes?"

"Lotteries are goods. You're buying a product. That's not the same as paying taxes."

"I pay taxes so you can go to school and I can drive you on a road there. They're products, too, right?"

"They're for the common good. Your lottery tickets? I don't think so."

"Don't argue with Dad," Marcos, her brother, eight years old, chimed in. Marcos, much to her exasperation, was in his daddy phase. Their father could do no wrong. Luisa had a vague memory being like that as a young child, but since then she challenged him about everything, as he was always reminding her. He brought it out in her and even baited her, though she always took the bait, such as the preposterous argument about the lottery. He called her Miss Very Serious *Jefe*. "Lighten up," her father would tell her. "Boys don't like girls who have no sense of humor." Nothing drove her more crazy than when he told her what boys expected of her.

Now he just sat in the middle of the dirt floor of the shed and stared at the disassembled lawn mower. She wondered how long he had been out here. On weekends he worked at the dairy until ten p.m. But during the week, he always made sure to have dinner as a family. There had been a memorial service for a local doctor who most of the whites in town saw. Her parents had always taken her to a free clinic in Greeley, because before her father worked at the dairy farm, they hadn't been able to afford anywhere else. Now he had benefits and his bosses were really good to him, but they still went to the clinic to save money. It was always crowded, and the drive took a half hour, and she wished she could just see someone locally. Her mother said they still had a big deductible even with insurance and the clinic was best for them. But Luisa suspected another reason was because her mother was afraid any local doctor wouldn't speak Spanish and she'd be embarrassed to talk in front of him. It didn't matter anyway now. At least for this doctor, who seemed to take care of everybody in the school but her. And she had more important things to think about. Five kids from her school had just disappeared. When she asked the principal about them—were they okay, where had they gone?—he avoided the question, saying there were some legal matters in process. What did that mean? Had they committed a crime? Been rounded up by ICE? "I think you need to return to class now, Luisa. We all appreciate your concern." Who was "we"? Not the vanished kids certainly. A total brushoff. No one would tell her anything. So now she was going to do something about it. She wanted to have a protest at school, a sit-in like what was happening around the country in the big cities with Occupy Ice. Of the four friends she texted—Carla, Anthony, Sofia, and Diego—only Carla said she "might be interested." What was wrong with these people? They could all be gone tomorrow themselves. Who knew whether somebody was really legal or not? One boy she knew, Bryan, didn't realize he was undocumented until he applied for a driver's license. His parents had never told him. Now he spent all his time worrying ICE was going to show up at his house and take the whole family away. He was furious at his parents, but they claimed they'd done it for his own good, so he wouldn't say anything to the wrong people. Like the DMV?

Meanwhile, her father had said he knew there were workers at the dairy who had fake papers. No one questioned them, especially Ellen who handled all the documentation for the farm and had said she'd find sanctuary for any of her workers before she let ICE take them. "Am I illegal?" Luisa had asked her father when she was ten. Some boys at school had teased her about not being an American. "No, *mija*," he had laughed, brushing off her concern. "Can you show me?" "Show you?" "Something that says I won't be taken away." He'd opened a locked file cabinet drawer and lifted out a folder. All the information was there: her name, her father's, her mother's maiden name, and Weld County as the place of birth. Relief washed over her. She'd been having nightmares, afraid that her parents would confirm her worst fears.

"Mom says to come in for dinner."

"Yes," he said, but didn't move. Just kept staring at the drop cloth with the oily machine parts in front of him. His face was sweaty, and it was too hot for him to be out here in the shed. He'd taken off his glasses and set them beside his hip. She didn't know how he could work since he couldn't see anything without them.

"Are you okay?"

"Yes," he said. "Tell your mother to come out here. I need to talk to her."

Luisa stared at him a moment. A shudder went through her, as if he'd just told her something terrible. She didn't know why. Something chilling in his voice, like a slug had come out of his mouth. "Okay, Papa," she said softly. She backed out the door, not taking her eyes off him.

12

"We got two more cancellations today," Rosa reported. "Another is putting you on probation. She says that if you dare print obscenities again, she'll cancel her subscription, which she's had for the last thirty-two years. Also, First Western Bank wrote that 'such a column contains words that many of our customers deem offensive.'"

"Send them an apology letter."

"You're not going to fire her, are you?"

"Of course not. It's absolutely silly, the whole controversy. I can't believe anybody would get upset about this. Have they no idea what's important…" Reuben couldn't finish. Who was he trying to convince? Rosa stood in front of him with her arms folded.

"It's really only been five or so cancellations," Rosa said, trying to console him, he knew, like one of her grandchildren. "You got three times that when you forgot to send Jolie to cover the last Welton High football game."

"They were 0 for 8."

"Exactly why you were accused of being disloyal."

"Okay, I learned my lesson. Thank you." He walked back to his office.

The job had too many loose ends, like a frayed piece of rope that a dog had relentlessly chewed. He could hardly keep track anymore. Why had he approved Jolie's column about "Kids Say the Darnedest Things"—with its mention of "hap-PENIS" and "*Screw something*, Daddy!" She'd passed it across his desk, and he'd automatically sent it on without so much as a glance. And who would have thought the town would be up in arms about it anyway. *You encourage pedophiles with these kinds of "innocent" remarks from children* an anonymous letter had read. The *Sentinel* had a long-standing policy of allowing letters to be published anonymously, so long as the paper could verify the submitter, a policy encouraged by the past publisher, the esteemed Brady Westcott, who believed it afforded readers the opportunity to really speak their minds. Never mind that was what free speech was supposed to be for in the first place. Meanwhile another reader vociferated, *There's a limit to what's decent and proper in print and this "cute" column definitely is out of bounds.* His favorite had been short and to the point: *This is a family newspaper that gets layed around the house.* Spelling notwithstanding, it was cause for celebration! His newspaper was getting laid!

He'd found himself in the awkward position of consoling Jolie. Here he had a perfect excuse to fire her, but instead he sat beside her one morning after her scandalous column broke and readers turned on the beloved author of the cherished Little Maddy columns.

"I'll tender my resignation, Mr. Rosenfeld," Jolie offered.

There, there, said Reuben. No, he hadn't actually used those words. He'd just said, "That's unnecessary." But he *might* as well have pity-patted her back and said, *There there* as she sat alongside him on the pilled orange sofa in the coffee nook and wept, while the mounted bison head above ("gifted" to Reuben and left behind by Brady Westcott), with its obsidian eyes, pitched horns, and flaring damp nostrils, bore down on them with a look of defiance.

"I've brought dishonor upon the *Sentinel*," Jolie said. And then confessed, as Reuben already knew, that Clement, the lab, had in fact *not* pulled Little Maddy from the window. She'd manufactured the entire incident *desperate to give my readers the excitement they've come to expect from my column.* She felt "sick to sin" about it ever since. Of course, at a real newspaper this would be grounds for immediate dismissal, but his wasn't a real newspaper—what kind of a newspaper printed anonymous letters! Nor did anyone ever read the paper for hard news, he rationalized, and such a dismissal would entail printing a retraction, which he couldn't bring himself to do because...because he would lose the little credibility the paper had left and get *more angry emails,* and he was "sick to sin" of getting them. So, he told Jolie that he'd suspected as much, that she must never fictionalize her stories, that it was a grievous violation of journalistic ethics, but that he was giving her another chance and that, damn it, he stood by her column regardless of whether a small if vocal minority was overreacting about some perfectly printable words. Plenty of people had written in support of her (though none had), and if he didn't have their emails that he could forward (she asked immediately to see them) this was only because people always took the time to complain but never to praise.

Jolie looked at him after he'd offered this baffling display of double speak and said, "Wow," and then: "Thank you, Mr. Rosenfeld, for standing right behind me." And Reuben went *There there* again, or communicated as much, and Jolie gave him a parting look of such admiring indebtedness that he blushed, mulling over with guilty arousal her choice of words *standing right behind me.*

He jogged during his lunch hour on the outskirts of town. Pastures and wheat fields he went by one week had green signs announcing "planning review" or "rezoning request" the next—a sure indication of imminent bulldozing. New developments went up so quickly it was as if they were plopped down like villages on a toy train platform. A Walmart Supercenter was scheduled to open on recently annexed land near the interstate. The downtown merchants in Welton, what was left of them, had protested to the town board, saying it would pull all their remaining business away. Welton needed to revitalize the downtown, not eviscerate it.

Reuben had written an editorial supporting the merchants and calling on the planning and zoning board to deny the permit for the 180,000 square-foot store, claiming it would squash competition, pay unlivable wages, pass over local suppliers in favor of cheap foreign goods, and create a traffic nightmare on inadequate roads. The editorial generated a mixed response.

Appreciative phone calls from Old Town merchants followed, along with new ad buys and a plan to feature coupons in the *Sentinel* during Merchant Discount Days, all lucrative boons of his stance.

From the other side he'd gotten pushback, championing all the jobs and tax revenue Walmart would bring to Welton. "And I might add," one reader noted, "that you're here only two years yourself and you want to close the door behind you, just another NIMBY!"

What was wrong with closing the door behind you? Didn't everything have its capacity? Elevators, restaurants, public bathrooms, concert halls—the number of wildebeests on the Serengeti? Why not towns? At some point, you had to say, Enough is enough, we're sold out, no more seats, no room, try the Midwest—they're having a fire sale on space. Find another lifeboat. It was a fact of life, yes, a selfish one, but so was all of survival. It was true: a town couldn't stand still, economically or geographically; it had to grow. Frozen development led to stagnation, unemployment, underfunded services, poor schools, torn-up streets, and even domestic violence. Desolation. A picturesque ghost town. Growth was inevitable and necessary, *yes yes yes*, but it just didn't make sense when he ran past an empty field with peregrine falcons soaring overhead that only yesterday had given him solace, refreshed his spirit, and now was being eradicated of prairie dogs, marked off with housing stakes, its wildflowers drowned in wet cement—the lovely earth being bulldozed under itself, smothered by its own.

In the afternoon, he drove to Tom's house. They'd almost moved here themselves, an irony that made him wonder if that slight change would have nudged Tom's fate off course for whatever reason. Somewhere in the universe's chain of events this would have proved just enough of a shift to throw off his death.

Tom's house was all closed up, the blinds drawn. The latest issue of the *Sentinel* lay in the driveway. Jack Watkins, Tom's brother, who lived in Colorado Springs and was the estate's executor, had called to thank Reuben for the tribute issue he'd published about Tom. Reuben had worked furiously on the article to get it done, writing about how much Tom had contributed to the community in so short a time. He'd given Jack the names of a few local realtors. The house had been willed to his daughters, who both had agreed to sell it.

A rock wall curved around the bottom of a terraced front yard. A stand of lithesome young poplars formed a boundary to the south and would one day offer a windbreak and shade for the house. The grass looked far greener than Reuben's. He had to move a sprinkler around their lawn, and all it seemed to do was quench the dandelions. Maybe it wasn't so bad after all to be one of these guys who went gunning for the incorrigible brown spot or two, neutralizing crabgrass, fertilizing the lawn into an emerald outdoor carpet. You could stand on your porch and watch the irrigation stations turn on just like the fountains at Caesar's Palace, a suburban lawn salute to greener days.

Or not.

He picked up this week's copy of the *Sentinel*. They'd been doing a free promotion in the area to get more subscribers. People had called him after the tribute issue and thanked him for speaking for the town; goodwill wasn't hard to earn here when he had his heart in it. He went up to the front door and glanced through the decorative glass. A rectangle of golden light, bright as a newly painted yellow toy chest, shined on the polished maple floors. The whole place looked airy and clean, orderly and peaceful, a show home of exacting taste.

He snapped a picture of the home's front. He needed to keep the story alive, not only to sell papers, cynical as that may be, but to make sure the case got solved. Wade was giving him very little. There was an important piece of debris from the crash site, but after two weeks Wade said no body shops had reported any vehicle damage not already documented on accident reports. "It's not going to be easy, Reuben. I know everybody is clamoring for progress. But we have a tough case. I'm hoping we'll get a break the usual way."

"And what would that be?" Reuben asked.

"Somebody's going to talk. And then that person will tell somebody else and then eventually it will filter down to us. But that may take some time. People are going to have to be patient. The reward will help."

Tom's brother, Jack, had put up a $25,000 reward leading to an arrest. It was why Reuben was up here at Tom's house at all. He needed to take a suitable picture of the house, because part of its sale, in accordance with Tom's daughters' wishes, was going for that reward money. Twenty-five thousand dollars was some very serious reward money, but Jack wanted Reuben, and the paper's readers when the notice came out, to know how steadfast they were about finding Tom's killer.

To get a better angle, he stepped onto a moss-colored rock in a landscaped patch of day lilies. He sized the image and clicked. And just as he did, a thought crossed his mind, one crazy enough that it just might make Ardith happy again.

13

No sympathy calls. No condolences. No public display of grief. She was an invisible widow. She wasn't part of the private ceremony for the family after his body was cremated and his ashes shipped back to Northern California to be scattered in the sea, a long-standing wish. At the memorial service for locals, she hid her anguish, unable to show he was anything more to her than the same great guy he was to everybody. Survival was all she could manage. Reuben picked up the slack once school let out for the boys, doing the shopping, taking Jamie to baseball practice, dropping Harry off at Ben's house—they'd become friends after all. Ben, who wouldn't take no for an answer and wasn't scared off by Harry's junior misanthropy. And Colleen had gone out of her way to take the boys canoeing, hiking, and swimming, finding time as a single mom and a midwife to do what Ardith could only wish.

Reuben was the one jogging and exercising now. He'd even joined a health club along the new shopping strip at the edge of Welton. He rose at six in the morning to ride his bike to the club, work out in the weight room, cross-train on the stair climbers and rowing machines, take a shower and be back home at eight o'clock to fix breakfast for the kids, and then run—jog—out the door to work. In the process, he'd lost eight pounds over the month since Tom had died. She, meanwhile, had gained weight, eating Girl Scout cookies and devouring avocado sandwiches while doing little more than cleaning the lint filter in the dryer on those days when Reuben didn't do the laundry for her too. He attributed his newfound energy to Tom's dying, "a huge wakeup call" that he knew would keep ringing in his ears forever. Some days she couldn't even find the strength to shrug her shoulders.

He suggested they go away on a vacation. It would be good for her, help her with her doldrums, as he put it. His aunt Mildred, still going strong, would come and stay with the kids. They could go to Mexico. Flights were cheaper this time of year. She tried to picture being alone with him for that long, the increasing pressure to confess, nothing to distract them from one another in their tiny ship cabin (a cruise being another possibility).

"I'll think about it," she said. They were in bed. She reached down to see if he was still hard so they could stop this excruciating conversation. He was. They had sex more now than when Tom had been alive. Lovemaking served the dual purpose of obliterating memory as well as working off her guilt. She felt jumpy and numb, all at the same time. Meanwhile, he couldn't believe his good fortune: *Whew. That was incredible.* He gazed at her with awe and gratitude (no doubt what contributed to his rushing around for her like a slave) and trust. She raked his back with her nails and threw bad Ardith farther out the window with each heated session. When it was over, she wanted it again, because she wouldn't have to hear anything but his heart racing next to her, his purring devotion that could deny the past and her own existence.

He started to move his head down and she stopped him, as she did every time he tried now. It was too sacred. Fucking was blunt and discarding—pieces of her fell away with dispassion. Licking was delicate punishment. She underwent spasms of pelvic longing so intense she wanted to crush her skull when she remembered Tom's supple mouth on her.

"I don't feel like that," she told Reuben, pulling him up like a confused puppy. "Let's just fuck."

She tried to get up in the morning to help him with the kids but trailed uselessly after him in her bathrobe. He bustled around, more cheerful than ever, whistling old show tunes as he washed the dishes by hand (the dishwasher was broken, again), hugging her goodbye for a long time, patting the boys on the head before he jogged off to work, full of surging endorphins and positive attitudes in light—or the shadow—of Tom's untimely passing. Today, Saturday, Jamie was going with a friend to a water park in Denver, and Colleen, once again, was taking Harry on an outing with Ben, this time to a skate park.

The phone rang. "Don't bother answering it," Ardith called too late.

Harry handed her the phone. "It's Ben's mom," he said, and Ardith felt a twinge of relief that maybe she was canceling or had run into some snag. The more Colleen did for the boys, the worse her sense of indebtedness became, until she feared answering the phone with another generous invite to take Harry somewhere.

"You have a minute?" Colleen asked.

"Yes."

"Are you somewhere you can talk?"

"Just a second." She went upstairs. Harry had glanced up at her when she stepped over him as he was watching TV. Was this about Harry?

"Okay," she said, once she closed the door of her bedroom. "Is everything okay?"

"It's about your exam."

"What is it?" It had been almost two years since her last wellness exam in Chicago, and she'd gone in to have a checkup after she met Colleen.

"I don't know whether this will be good news or not."

"What, for heaven's sake?"

"You're pregnant."

"Pregnant?"

"It crossed my mind during the exam because you mentioned you felt tired and your breasts were tender. I didn't want to say anything at the time without checking. But I tested your urine and, well, sure enough."

Ardith held the phone in her hand, unable to speak.

"So, are we happy?"

"I…"

"Or maybe not," said Colleen. "I guess it's an oops then."

Colleen waited through a long silence, then said, "Are you okay, Ardith?"

"Yes, yes. I just need time to take it in."

"Of course."

She sat in a daze after she got off the phone, her hand instinctively rubbing her belly. It was Tom's baby. Reuben had gotten a vasectomy eleven years ago, right after Jamie was born.

She was eight weeks along. Yesterday, Colleen had given her another exam, and through counting back to her last period, they'd determined she'd gotten pregnant in early April. Colleen had offered clinical information, including reassurance that the Xanax, which Ardith immediately stopped taking, had not harmed the baby. The fetus was just over a half inch long at this stage. The spot bleeding Ardith had been having—and what she had mistaken for a light period— didn't indicate any complications. It was not unheard of to have a little bleeding during the initial stages of pregnancy. The big question was did she want the child?

"I haven't told Reuben yet." She meant she hadn't told him everything—anything!

"Does Reuben want another child?"

"I don't know."

"Do you?"

Her face flushed. They'd been sitting in Colleen's waiting room, after hours. Colleen had squeezed her in at the end of the day. Ardith looked at the photographs on the bulletin board of all the babies Colleen had delivered, the stacking toys and blocks in the wicker basket, the pile of parenting magazines, the discount coupons on the counter for Pampers and baby wipes. She'd never dreamed of going through this again.

"I know it can be a hard decision when you have an established family," Colleen said. "We don't have to talk about it now, especially since you haven't told Reuben yet."

"I can't," Ardith said.

"Can't what?"

"I can't have an abortion."

"That's understandable. I've seen very few married couples in your position who can."

"It's Tom's baby. Tom Watkins."

Colleen stared at her. "I don't understand."

"You do," said Ardith, squeezing Colleen's hands. "*You do.*"

They sat in one of the most uncomfortable silences of her life. She wasn't sure she would have ever spoken again if Colleen hadn't taken her hands and moved closer beside her on the couch. "How can you be sure it's Tom's?"

"Reuben is…"

"What?"

"He had a vasectomy after Jamie was born."

"I had no idea anything was going on. How do you keep a secret like this in a small town?"

"We were jogging and tennis partners. I thought everybody would suspect."

"Maybe they did. But nobody ever said anything to me. You just thought of Tom as this big-hearted guy who cared for everybody."

"He did."

"Some of us more than others."

"You think I'm awful."

"I'm just thinking aloud here, getting used to all the implications of this news…"

"It sounds so terrible the way you're saying it."

"No one else knows?"

"I haven't told anybody."

"Ardith, you have to consider the circumstances. This is no ordinary situation. It never is but this—"

"I *know.* All I can think about are what clothes I'll buy, how I have to get a whole new layette because we gave away all our baby stuff before we moved. Then I stop myself and realize I'm having this fantasy about a true event. It's Tom's baby, he's dead, and I can't tell Reuben because I'm afraid he'll want me to get an abortion."

"It's your choice either way. But if you do decide to abort, it can be a private matter."

Ardith felt a sudden dreadful freedom at knowing she was right. She could get it done secretly and be home the same evening. Tom had wanted to make love without a condom, just once, so they'd done it right before her period—or so she'd thought. It was reckless, but she had wanted to please him.

What was the point now of beating herself up?

"You don't like that idea," Colleen said.

"I can't. It's the easy way out."

"And what's wrong with that?"

Ardith just stared at her, unable to answer.

"Oh, I see it all over your face—what he meant to you."

"If Reuben kicks me out, can I stay with you for a while until I get my footing? I could get a job and pay rent and share all costs."

"We're getting *way* ahead of ourselves here," said Colleen.

"I know I am, but I have to think of the worst possible thing in order to have a plan so I can do this."

"Well, in a word, yes, use me as your plan. But…"

"But what?"

"Will you please tell Reuben soon if you decide to keep the baby? It will be better than if he finds out for himself."

That afternoon Wade came over. Ardith watched him again try to walk up to the front door and then, realizing his error, go around to the side of the house. The door to nowhere. They had installed a locked deadbolt so Jamie, who sometimes sleepwalked, wouldn't try to open it and fall to his death three feet below. That door represented everything about her impossible life right now. You could open it and look out but go no farther, forever stuck on its teasing threshold.

She knew why Wade was here. She'd been expecting him for a while. Still, she carried on with the charade and said, "Reuben isn't here."

"I know. Is there somewhere private we can talk?"

The boys were gone so she led him into the detritus of the living room, Jamie's sports equipment everywhere, the usual

piles of laundry unwashed or in need of folding, runner magazines, Reuben's latest obsession, an especially galling reminder
of Tom. Her husband had usurped the activity that had bound
her to Tom. "Sorry about the mess," Ardith said. She wasn't
really sorry, she just knew that was what you were supposed
to say. Mothering and wifering, or whatever it was, along with
housekeeping…that ship had sailed, and she had dropped to
some chronic level of intractable indifference. The only thing
she wanted to think about was this life inside her, clutch it fast
and draw every last breath of hers to it.

"I just have a few questions," Wade said.

She liked Wade. He had made them feel welcome when they
first came here, telling Reuben, unlike many others who had the
opposite view, that the town needed some fresh perspective.
She just wished he'd lose a few pounds, because the thought
of Wade dying, or anyone else, could make her burst into tears.

"It's been challenging, Ardith. I won't hedge about that.
We've had some help from the state bringing in their experts,
and I'm glad for it. But we don't know much more than we did
the day Tom died. There are thousands of hit-and-run deaths
in this country every year, the majority of those are pedestrians
or bicyclists like Tom. I'm sorry to say a lot of those cases don't
get solved." Wade stopped. "Could I trouble you for some
water? You don't happen to have any of that lemonade Jamie
made me last time?"

"I don't—"

"I'm kidding you. Water will be best."

When she came back, he had stood up and was examining a
photo on the mantel of the four of them on a trip they'd taken
to Hawaii when both boys were small. She looked so much
younger and lighter of spirit then, and indeed it had been one
of their best vacations, Harry old enough to snorkel and impossible to get out of the water. He wanted to live underwater,
he told them, with his usual seriousness.

Wade gulped down half his glass. "I've tried to keep you out
of this. I had hoped we'd have this all wrapped up by now. We'd

catch a break from a witness that saw something. A surveillance camera would spot the vehicle. Or the perpetrator would walk in to clear his conscience. It does happen. Not this time. I'll tell you what my hunch says. This was random. Somebody was driving along a dark county road, turned into a curve too fast, and clipped a bicycle. Tom wasn't run down on purpose. Still, there's always a possibility it was intentional."

A leaden heaviness set in. She'd escaped it temporarily with the news of the baby, but now, listening to Wade detail this scenario of Tom's death, it had returned. There was something new, however, some small protest rising at having to hear this, as if she wanted to protect her baby's ears. "Why would anyone want to hurt Tom?"

"I'm not saying they would. In fact, I think it's unlikely. You drove home that night yourself."

"Yes."

"And Reuben and the boys were with you in the car?"

"That's right."

"And you and Tom had been seeing each other?"

"We loved each other." She'd blurted it out helplessly. She'd never even said the words to herself. Of all people, Wade. Her eyes welled up.

Wade pushed past her confession; it had meant so much to her and so little, she could see, to him. "Did he ever mention anyone who had a gripe with him? Say, a disgruntled patient or an angry business associate. Anybody at all who may have carried a grudge and intentionally been on the road that night looking for him."

"Not that I know of."

"And Reuben? Did he know?"

"No. And he still doesn't."

"Reuben never showed any suspicions about you seeing someone?"

"No one knew. Reuben least of all."

"What do you mean by that?"

"I don't know. He's just a trusting person." She was

embarrassed at how it sounded, as though she could easily take advantage of Reuben.

"You haven't seen him acting any different lately then?"

She suddenly realized what Wade was angling at. It was so preposterous that she started laughing. "Are you asking if Reuben had a motive enough to involve someone in killing Tom? That's ridiculous."

Wade stood up with what appeared a mild rebuke. "This all stays between us, Ardith. I have no interest in hurting anyone. But if you think of anything at all that could help this investigation, no matter how insignificant it might seem, please contact me. I suspect you had more of Tom's ear than anybody else around here."

After he left, she sat cross-legged on the floor in front of the piles of laundry. The visit left her feeling as unclean as the unwashed bundles. She sorted the whites and colors, grabbed some stain remover and went about the business of treating the ample spots on everybody's clothes, including hers. If she kept Tom's baby, she'd soon have more to wash than ever and wondered where she'd ever get the motivation to do so. Things would have to change. The boys would need to take more responsibility. And Reuben… The thought stopped her cold. As if Reuben just fit neatly into the whole scheme.

She stood up and walked around the piles of laundry like burial mounds. Upstairs she curled up on the bed and fell into a deep sleep. Voices below soon awakened her. The boys were home and Reuben would be shortly. Dread came over her about the excuses she'd have to make about why dinner again was pizza. "Mom?" Jamie called from downstairs.

"Coming," she called back. She remade the bed and then went into the bathroom and washed her face. She pulled back her hair and stared at herself in the mirror, her face pinker. With Jamie and Harry her face had broken out. Maybe it would just glow this time.

"We're so hungry!" Harry yelled up. She rubbed some moisturizer on her chapped hands and then went down to face her children.

14

"Where are we going?" Harry asked.

"You'll see," said Reuben.

Jamie leaned over from the back seat. "Is this surprise for all of us?"

They'd just come from Jamie's baseball game. Jamie had gone three for three, his last hit a triple. More remarkable had been his fielding. Playing short stop, he dove for catches. And even ones he couldn't grab he was still able to knock down. A parent of a teammate had shouted out, "Give that kid the golden-glove award!" and Reuben had squeezed Ardith's hand, wanting her to enjoy the moment. She nodded, the kind of overly enthusiastic nodding someone does when you catch them not paying attention. As for Harry, he had wanted to go shopping with Ben to get new hiking boots for Ben's trip to Alaska (he would be visiting his father), but Reuben had in-sisted he come with them to Jamie's game, so they could all be together afterward.

"Yes," said Reuben, "it's a surprise for all of us." While he drove, Ardith looked at him with a mixture of curiosity and, he thought, worry. She had on a baggy gray sweatshirt that he knew she was wearing to hide her weight. She'd gone from starving herself to stress eating. The snug little running outfits were gone, her cheeks puffy, her eyelids heavy all day. "But mostly it's for Mom." Reuben patted her knee. She'd been more withdrawn than ever. He saw dread in her eyes when she got up in the morning. She'd been distracted over…he didn't know. She wouldn't tell him. "What?" seemed to be her favorite word. She was completely aphasiac at times, maybe from the Xanax, which she claimed to have given up. She cried frequently, but when he asked, pleaded, gently coaxed her to tell him why, she just said, "Stop trying to fix me!" He was so damned confused he'd thought of driving her to a therapist without telling her.

"Is it bigger than a shoebox?" Jamie asked.

Harry hit him in the back of the head. "Fool. Of course, it is. We have to drive to it."

"Stop that, Harry," said Reuben, knowing Harry was picking on Jamie because of the praise heaped on him after his game.

"How long's it going to take?" Harry asked.

"You'll see." He purposely made a detour, circling around behind the water filtration plant and then past Welton's old sugar-beet mill. The equivalent of blindfolding and turning them around three times.

Ardith said, "I'm feeling a little nauseous."

"You want to stop?"

She shook her head. "I'll be okay if it's not much longer."

"Are you coming down with something?"

"I might be," said Ardith. "Are we going to be there soon?"

"Very soon. Everyone, close your eyes for the next couple of minutes. No peeking, Harry."

He made a left turn into the back of Eagle Crest and then a right on Dahlia and another quick right onto Laceleaf, a pretty name, he thought, for their new street.

He turned into the driveway of the three-car garage. "We're here. What do you think?"

"What are we doing here?" Harry asked.

"This is our new home."

Reuben looked at Ardith. Her mouth gaped open. Blood rushed to her face.

"What—what are…"

"I bought it. It's a long story, but after some back and forth, Tom's brother, Jack, and I worked out an agreement. Tom's daughters wanted a quick sale, and I took advantage of the opportunity."

"You…you bought Tom's—"

"I put two thousand down in earnest money. We can close in five weeks, if all goes well. I made everything conditional on selling our house, which won't be hard if we price it right in this up market. The payments will be more than what we make on our mortgage now, but we won't have the infinite repair bills we've been looking at. Actually, we'll come out better in the long run. The house appraises at thirty thousand more than what we're paying for it. Tom's brother said he'd keep clear of listing it until we decided for sure. I just surrendered finally, Ardith. We're never going to make our place livable. It's what you wanted, isn't it?"

"You're crazy," said Harry.

He'd been expecting surprise, even astonishment, but not outright mutiny. Everybody hated the present house, even Jamie, who dreaded all its creaky noises. Whipping its poor, run-down existence had become family sport.

"What do you think, Ardith?" he tried again.

She was weeping.

"A dead man lived there," said Harry.

Reuben drove home. Only Jamie had been willing to get out of the car and even look at the house. Earlier, he'd gotten a key from Tom's brother, Jack, who had driven up from Colorado Springs. They'd even discussed an option to buy all the furnishings. Reuben had tied a bouquet of silver balloons to the front door that spelled out WELCOME HOME. To show off the marble entryway, he'd left all the lights shining inside.

Nobody wanted to come inside, not even Jamie, who said, "I think I'll stay here with Mom." (Who was crying her head off.) What had he done?

Now Harry was trying to explain it to him. "It's creepy to think about living there."

"Why? He was a wonderful man. We're not talking about an ax murderer who left behind bloodstains in his workshop."

Ardith whimpered.

"I mean nobody died in the house."

"The Navajos burn down their hogans after people die in them," Harry said.

"We're not Navajos!"

His son snorted. "You still don't understand."

"I do understand. I understand I made a decision, and everybody, out of some superstitious fear of the place being haunted or jinxed, hates the idea. We have a chance to live in a new home at a terrific bargain, with working plumbing, lights that don't blink when you turn on a hairdryer, and usable garages, and you want to stay in our old, and I mean falling-apart, house." He was mainly talking to Ardith who had withdrawn into the corner of the car, no longer crying but mashed into the whippet-sized space between the seat and the window, motionless and folded in on herself like a wounded bird. What did she want? What the hell did she want? He couldn't even make her happy by buying her a new house!

"You just don't buy a house as a surprise," Harry said. "It's common sense."

"You're telling me about common sense?"

"You don't get it."

"*Please*. I'd be proud to live in a house that was owned by—"

"A dead man," Harry said.

"A doctor and a friend and as fine a man as you could hope to be."

He heard Jamie wheeze in the crashing silence that followed.

"I have your inhaler," Ardith said in a faint voice.

Jamie took two quick puffs.

"What happens to the money you put down," Harry asked, "if none of us wants to live there?"

"Just be quiet for a moment," Reuben said. He was listening to Jamie's labored breathing. "You okay, buddy?"

"Take another puff," Ardith told him. She turned to Reuben. "Go to the hospital."

"You doing okay, Jamie?" Reuben asked again.

"I'm…I'm having trouble." He took a long, ragged breath that sounded like broken glass being swallowed.

"We need to take him to the hospital," Ardith insisted.

Ardith sat down in the waiting room while Reuben haggled with a receptionist about insurance. They had a huge deductible. She wasn't sure how much, she just knew it paled compared to the group plan they'd had through the *Tribune* in Chicago. Easier to worry about these things, high deductibles and meager benefits, than to think of having a baby and living in Tom's house.

The house had loomed like a giant gravestone while they sat in the driveway and listened to Reuben's campaigning. Only Jamie's asthma attack had snapped her out of her shock.

Harry had gone downstairs to the cafeteria to get a snack. Their doctor, who barely looked thirty, came into the waiting room with the test results. "We have some ragweed still out and the summer grass and weed pollen. My guess, though, is that Jamie's asthma is exercise induced. Has he had attacks after playing hard before?"

He'd come home a couple times wheezing after flag football practice in Chicago. "I think he has once or twice," Ardith said.

"He needs to use a preventive inhaler before any active exercising, and then use another one to treat the problem if he has any tightness. A lot of this with kids Jamie's age is trial and error with different medications. Don't worry, we'll find the right combination for him."

"Should he stop playing?" Reuben asked.

"Not at all. That's a lot worse for a kid than any attacks he might have that we can control. He's fallen asleep back there, so we're just going to let him rest for a while and observe him for an hour. I'll check him again before he goes home. Why don't you go into the lounge down the hall? It's more comfortable than waiting out here. We have some tea and coffee set up. I'll have the nurse come out soon and talk to you about the sample medications I'm sending home."

Harry came back up on the elevator with a Snicker's bar in his hand.

"That's what you got to eat?" Ardith asked, after the doctor left.

"I wasn't hungry for anything else." He sat down in his cargo pants and baggy flannel shirt, even though it was June.

"We're going to the lounge," Reuben said. "Want to come?"

"I'll stay here." He stared up at the TV that was showing a chef making meatballs on the Food Network.

They walked down the hall together. Two leather couches at right angles took up half the small room. A rocker sat next to an end table that had a decorative box of Kleenex, as did the glass coffee table. In the corner, on another taller glass table with polished metal edging, coffee and tea waited to be made. The look was one of sterile chic. Ardith guessed this was where doctors consoled people about their loved ones, giving them the devastating news.

Reuben took her hand. "I wanted to surprise you. Instead it turns out to be the stupidest thing I've ever done."

"It wasn't stupid," she told him. She couldn't seem to unclench her hands. He took them in his own and gently opened her fingers.

"You're so unhappy lately. I've been wracking my brain trying to think how I can help. I thought it would free you." She was shaking now. "Are you cold?"

Ardith shook her head.

"Are you worried about Jamie? This ER doc seems to know what he's talking about. We'll get him on the right combination of medication and find someone regular for him to see, even if we have to drive to Denver."

"I know."

"Is it the house? I'm sure I can get the earnest money back. It was just a handshake with Jack."

"I'm going to have Tom's baby."

Later Reuben would think: Why didn't I react? Why didn't I do more than *sit* there? Why didn't I get up and punch the wall, kick the coffee table, walk out? Why did I simply say, like the stupid schlemiel I am, "Are you sure?"

15

His father had ulcers. All the Jewish men of his generation did. Aggravation and ulcers. Today doctors knew that ulcers came from an infection, not stress. You didn't hear mothers yelling at their children, *You'd better behave or you'll give your father an ulcer!* You only heard about exercise and meditation. It was good for you. It kept you calm. It made you see things clearer. No more bleeding ulcers from taking it all inside. Now everybody was a runner and a meditator—good, clean, healthy living.

Once when Reuben was a boy and his older brother, Harry, was still alive, they'd both been at the butcher shop when a former employee who had swept up and made deliveries for their father came in drunk. He claimed he'd been cheated all those years he worked for Reuben's father. He wanted what was owed him. Reuben's father stood behind the counter, with its white basin scale and lighted dial, and the display case filled with unskinned chickens, sides of ribs, scalloped mounds of sirloin, links of sausage, and slabs of cow tongue, and stared down his ex-employee. The man wasn't going to challenge Reuben's father. Why would you challenge a butcher with eighteen knives and cleavers in front of him?

"Go home. You're drunk, Jerry," their father said quietly.

"My money."

"Go home."

"Pay me what I got coming to me and then we call it even."

"Jerry, you haven't worked for me for two years. Look at yourself. You're a drunk now." Reuben's father turned his back to chop a chicken.

"Rot in hell, you goddamn Christ killer!"

And then Jerry stormed out. Reuben was in the back with Harry, who was doing his homework. Reuben, six years old, was reading a picture book about volcanos given to him by his aunt Mildred and uncle Simon. Their father came back, his shoulders heavy, the smell of chicken fat on his hands, his gray wool tie knotted tightly under his blood-spattered white apron. He took Harry and Reuben aside; Harry was already in third grade and working on fractions; their mother, pregnant with Stan, was out shopping for Hanukkah presents; everybody was fine, happy. It was five years before Harry would die, and their father said to his boys, "That's why you never want to marry a goy. One day, you'll be going about your business and she'll turn on you and call you a dirty Jew. Just like that. Just like that."

Ardith read: *Week 11: The baby has all its major internal organs though they still have not fully developed. The eyes and ears are growing, and the face is taking on a human shape. The baby is just under two and a half inches and weighs fourteen grams. A D&C (dilation and curettage) can be performed safely in a doctor's office or clinic by a qualified physician ... possible side effects may be dizziness, nausea, hemorrhaging...*

"What do you want? Tell me what you want from me?" It was their fifth argument in as many nights. Reuben wanted her to decide whether she was going to have the baby. He said he wouldn't leave her either way. "But you won't love the child," she said. "You won't love the baby as if it were ours."

She could move in with Colleen. Every week her stomach would stick out more. People would talk. A small town. A scarlet *A* for Ardith.

Her due date, Colleen had told her, was December 20.

The day in April when she and Tom had conceived, Jamie had brought home a note that a mountain lion had been sighted in a field not far from the elementary school. Parents were cautioned to make sure their children walked to school in groups. At a school assembly, the students received instructions what to do if the mountain lion came near while they were at recess. Someone should shout to the teacher, who would then use her whistle to blow a single long blast, at which point all the children were to crowd together in a pack behind her, and then, slowly and calmly—absolutely no running!—walk back inside.

Reuben had interviewed Ardith for a quote. He'd needed to run something in the *Sentinel* about the mountain lion. She'd just gotten home from Tom's house, flush with pleasure and (she was unaware) new life. Feeling talkative and thrumming with desire, a magpie intoxicated by an interview, she went on and on about how when they'd moved from Chicago she never imagined protecting her children from dangers like this back there—just the urban variety—and she hoped they wouldn't shoot the poor creature—she'd read somewhere that each mountain lion needed twenty-five square miles of territory— but she worried for her children, too, who walked to school every day past open fields not far from where the lion had been sighted. Reuben had to stop her; he could only use a single sentence for "Heard on the Street," along with three or four other people's responses.

That afternoon, carrying a heavy-duty, truncheon-like flash- light, she met Jamie halfway home from school. He wondered what she was doing there.

A day later, but after her comment had already been pub- lished and posted on the *Sentinel's* web and Facebook pages, it was discovered that the mountain lion had actually been a golden retriever. Ardith was mortified, her reaction bespeaking such alarmed and vociferous worry, surely that of a city person overreacting. For days afterward, Harry would sneak up to her. "How 'bout them golden retrievers?" and curl his hands into claws. Though she'd glare at him and push him aside, she'd also—she didn't know why at the time—turn her belly protec- tively away.

"Raise our baby? What do you mean our baby? What do I have to do with it?" He was ranting. He'd go on like this and Ardith would let him. What choice did she have, what right to stop him? "*His* baby, you mean. How can I think of it any other way? How do you think I'll feel when people say, 'You must be so proud!' or 'He looks just like...somebody!' Did you even think to use any protection? Or were you *trying* to get knocked up?"

His most bitter lashing had been the story about his father warning his boys never to marry a gentile. It was the only time she'd felt justified and furious enough to fight back: "How could you say that? I've never said a word, done anything in the world to give you reason to think that. That's the most awful thing you've ever said to me, and I'm sure your father would be ashamed to have you using him to make such an ugly point. Your father loved me, and regardless of what I've done, he would never have said such a thing, and you know that, Reuben, you know that!"

Symbolically, he told her, he'd meant it symbolically, not literally. She'd humiliated and betrayed him.

"Then call me a cheat or slut or whatever you want to call me but don't make horrible accusations about me being some anti-Semite, because such words will kill us for sure."

"I'll go with you," Colleen said. She'd asked Ardith to come into her private office for a talk. "I know the doctor who does the procedure. She's very warm and sensitive and will make you feel comfortable."

"I don't know what to do," Ardith said. "The damage has already been done between Reuben and me."

"I'm obligated to make a case for the other side. You understand that, right?"

"What *is* the other side exactly, besides getting an abortion?"

"Your marriage. Your kids. Your present family. It will make things a whole lot easier to get through this period. It's your prerogative to have it done safely and quickly, and to keep it to yourself. You wouldn't be the first woman to do so."

Colleen waited.

"I know what you're saying is true."

"But I'm putting my nose where it doesn't belong?"

"No, I appreciate, more than you can imagine, your advice. All your help."

"Is it a moral issue for you?"

Ardith shook her head.

"What is it then?" Colleen asked.

She squeezed back tears. "It would be killing Tom a second time. That's how it would feel."

"It was different, that's all, just different. I don't know, just different. No, I'm not trying to spare your feelings. It was just different, that's all I can say. It felt different. Not better or worse. It's all connected for me. I can't separate it out like a man. I'm not just telling you that. I'm not afraid of hurting you. You'll just have to believe me. Different, just different."

"I don't know how to describe it. You keep wanting me to say it was better. I won't."

"At his house. Once a week. On Wednesdays. Just the usual way. The usual. I'm *trying* to answer your questions. I told you I would tell you everything. I *am* being honest. You're making me say things so you can hate me more!"

"Yes, yes, yes, okay, *yes*, I came. Is that what you want to hear?"

"I'm not putting pressure on you one way or another, but the kids are going to start asking questions soon. You tell them what you want. If they ask me? I'm not going to lie. I'll tell them your mother became pregnant by Tom Watkins before he died. Because it's the truth. I don't see how it's best for them to pretend I'm the father. No, I don't. Since when has a secret ever been good for a family? I'd rather not have our family's history based on a lie. No, I'm not doing it to punish you. Humiliate you either. That's right, it's a terrible burden for us all to bear. But since when are principles always convenient? I'm sorry, I don't see what else there is to do but stick to the truth. Well, that's your opinion. But what you call being rigid I call being clean. I didn't. I didn't say anything about not being Jewish. You're getting hysterical. Being clean doesn't mean not being Jewish. No, it doesn't imply that you're dirty. I am not trying to take my foot out my mouth. Clean is not a condemning word. Neither is purity. How are you supposed to have a marriage that's impure? If that's what you think, fine. Maybe I do sound to you like the Taliban, but I'm just trying to have some integrity. No, I'm not trying to put pressure on you one way or another…"

1) Sex
2) The house
3) Money worries
4) Tom's penis
5) My procrastination
6) My self-absorption
7) Your having slept with only two other men before we got married
8) The professor (see above) who dropped you in college
9) Marrying young
10) No present job
11) Life in a new place
12) Being an only child
14) Your father dying when you were in high school
15) Obsession with father figures
16) Taking care of your invalid mother
17) Sexual fantasies of other men
18) Sexual fantasies of doctors
19) Sexual fantasies of being a rich doctor's wife
21) Boredom
22) Harry
23) All males in the family
24) Independence
25) Feelings of being smothered
26) Low self-esteem
27) Lack of respect for me (and yourself)
28) Career disappointments
29) Fears of aging
30) Love

Reuben handed her the list. She was supposed to circle all

the reasons why she'd cheated on him. She could pick as many as she wanted; feel free to add others on the back. If she could circle, then rank them in order of most to least influential this would be helpful. Don't circle a reason just because it might be less personal and hurtful, e.g. "money worries." She might want to elaborate on some choices. "Independence," for example. That could mean physical independence (escaping the house) or financial (a wish to have her own income) or psychological (feeling controlled by another person) or social (did she feel trapped by always being seen as a wife and mother?). She should take her time with the answers. Oh! If she assessed two or three items to be of equal weight, she could put an asterisk next to them to indicate "not significantly more important than the above." He handed her a number 2 pencil, in case she wanted to erase, and then shut the bedroom door behind him.

She wrote THIS IS FUCKING CRAZY across the list. Then she looked down and saw number 30, circled it, and tore the paper into furious tiny pieces.

An entire day passed without his interrogating her. After Harry and Jamie were asleep, Reuben asked if she wanted to sit outside with him in the backyard. He got himself a beer and inquired about her most recent visit to Colleen. Ardith told him everything was fine. He took a sip of his beer. People in town knew she was pregnant but assumed it was their child. A patient in Colleen's office had overheard Ardith mention the baby. No, he didn't know who it was that had overheard. What did it matter? Ironically, people couldn't be happier for him. Nothing like a baby to celebrate a family's joy. Unfortunately, it wasn't his baby and never would be, because he had no intention of adopting a child conceived out of an affair. He told Ardith that he would stay until the baby came, so as not to cause either of them the embarrassment that would surely follow his walking out on her. Then he'd find a place in Welton or maybe move to another town close by, Fort Collins, Greeley, maybe even Denver, barring a difficult commute. They'd figure out what to do about the boys. Living with him might be the best option while Ardith raised the baby. She shot him a warning look but otherwise remained limp, listening without any real strength to fight him back. He didn't care that he was being harsh. She'd made her decision to keep the baby, he said, and he'd made his not to be the father. He didn't care either that he'd originally told her he would stay if she decided to have the baby. That was weeks ago. He'd changed his mind.

"By the way," he said. "I'm wondering what you're going to name the baby."

"Why?"

"Have you thought about the baby's name?"

"I don't have a name picked out yet. Why?" Was he going to suggest something?

"I mean the last name. You won't use Rosenfeld, will you?"

She was speechless.

"The kid's going to look very…he's going to look different from Harry and Jamie. I'm not comfortable with him being named Rosenfeld." He paused. "If that's what you were thinking."

"I… First of all… Listen…" she sputtered, unable to get anything more out.

"You're angry," Reuben observed.

"You're acting insane!"

"Is it such an unreasonable request? I mean, when you think about it? He's not going to be a Rosenfeld. It's a family name—"

"Stop saying he! How do you know what he's—*it's!*—going to be? How the hell—" She waved him off, fled to the bedroom, and buried her face in the pillow, coughing and sobbing and dreading more of these punishing talks with him.

It was his family name, Rosenfeld. That's all he wanted to say. It belonged to his kids. Not somebody else's. Forget the stuff about how the child would look. He'd only meant to persuade her that a kid should look like his name and given the father, this child was definitely not going to be a Rosenfeld.

Upstairs he could hear her crying into her pillow. She turned around sharply when she heard him. "What do you want?" she said.

"I'm sorry. I meant to say something else."

"Nothing! Please don't say anything!"

"I meant about the name business. I see your point."

"Just leave." She had turned away from him.

"So, listen," he said. "You use whatever name you want."

No response. She just wanted him to go. She'd stopped crying but was playing dead, as if that might make him leave.

Lyle, Ellen, and their daughter Isadora came over for a Fourth of July barbecue.

Ellen made a fuss over her being pregnant, giving her repeated hugs. As far as Ardith could tell Ellen knew nothing more. Colleen was to be trusted in her professional capacity. "I had no idea you two were even considering another child!"

"I guess we didn't either," Ardith said.

She could hear Lyle making guy remarks to Reuben ("Way to go, you sly old dog!"), and Reuben's monosyllabic responses. He'd been businesslike, cooking salmon and bratwurst on the grill, dodging the present conversation with Ellen. No one knew he'd had a vasectomy.

They hadn't all been together since Tom's death. Ardith felt the subject lingering over them like a low fog, the four of them trying to poke their heads up through it with talk of other things, the kids' summer activities, Isadora's music camp, Jamie's baseball despite his asthma, Harry's fast friendship with Colleen's son, Ben. And about the dairy farm—a developer had approached them with a tempting offer to sell. Soon they would be ringed by a massive development of thirty-five-acre ranchettes. They might as well sell while the money was there, the developer had suggested. "The noose is tightening," Lyle said, but they had no intention of selling. They'd keep farming until they went belly up. Tom's name did come up when Lyle asked if there was any news about the case.

"Not that I know," Reuben mumbled. Ardith said she hadn't heard any either. The lack of progress left her frustrated and angry and wanting closure, unable to put Tom to rest in her mind.

Isadora, her brown hair cut short, her overalls on, asked to touch Ardith's stomach.

"Certainly," said Ardith, "but it's much too early to feel anything."

"I know," Isadora said, and put her hand on Ardith's barely protruding stomach. "Neat," she said. She smiled up broadly in a way that suddenly made Ardith wish for a girl to share such moments.

Reuben got blankets, bug spray, and some light jackets for the kids and they all went off to watch the fireworks downtown over Lake Finnegan, everybody except for Harry and her. Ardith made an excuse that she wasn't feeling well enough to go to the lake—the pregnancy. She could catch the fireworks fine from here. Harry didn't want to go either. Unless he was with Ben, he didn't like to go anywhere. They spent much of their time up in Harry's room talking and listening to music, not getting outside as much as Ardith would have liked, but in all honesty she was so caught up in her own problems she was just glad he had a regular friend like Ben, who was a nice boy.

Harry was whittling a stick. Peach fuzz lay on his upper lip and his brow jutted out in a more adult tilt—an awning shading serious thoughts. His voice was cracking too, his feet and hands enlarging. When they stood next to each other, he wasn't that much shorter than she, nor was he always standing on his tiptoes as he used to do to make himself look bigger. Braces: she needed to take him to an orthodontist. She'd completely forgotten about the summer fitting he was supposed to have.

The fireworks started in the distance, successive booms, and then streaks of copper, red, and blue. Harry swatted at a mosquito on his arm. She took a deep breath. "How much do you know?" She tried to control the quavering in her voice to let him know it was okay to tell her.

"About what?"

"About the baby."

"It's not Dad's," he said matter of factly.

Ardith looked down at her lap. But Harry wasn't one to feel sorry for anyone and make this easy. She prodded him again. "How long have you known?"

"You don't want to know."

"I do, Harry. Tell me."

He ran his hand across his hair that had grown out and looked at her with his deep green eyes. She held his gaze. "I saw you."

"You saw me? What do you mean?"

"The day I lost my tooth."

Ardith's breath caught; for some time, she'd felt there was unfinished business about that tooth, but she'd pushed it out of her mind as the tooth regenerated its roots and turned healthy again. She tried not to let her voice betray her fears at hearing— it may have been the only opening she was going to get with Harry. "What happened?"

"Ricky's brother picked us up that morning—"

"Picked who up?"

"Me and Ricky."

"At the house?"

"Wherever, yes, it doesn't matter." A thousand questions erupted in her head but she didn't want to scare him off with her alarm or he would never tell her. "I'm sorry, honey, go on."

"We saw you jogging with him and your car up by his house."

She had parked on the street that day, figuring it would go unnoticed. Tom's new boat was in the garage. They'd done a run around the soccer fields and a south trail and then back up to his house. "Is that all?"

Harry slapped the spatula against the picnic table that she'd covered with a red-and-white-striped paper tablecloth. He did it again. Ardith put her fingers gently on his wrist to stop him. "What else, Harry?"

"You *really* don't want to know."

"Yes, I do," though she didn't but felt he had to tell her, for his sake as much as hers. "I want to hear everything."

"He kissed you. At his door."

"Is that all?"

"Is that *all?*"

"I mean, did you leave after that." She had a flash of Tom lifting her by her bottom onto the kitchen counter, then pulling up her powder-blue linen sweater. The blinds were open. She remembered having a moment of worry but had pushed it away because it excited him seeing her topless in the broad daylight sitting on his kitchen counter, her chest flushed with urgency.

"Yeah," Harry said. "We left."

Tom had kissed her neck and breasts, and she'd raised her arms so he could slip her sweater off all the way. Now, despite his denials, she pictured it all through Harry's eyes, without sound, without her low moans, without her cries of encouragement and want, without her nipples springing erect under the knowing tip of his tongue. Harry could have seen everything, a peep show of his mother with her legs wrapped around a man's waist and her cries of pleasure so deep and insulating she didn't even feel the hanging sauce pan bang against the back of her neck as Tom thrust into her. The bruise there the next day had surprised and shivered through her.

She felt sick. She excused herself and went to throw up in the bathroom and then splashed water on her face and washed her hands.

When she came out, the fireworks had begun. Harry sat at the picnic table, watching the rockets whistle up and explode. She stood a moment next to him, looking up as a rocket erupted and rained down glittering purple tendrils. "I'm so sorry, Harry. I had no idea."

He shrugged and kept staring up into space.

She wanted to keep him talking. "What happened after that?"

"We went down to the junkyard. Vic wanted to smash the owner's fence because the guy had ripped him off on some kind of bum car part. I was just sitting in the truck, unable to think straight and having to listen to Vic"—she heard the catch in his voice— "say things about you."

She watched Harry dig at the paper tablecloth with his nails. *I should have him cut his fingernails*, she thought because it was unthinkable to imagine how Vic talked about her in the truck in front of Harry. "Why did you"—she made her voice as neutral as possible— "go with him in the first place?"

"He said he would pay us to do him this favor. 'Yo, do me a solid, bro,' he told me when he and Ricky showed up. Ricky knew I was home because, well, because Ricky was always home, and I had told him the day before I was thinking about cutting school too because I was so bored."

"You did it for the money?"

Harry looked away. "I don't know why. Vic made it sound like something cool and, you know, courageous, like we were the good guys helping him even the score. We got down to the junkyard, and he handed Ricky and me a couple of baseball bats. We followed him across the mud flats. It was really deep mud because the junkyard was in the lowlands and there was a spring runoff. Vic started wailing on this wood fence with a crowbar and screaming at us to do the same thing with our bats. I took a few weak hits, scared that he'd hit *me* if I didn't. Then I beat it with all my might. I was angry." He looked at the ground. Ardith nodded. Anger, of course, it was good he was angry. She pictured his savage swings at the fence, at her and Tom. "Then I must have gotten too close to Vic because I got wacked in the mouth with the crowbar when he brought it back for windup behind his head. A dog started barking and Vic took off back to the truck. I don't even know if he realized what he'd done. But Ricky saw and stayed with me for a few minutes before he got scared and tore off with his brother. I crouched down and scooped up a bunch of cold mud and pushed it against my mouth to stop the bleeding, I don't know why, just instinct, and it worked, making it hurt less. The tooth had fallen between my bottom lip and gum and that must have been why it stayed good. At least the dentist said so. You're supposed to tuck it in your cheek." He put a hand up to his mouth where the tooth had been knocked out. "I started walking home after that. Then Wade drove by. Somebody might have driven by and seen me and then called him. I don't know. He said I should call you, but I told him to call Dad instead. I knew where you were."

Ardith saw Tom push himself into her—not a sound, thought, or care in her head. Just all silk and butter.

"When Dad came out, he just looked at me like I was shit, complete shit. He didn't even try to believe me when I said it wasn't my fault. I meant everything, not just hitting the fence, but *everything*, what I'd seen, but I couldn't tell him that. I just wanted him to take my word for it and know how I felt. I couldn't even begin to explain. He couldn't have picked a worst moment to be himself. I hated him."

"You mean you hated me."

Harry shook his head and she thought he was going to cry, something she wished he'd do so she could too. But he didn't. "Things would have been different if he'd been nicer to me. He'd picked the wrong moment not to get it."

"How could he understand, Harry? He didn't know what you'd seen. He didn't even know Vic had been there! Why didn't you tell him and Wade that at least?"

"Because I was scared shitless of getting my brains beat out! Vic has cut guys with knives. He owns guns. This junkyard owner just gave him a bad alternator or something and wouldn't refund his money—what do you expect from a junkyard? You should have seen Vic go nuts on his fence. Even Ricky says he's a psycho." He shook his head in disgust. "And what was I supposed to do? Leave out the part about you? You don't think Vic would have made something of that if I'd opened my mouth about him?"

"Where is he now?"

"He left town. That's the only reason I'm telling you this, because I know he's not here to hurt me—or us."

Us.

"Harry?"

"What?"

"Do you hate me now?"

"I don't hate anybody," he said, which wasn't what she'd asked exactly. There was a long baleful moment, like the pause before a twenty-one-gun salute, as the finale was readied. Nothing filled the silence.

Ardith said, "You don't have to pretend to be understanding. I don't even understand what I did."

"So are you going to get a divorce?"

"Tell me what you're feeling about all this. Maybe I'm not the right person to tell. But you're going to need somebody to talk with, don't you think?"

"What's going to happen after the divorce? To us, I mean. Jamie and me."

"Harry, we're so far from that stage—"

With the explosion of the finale, she saw the flash of the exploding rockets on his face, all his ferocious resentment and mistrust. "Are you?" he said. He turned away to watch the contrails of shimmering gold and electric blue explode from a starburst.

16

"What's wrong with him?" Luisa asked her mother, twice now about her father, only to get the same answer, *Déjalo en paz.* But that was the problem. Leaving him alone only made him more alone. He went to his job and when he came home he sometimes didn't even take a shower, just went straight out to the shed. She wasn't even sure what he did out there anymore. Her mother would go and talk to him and then come back shaking her head. But nobody would tell her what was going on! Only that Luisa shouldn't ask so many questions. It was nosey.

Nosey? If you couldn't ask your own family questions, who could you ask? It was like trying to talk to the principal of her school about what happened to the five Muñoz children. All she got was silence. Concentrate on your schoolwork! her mother said. Well, school was out. Hadn't she noticed? And anyway, she was trying to find a job. Not a lot of work around for a fourteen-year-old, and she didn't want to go with her mother to clean houses. Or she might have if one of her clients hadn't said to her mother that Luisa looked a little young to be scrubbing toilets. After that her mother got scared she'd be reported to…somebody. It didn't matter because there was always a government agency out there waiting to catch and prosecute you. And lately her mother had gotten even more paranoid about that possibility, throwing a fit when Luisa said she was going to participate in an Occupy Ice protest in Greeley. "No!" her mother had screamed at her. *Nunca jamás.*

Even her brother was getting freaked out. Marcos was used to their father making jokes and wrestling with him and getting into squirt gun battles. "Papa, chase me," he would say. And run screaming around the obstacle course of furniture while their father pretended to maul him like a bear. Luisa had found it beneath her to participate—she was in high school next year, after all—but now she would have given anything to see the two of them acting like a couple of *bobos*.

"He could be seeing someone," Carla suggested. "Men get very mysterious when they're cheating on their wives, very secretive." They were sitting on a picnic bench in the park eating ice cream cones from Ollie's Soda Fountain. Carla was looking for work too. The Metrolux theaters out near I-25 hired kids their age for the refreshment counter. Luisa wanted something closer to home—who would drive her all the way out to the interstate anyway? Her father took the truck to work and her mother had the old Subaru. And anyway, she had to babysit Marcos all summer unless he went to a camp like their father had promised him. But nobody had said anything about that lately and their mother had told him to stop asking his father.

"My father would never do that," said Luisa. Carla's theories for why boys and men behaved the way they did all had to do with sex. She sometimes worried, given Carla's preoccupations, that her best friend was going to get knocked up before she turned fifteen. She could only imagine what her own mother and father would do to her if she became pregnant. Not that she had even kissed anyone except for Diego, whose mouth was like a runaway hamster trying to get to her breasts before she pushed him away. She wasn't even sure she liked boys, or not the ones who always hooted at her and cupped their hands under their chests. Unfortunately, her breasts had become almost as large as her mother's, and when her mother took her bra shopping, she'd covered her ears not wanting to know her size. She worried if they kept growing she wouldn't even see her feet. She hated that boys only stared at her chest when they talked to her, not to mention the creepy looks from men. When she complained to Carla, who had the opposite problem and hated being flat chested—she had shoplifted a pushup bra to give herself cleavage—she just laughed. "I wish." And then gave Luisa some trashy article ("Studies prove it!") about ten moves you can do that drive guys crazy. Number one was leaning forward while arching your back. Sick.

"Oh, wow," Carla said. "Look who it is. The weirdo."

Luisa lowered her sunglasses. There he was, backlit so he looked more like a ribbon of light than a skinny boy sitting on his bike playing with his phone.

"Hey, white boy!" Carla shouted. He looked over at them, took out one of his earbuds. "Come over here."

Luisa elbowed her and hissed, "Why'd you do that?"

He got off his bike and walked over to them. "Did you say something?"

Luisa had never heard him talk before. His voice wasn't what she expected, softer and more relaxed, like he was ready to tell somebody a bedtime story, not gruff to match what she'd imagined to be his personality.

"You got any smoke?" Carla asked. She was always trying to bum weed off people.

"I do not."

Carla laughed. "You 'do not'?"

"Correct."

"Well, can you get some for us poor girls?"

"Your ice cream is melting," he said to Luisa. The first time he'd looked at her. She licked the side of the cone, embarrassed.

"What's your name?" Carla asked.

"I could tell you, but I'd have to—"

"Kill me?"

"Worse than that."

"Ooo, I'm scared."

"Better we stay anonymous then."

"You are weird."

"That seems to be the consensus."

"I like your eyes though."

Carla kept flipping her hair back over her shoulder, shamelessly flirting.

"I'd better go," he said.

"Hey, no-name boy! If you bring us some weed, we'll let you hang with us."

"Here's the thing: I don't have any money. I don't smoke.

And I don't hang out a lot." He turned to Luisa. "You're dripping again."

She didn't know why, but she stuck the cone out to him. His long lashes blinked twice, and he wrapped his hand around hers, pulling the cone, and her hand, toward his mouth and then licking the drops off.

"Gross," said Carla.

His hand, still wrapped around Luisa's, which was wrapped around the cone, finally let go. He took out a small notepad from his back pocket and a charcoal stick. He flipped open the pad, scribbled on it while they watched him in silence, then tore out the page and handed it to Luisa. It was a sketch of a dripping ice cream cone, detailed down to the waffle squares. "How did you—"

"Bye," he said. He got on his bike and rode away.

She showed the sketch to Carla.

"I told you," said Carla. "*Super* weird."

17

The summer turned hot. Harry hung out with Ben at the pool or at the new library where there were some ramps to skateboard. He watched his mother starting to show and sometimes imagined horrible things that could happen to the baby, including how little its head would look in a guillotine basket.

"That's neat your mom's having another baby," Ben told him, and Harry smiled, clenched his teeth, swallowed past the moment. "I would have liked a brother or sister, but my mom can't have any more children. She takes second best delivering them." Ben's father lived in Alaska and Ben was going to visit him soon. He'd remarried. "I don't really get along that well with him and his new wife. She's too strict."

Ben's mother took them lots of places during the summer, Water World and Elitch's in Denver, up the Poudre Canyon camping and rafting, to Wyoming for Frontier Days, to skate parks and movies and a concert at Red Rocks. Harry's dad was hard-core into exercising when he wasn't at the paper, and his mother was throwing up a lot from the pregnancy and resting in bed. She'd said she'd feel better once the first trimester passed and then they'd do things, but even so they didn't do much together. She bought baby clothes and fixed up part of her bedroom into a nursery and sat on the porch a lot and rocked by herself. He saw she was miserable at times and he saw too that his father was miserable in his own way and he wanted sometimes to say a nice word, but everything came out snapped off, as if he had crocodile jaws with four thousand pounds of pressure behind them, even when he said pass me the salt on those rare nights they all ate dinner together. The bright spot was hanging out with Ben and his mom, and he thought he would ask if he could go live with them and then the baby could have his room when it was born. But every time he was about to ask, he'd see his mother's face draped in sadness like a black hood, and he'd shrink away from her, shrink far away.

He wished he could be as ignorant as Jamie, who couldn't wait until the baby came. Once, on the verge of telling him, just to shake things up, just to make Jamie a little crazy too, Harry said, "Do you know where this baby came from?"

And Jamie, annoyed at the suggestion of his naivete, answered, "Duh, I guess it wasn't a stork."

"That's right," Harry said. "Most def. Not a stork," but left it at that.

18

Reuben added a mile to his now daily six-mile run and woke up half an hour earlier so he could be at the fitness club right when the sleepy-eyed receptionist opened the doors. Okay, so he was a fanatic. He'd stopped eating meat altogether. Every morning, on an empty stomach, he forced down a bitter-tasting Chinese mushroom tea purported to do everything from slow baldness to eliminate wrinkles to open cholesterol-clogged veins. And he'd driven to Boulder to have a colonic. If he could evacuate all the toxins from his system, as the naturopath in Boulder had tried to do by giving him a coffee enema to flush out his liver and a bowel tonic to get the sludge out of his colon, so much the better for keeping his head on straight. Ardith had been right. He did want to purify himself of her, only it wasn't motivated by believing she was dirty. He wanted to flush away years of desire. "Picture your colon returning to the healthy pink color of a newborn," the naturopath had practically chanted as he ran for the bathroom. Of all things to say—a newborn. He could only picture the black, tarry residue of his own bitterness clinging to his inflamed lower intestine.

Ardith wanted the baby. That was that. She was into her fourth month come the first of August next week and clearly showing now. He wasn't talking. When people congratulated him, he simply nodded. If you kept your mouth shut long enough, folks shaped your silence like clay into a familiar form. His reticence they interpreted as anxiety, the aging papa of two older boys, starting over. Chummy looks from men, approving ones from women. The president of First Western Bank had sent him a congratulatory fruit basket. Even Dennis Olberg, the postmaster, had stopped stiffening in displeasure when he passed Reuben on the street and instead muttered his congratulations one day.

Now he sat across from Wade, watching the chief consume

the last bites of his banana cream donut. Reuben didn't even want the plate near him. It made him nauseous to smell the powdered sugar.

Wade patted his mouth with a thin square of industrial-brown napkin. Dot did not splurge on niceties. The one-room coffee shop with its hand-painted welcome sign, wobbly tables, plastic orange chairs, and rattling air conditioner had been reviewed by Jolie, who declared Dot's *a haven of homespun simplicity!* Generously allotting it three stars. Dot served straight coffee, no fancy flavors, no espresso, though she was sure to get competition now from both the Starbucks on the east side of town and the new coffee house at the opposite end of Main Street (Dot's sat doggedly in the middle) that had just opened in style with tall tables, ample electrical outlets, overstuffed chairs, soft lighting (buzzing fluorescents at Dot's) and leafy oxygen-pumping plants.

"A man doesn't like to eat alone, Reuben. If you insist on sitting there glowering in judgment you could at least bring something to munch on, even if it is that rabbit food you eat now. I'm sure Dot would give you a special dispensation to bring that stuff in here, if you don't mind being laughed at."

"Thank you, no. I'll just continue having water." Reuben lifted his bottom and pulled out the hems of his nylon jogging shorts chafing at his thighs. He felt fussy and famished.

"I never had kids," Wade said. "I probably wouldn't eat like this if I did. But who do I have to stay around for anyway? You don't mind me having a little pity party here this early in the morning, do you?"

"Go right ahead." Wade had never said a word to him about Ardith's pregnancy. He knew the truth, of course, and had no doubt kept it to himself. Ardith had told him about Wade's visit, his absurd probing for any hint of Reuben as the spurned, vengeful spouse. But out of politeness (or just pity) he'd never brought up the subject.

"I drove down to Longmont last night and met my ex-wife for dinner. She's living there now with her niece's family, helping to raise their kids. I asked if there was a chance in hell of us getting back together, and she said, 'Do you want the short answer or the long?' I said the short one. 'No,' she said. 'What's the long one?' 'Our marriage.' However, she did tell me that if I got myself into a program and stopped overeating, she'd agree to talk with me. I appreciate her holding out that small thread of hope. You'd be surprised how little and yet how much it takes for a man my age and size to get up in the morning."

"Are you going to do it?" Reuben asked.

"What's that?"

"Lose weight."

"Losing weight—that's not the problem, my friend. It's overeating."

"There are places to help you with that. Groups too."

"As I've been told. And tried. And failed."

He knew Wade wouldn't take him up on it, but he offered anyway. "You could work out with me."

"I have to say I appreciate the offer, Reuben. Will I do anything about it? I don't know. I suppose it depends how much goodwill I can summon up on behalf of myself. That's never been my strong suit. I'm better at doing for others. Which is why I wanted to speak with you. I need your help reminding people about the case. I'd like you to run a follow-up in the paper."

"I will if you have something new for me. I can't just keep saying the investigation is still in progress."

"I'll have something new if we can get people talking again and telling us what they might have overheard."

"Give me something, Wade."

"Somebody saw Tom."

"What?"

"An old couple, the Hensons, live about a mile from Lyle's farm. The husband has dementia, but the wife is still sharp. They're one of the few houses along that stretch of road, less than twenty-five yards from where Tom was killed. After it first happened, I went straight out there and asked if they had seen anything that night. They said they'd been on the front porch because the weather had turned warmer and it calmed her husband to be out there. They'd gone to bed about ten thirty, a half hour after we determined Tom had been struck. So, they definitely had been out there. Still, she just shook her head about any bicycle, and her husband only smiled pleasantly at me. So I left.

"Last week I realized I may have been asking the wrong question. I went back and after reminding the wife that I'd been there a few months ago, I asked this time if they'd seen a light that night, like a flashlight? 'Oh, yeah,' she said. She'd seen a light. She thought that was somebody walking along the road with a flashlight. She hadn't thought to say anything about it because I was looking for a man on his *bicycle*. Of course, it was pitch dark and they wouldn't have seen a bike go by. But that light was from Tom's bike. Then I asked if she'd *heard* anything that night, and she said, sure, a squealing sound, like bad brakes not a minute later. She thought shortly before that she'd seen a pickup truck go by. I don't know why she hadn't told me this the first time, maybe because she had something else fixed in her mind, but once I mentioned a light the whole package of the pickup came with it."

He felt sorry for Wade. Just ten years ago, Welton had five thousand residents. Now it had almost three times that many, and what had amounted then to mischief, teenagers with baseball bats driving by mailboxes and decapitating them, had become more serious crime: burglaries, domestic assaults, vehicle thefts, arson. Reuben published the rising rates every week. But it was solving this hit and run that appeared to obsess Wade, and despite calling in additional resources from the state, he was no further in cracking it than he had been on the first day, reaching for straws now.

"Wade, I've talked to a lot of reporters in my time who have worked on some hardcore cases. If I told some of these crime reporters what you just proposed to me as a lead, they'd laugh me out of the building. You go back months later to an old lady with a husband suffering from dementia and ask about a light she may have seen, and she says, 'Oh, yeah! I forgot! *That* light!' And then she remembers a pickup and brakes squealing, after being prompted about some noise, and this is the new evidence I'm supposed to put in the paper? I wouldn't even know how to write this up."

"A witness reported a suspicious pickup in the area," said Wade. "That's all you have to say."

"And then you get calls about every pickup in the county?"

"That's the idea. Until we find the right one or get a nudge in that direction."

The sugar in the air itched Reuben's nose. Maybe it was all somatic, some pseudo-allergy. He had to question how much of his own skepticism—or maybe more to the point, hostility—arose because they were talking about Tom. Wade's zealousness ran counter to his own drive to just bury the man once and for all and never think about him again. "All right. I'll write something up. Just don't get your hopes high."

"You leave the hope part to me, Reuben. I owe it to Tom's family to see this through to the end. And to others, I suppose." Wade's last words hung in the air long enough for Reuben to look away. "And, no, I'm not insulted you just ran roughshod over my qualifications as a law officer."

"My apologies."

Reuben's cell phone rang. Wade laid two dollars on the table and then opened the door. Its three brass bells jingled awake. He gave Reuben a backward wave as he stepped into the drilling sunshine of a high-altitude summer morning.

"Hi."

Hearing Ardith's voice, he realized he felt sorry for her. God was he ever confused. Her unhappiness pained him though, he couldn't deny that. What did this mean? After twenty years of marriage, the circuits got so crossed that you shorted out all common sense. "Your brother called to say hello."

"How's he doing?" Reuben said.

"Fine. I spoke with him for a while. They'd like to come out in early December for a couple days and then go up skiing. I told him it was okay to come."

"He'll want to know why the house still looks as bad as it did a year ago and then he'll ride me about it until I blow up at him."

"Then you'll sit down, devour a bowl of popcorn together, and make up with each other, like you always do."

Shit, she knew him. "Something like that."

"Can you get somebody over to fix the porches at least by then?"

He sighed. "All right."

"Reuben?"

"What?"

"What do you want me to say?"

"What do you mean?"

"I'm going to have a baby. When should we tell them?"

They'd told Jamie that Mom was going to have another baby. He didn't even think to question who the father was, of course. He lived on the surface, like Stan in that regard: you trusted your family; they did good by you. As for Harry, Ardith had spoken with him on the Fourth of July and told him Tom was the father. Harry looked at him now, he thought, with pitying derision, or maybe that was just his own projection of how he thought his son viewed his cuckolded father.

Reuben walked outside with his phone and stood in the alley. A woman rooting through a dumpster reminded him that he was scheduled to run another article about (un)affordable housing and the increasing homeless population in Welton—the less feel-good stories for which he carried around a quota in his head. The paper's readers, according to a recent survey he'd circulated, wanted more positive stories about Colorado life. "I'm going to leave that up to you," he answered Ardith.

"So, what are you going to say?"

"I'm going to say Ardith is having a baby."

"Are you going to tell them the truth?"

"Do I have a choice? Stan knows I had a vasectomy."

"Oh."

"Get it?"

There was a pause. "You could tell him you had it reversed."

"I'm not going to do that."

They waited in a strained silence.

"Maybe Stan won't remember," Reuben said, although he knew his brother would. He'd had his vasectomy shortly after Reuben's. "Or maybe he'll work it into some brighter picture of happiness anyway. His idea is that we grew up in a close-knit family, which is why he's made his house into a gallery of pictures of Mom and Dad and the three of us all-American brothers, family revisionist that he is."

"You could put some pictures up too, Reuben. It would be good for Harry and Jamie to know what their grandparents looked like."

"They know. They've seen."

"Including your brother Harry. You have one picture of the three of you together, and it's packed away."

"Well," said Reuben. He suddenly had run out of steam, his insides aching and twisting. They hadn't talked this long without fighting since he'd found out. It felt worse now to have done so, the gentle words like a surgeon's tender cuts, or like his father's diligent, skilled butchering. "I've got to go," he said. The homeless woman gave him a wary look, then turned back to her work.

19

Their waiter came over and asked if they wanted more coffee.

"None for me," Ellen said.

"I'm drinking decaf," Ardith told the waiter, and he danced off to get a different pot.

Ellen asked, "Are you feeling all right? You're not having any more morning sickness, are you?"

Ardith shook her head. She felt so alone lately that she'd woken up this morning knowing she had to get out of the isolation any way she could, with whatever small steps she could make herself take, and she'd forced herself to call Ellen.

"What is it, then? You look glummer than our three cows with mastitis."

"I was just thinking how to tell you something."

"You know, 'Just do it.'"

"Why didn't you and Lyle ever marry?" Ardith asked instead.

"We never saw the need. It doesn't matter now, anyway. We're married by common law, I'm sure, after twenty-five years. We had so much trouble having Isadora, and then when we finally did—we always said we'd get married after we had a child—it seemed almost bad luck to go ahead and fool with the arrangement. And, to be honest, I never pictured myself a married woman. I still don't, in name at least. I wasn't even sure I wanted to be with a man, let alone old foot-in-the-mouth Lyle. But things go on, day by day, the cows get milked, I keep the books, Lyle trudges through the mud and muck and gets the cows unstuck and into the milking barn. He's up at five every morning. Freezing cold, blistering hot, it doesn't matter. He loves what he does, and I've loved him so long in spite of his abrasiveness that I wouldn't know him without it. And he's a cream puff to Isadora. For her, he'd take a bullet in a second.

It makes me feel safe to see him out there forking hay. I like that he knows who he is."

"I had an affair with Tom Watkins. It's his baby I'm having."

The waiter came by and, with a flourish, filled Ardith's cup with coffee. "Anything else?"

"No, thank you," Ardith said.

"Okay, I was always curious how long I could hold my breath. When...are you all right?"

"All right?"

"I mean, how could this all be going on?"

"It just is," Ardith said. "I fell in love."

Ellen laughed, but it had a hysterical edge.

"It's okay. You don't have to say anything."

"I don't know what to say. I hardly know where to start. Does Reuben know?"

"Yes. It's been difficult, an understatement."

"I can only imagine."

"I told him I was going to tell you."

"I can't believe it. I'm so sad about Tom all of a sudden. The whole situation... I don't even know who to be upset for anymore! How do people get involved in such things?" Ardith didn't answer. She didn't know herself. Ellen took a tissue out of her purse and wiped her eyes. "I won't say anything to anyone, not even Lyle, if you don't want."

"I'm wondering if you could be my coach."

"Your coach?"

"When I have the baby. Colleen will be there to do the delivery, but I don't want to be alone, and obviously I can't ask Reuben. I knew I wanted to ask you, I just wasn't sure how."

"Of course." She came around to Ardith's side of the booth and slid in beside her, studying Ardith.

"I'm okay," Ardith said, with a laugh. "I've had a while to get used to it."

"Well, I'm a wreck, as you can see. But I'll be a rock when the time comes. I just need some time for it to sink in."

"You can still be excited for me."

"I know, I don't mean that I'm *not*…"

"It's a shock, I realize."

"Can I ask you something?"

"Of course."

"Don't be insulted."

"I won't," Ardith said, knowing what was coming.

"You never considered having an abortion?"

"No. Not really." Ellen nodded intently, waiting for more. "I just didn't. That's all. I didn't have the guts for it. Or maybe the common sense. That's not true. I wanted the baby and I believe Tom would have wanted me to have it."

"Wow," said Ellen—the word, for Ardith, seeming to emphasize the "ow" part.

She hugged Ellen, telling her not to worry; it actually felt good to be the one doing the reassuring. "I'd better go home. I'm trying out Harry as a babysitter for Jamie. So, it's okay that I told you? You don't feel too burdened?"

"Of course not," Ellen said. "Knock 'em…knock 'em down," she settled on, thinking better, apparently, of bringing up the dead at this moment.

20

Luisa spent the last part of the summer helping her mother clean houses, her mother's need for her greater than her fear a client would call the Department of Labor. It was hard work and harder on her knees, but even worse, she hated to see her mother doing entire floors by hand. "You don't need to do that," Luisa told her. "Use a mop. You're killing yourself." A doctor had told her mother she was going to lose what was left of her cartilage if she kept going like this, and she was only forty! But her mother was stubborn; it was the way she'd always done the floors because they never looked as good mopped. The doctor had been blunt. "You can't keep doing this, Martina." And had she listened? No. Instead she'd gone online and bought bright red kneepads. When they came, she showed them off to Luisa like a shiny Christmas present. "I am good, okay?" But knee-pads or not, her face was squeezed tight while she scrubbed, and now something was wrong with her hip that made her limp.

"Sounds a lot like my mother," Carla told her. "Won't listen either to what's good for them. And they're the parents." Luisa hardly saw her over the summer. Carla spent all her time with her new boyfriend, Donny, who was twenty-two. He worked in the oil fields in Greeley and was making good money and spending it lavishly on Carla, who now talked about dropping out of school. Her parents didn't know she saw him, and she'd sworn Luisa to secrecy. Luisa had told her, "Don't be dumb. You'll drop out of school, this guy will dump you, and then where will you be? He's eight years older than you. That's statutory rape, by the way."

Carla blew past the comment. "We love each other. He's got a good job. He's responsible. How many people do you know his age who own a home and drive a Camaro ZL1?"

"How many people do you know are twenty-two and making

it with a girl in ninth grade? Can't he get anyone his own age?"

"Too bad no older guy is interested in you, huh?"

Luisa shook her head. "You wanted to go to college, maybe be a nurse or doctor and have your own money. You hate how your mother always has to beg your father for money."

"Donny's *not* like my father. And who are you to give me advice? I'm making bad choices? Your own family is a goddamn mess. Your father can't even get out of bed these days."

Luisa slapped her.

"Bitch," Carla said, holding her cheek. She walked away, and that was the last time Luisa spoke with her. She'd texted and called and messaged and sent a video on Instagram of the two of them on a roller coaster when they were twelve, but Carla had blocked her and when she went to her house, she was never there. Her apologies went unanswered. When classes started in the fall, Carla turned away from her in the halls and disappeared right after school, probably to Donny's.

The sad thing was Carla had been right about her father. It was just painful to hear it. He was given time off from the dairy farm, but a few days had turned into a week and then two weeks. Ellen had come out to talk with him, and, along with their mother, the three of them had sat in the kitchen speaking in low voices. Luisa had listened on the steps. Ellen wanted him to see a doctor, a psychiatrist, and her father had nodded silently. Ellen, who spoke Spanish better than Luisa did, translated some of the medical words for her mother: *entermedad*, *antidepresios*, *genético*. He'd gotten medication and he was well enough to work at the dairy, but he didn't seem better, just different. He walked through the house like a zombie now. At least before, he would raise his voice, especially at Marcos, who just wanted attention from him. When Marcos pressed to go fishing or play catch or make an obstacle course of the furniture, he would only say in a weak voice, "Maybe later." Later never came. She had given up asking her mother why the medication wasn't helping more. Her mother would only say their father had *problemas emocionales*, a phrase Ellen used about him.

In the meantime, on weekends, she still helped her mother.

She scrubbed toilets and folded sheets. She wiped windowsills, pulled hair from drains, and arranged stuffed animals in the kids' rooms of clients whose houses had bedrooms to spare. Sometimes the owners were there, and they'd take her aside and ask about her favorite subject in school and try to get to know her, but she was always cautious about saying too much. Lately, she didn't trust anyone. Any openness she'd once felt had withered like old fruit. Between her father's oddness and her mother always hushing her, she'd grown timid around people, especially white people.

"Your mother's one of the good ones," Mrs. Samuels told her one day when they were cleaning her house. "We need more like her."

Good ones? Compared to all the other lazy Mexicans? Who, by the way, *were* Americans like her mother.

"And *you*, Louise. So nice to see someone of your background not afraid to work hard!"

At one time, she would have fought back, got in the person's face, older white woman or not. At the very least told her it's *Luisa* not Louise. But she didn't have the energy. And anyway, her mother—who understood English perfectly well, even if she chose not to speak it, maybe because people like Mrs. Samuels assumed she couldn't—had given Luisa a warning look. Keep quiet. Do your job and let's go home. *No hagas problemas.*

21

Ardith couldn't fall asleep, and when Reuben climbed into bed next to her—the first time since he'd started sleeping on the couch—she turned on her side to face him. "Hi," she whispered.

"I thought you'd be asleep."

"I'm not. Is that okay?"

He carefully unfolded his legs under the covers as if to avoid even brushing her.

She'd made up her mind to ignore his rigidity, to do whatever it took to welcome him back to their bed after encouraging him to do so. He'd stayed downstairs in the kitchen reading until Jamie and his friend Danny had drifted off to sleep. Harry had gotten the news that afternoon that Ben was back in town, and he'd raced over there to see him and had wound up having a sleepover. She'd almost wished Jamie wasn't here either. They needed the whole house empty to say a few real words between them.

Ardith rolled over to his side and put her hand on his chest. The graying hair felt fuzzy and soft, a little like the fibers on the wool baby blankets she'd run her hands over in a store this afternoon, looking to get ready for the winter birth. She forced herself to think about quilts and almond-scented candles and not that he might reject her. He moved over toward her. She hoped they would make love quickly, before either of them thought too much about it. Her own sudden twitch of interest came when he slid his knee between her legs and then sunk his mouth over her nipple, her breasts fuller every day. She rolled on her back and helped him inside her, not entirely ready, but she wanted it quickly. "I want you to come," Ardith told him. And she braced her hands against the headboard and offered him the resistance he seemed to want. As the headboard banged away—she prayed Jamie and Danny were fast asleep—she caught her breaths in between Reuben's fierce thrusts. He stopped. Then rolled off her.

"Did you come?"

"No," he said.

"You can't?"

He shook his head. "I don't think so."

"What's wrong?"

"Look," he said. "I don't think this is going to work. I want to move out."

"I thought—"

"That things would be fine? That time would take care of all?"

"We could try, Reuben. I'll do anything you want. We can go to counseling. People come back from these things."

"I can't, Ardith." He said it so reasonably, without any spite or the now-familiar malice, that it hurt her worse than if he'd spat it out. "I would if I could, but I don't have it in me. The baby…it's not even born yet, and I already feel monstrously bitter toward it."

"You might feel differently, Reuben, once the baby comes. We need some time to work all this out. It takes years to recover. I know it's not going to happen overnight, or even in a few months. I've told you and *told* you I'm willing to do whatever it takes to make things right. In the meantime, maybe we can find out how we got here in the first place."

"How we got here? You had an affair and got pregnant by another man, that's how we got here."

She kept silent, rather than provoke him further.

"I don't have years anyway," he said. "I don't want to spend years recovering. I just want to get out. It's not good for me, it's not good for you, and it sure as hell isn't good for the kids and this new child. Maybe I'm someone who is better off alone."

"Reuben, you don't really believe that. You want me to plead? I'll do it. I don't know what I'd do if the situation were reversed, but I wouldn't run away. I'd give us a chance. Do you hate me so much that you can't try to forgive me?"

"What is it you want, Ardith?" He propped himself up on his elbow and looked at her. "You don't love me anymore. You'd like to, you wish you could, it would make things easier for everyone, but that bridge isn't there for us. I know it and so do you."

She felt a cleaving in her chest. Her eyes burned with tears that she tried to hold back. "Please don't say that, Reuben. I don't know if that's true. I'm just confused."

"No, you're not. You're in love with someone else, who happens, miserably, to be dead. You won't get over that so easily as you'd like. That's going to be more punishing to you than anything I could say or do. I just want to get out of the way. It rips my guts apart to see that on your face every day."

She put her hand on his shoulder and tried to pull him down toward her, but he remained stiff, his elbow locked. "We can work it out. If you give me some time—"

"You can't grow a new heart for me, Ardith." He touched her hair, and the consoling gesture wrenched loose a sob from her. "We've got the kids to think about, most importantly. How it's all going to affect them." He took a deep breath. "We've been headed this way for a long time. I was just too stupid to see it."

Jamie stood in the doorway, silhouetted by the hall light, in his pajamas, his hand on the doorknob.

Ardith sat up and wiped her eyes. "What's wrong, sweetie?"

"I had a bad dream."

"It's all right," she said, "go back to bed now."

"Can I sleep in here?"

"Your friend is downstairs, Jamie. You don't want Danny to wake up alone, do you?"

"Can you walk me back down? I keep hearing noises."

"I'll do it," said Reuben. Ardith felt him slipping his underwear back on under the sheet. When he lifted himself from the bed, she reached over for him and grabbed his wrist, but he gently, if decisively, pulled away.

PART 2

22

Reuben had done it for Rosa. Joined the Rotary and forced himself to attend the lunches. Fed up with his moping (who wasn't?), she had read him the riot act. "You have to be more aggressive. You can't wait for advertisers to come to us. You can't thumb your nose at the segment of the community that keeps us alive. You need to go to Rotary meetings to make nice with the businesspeople."

"Rotary?"

"You can do it. I think you should restore the 'From the Pulpit' section too. People liked that."

So Christian. And one of the first things he'd gotten rid of when he took over. "Do we have to?"

"If you want to appeal to the regular folks." She'd had her hair done up in floppy hennaed waves that glinted red sparks, and Reuben wondered if it was too late and too shameless to compliment her on the new style. He would be lost if she ever quit on him. "You should run an anniversary piece about the paper's history. Brady Westcott used to print that every year and it reminded readers why the paper is important."

"These are all possibilities—"

"We should do something for Hispanic Heritage Month. We don't hear enough of those voices in the paper."

"Absolutely."

"And you need to get off your high horse."

"What high horse?" If anything, he'd been on a miniature mule since he'd come out here.

"The G-word. Yes, growth's a big deal, but people have everyday lives too. Whatever happened to the 'Recipe Box'? That used to be one of our best-read sections. You'd be surprised how much more a good German potato soup matters to people around here than another story about annexation."

So, now he sat in a Rotary meeting at the new Holiday Inn that had opened out by the interstate. He could do a story on Welton's various service organizations: *Lions devour Moose and Elks at Rotary luncheon! Masons imprison Optimists in brick fortress!*

The president of the First Western Bank stood at the podium presenting a fifty-dollar check to the eighth-grade girl who had won the Rotary's essay contest on the topic of "Why Drugs Must Be Kept Out of Our Schools." Reuben had agreed to publish the winning essay in the *Sentinel.* He'd groused a bit when the club had approached him about the topic: "Isn't that an old subject by now?"

Mike Uphoff, the town manager and president of the Rotary, had folded his hands across his stomach. They'd been sitting in Reuben's office. "Drugs," said Mike solemnly, "are never old news, Reuben. Never."

"Why not an essay about guns? How about 'Why We Need to Keep Guns Out of Teachers' Hands—and everyone else's by the way.'"

"Guns are more controversial," said Mike.

"Exactly."

"People have differing opinions about guns. It's a personal matter."

"Whether a teacher accidentally shoots a child on a playground? That's a personal matter?"

"Best left to another organization to sponsor that topic."

"How about the NRA?"

Mike (was he a member?) found no humor in this. "We're a nonpartisan group, Reuben. We're here to serve the community. Period." A few seconds later, Mike added a gentle goading: "Of course, if it's really an imposition, another publication might want to help."

What more could he say? Mike, as town manager, could make his job even harder. He agreed to do the story announcing the timeworn topic of saying no to drugs. "We'll see you at the lunch Monday," Mike had said pleasantly after Reuben conceded, all chummy again.

"So, in making this award," the president of First Western intoned, "we're honoring all those young people who do in fact say no and mean it. It requires strength and courage to make healthy choices. When our young people today face so many difficult challenges—"

Postmaster Dennis Olberg farted. Not the kind of fart you could overlook but a really profound gastrointestinal deployment. So resounding an ill-timed interruption that Reuben burst out laughing. No one else seemed the least bit disturbed. Perhaps Dennis farted regularly at these lunches—all that homebaked bread with walnuts or whatever super fiber his wife used.

Recovered, he leaned back in his chair, rubbed his face, reproved himself to get a grip, more sleep, less stress, better living conditions—he'd been staying at Lyle and Ellen's farm—and continued to listen to Pete Morgan, First Western's president, finish up his congratulations to the neurasthenic eighth grader in her tan jumper, her thin, pale arm extended like a sleepwalker as she took the check and received a round of applause.

Everyone stood up afterward and shook hands. Chauncey Griggs, who owned the town mini-mart, held out his hand. "Great job," he said to Reuben. "Looking forward to reading the essay in the paper."

Reuben already had seen a copy. Its virtue was brevity. He could devote less than a quarter page to the thing. The essay praised the role of parents and credited the influence of a strong Christian background (which Reuben insisted on changing to "religious") and the support of caring teachers for her staying away from drugs. Frighteningly unoriginal, though spelled better than all the other entries, the old copyeditor in him couldn't help admire, the piece would have been a total loss had she not come up with a good acronym, PIG—pride in yourself, interest in others, goals!—and a catchy last line: "Keep your kids on track, not making tracks," which redeemed the rest of the piece—though not surprisingly he had to fight with Mike, his co-judge, who worried the wordplay might send the wrong message. "It's the only decent line in the whole damn thing!" Reuben exploded, fed up. "I won't publish anything at all if we have to take it out!" Alarmed by his vehemence, Mike backed off.

"Just wondering," Chauncey was saying now, not letting Reuben leave—didn't the mini-mart have customers waiting?—"how you spell your first name?"

"Pardon?"

"With an *i* or *e*?"

"An *e*—two of them."

"Funny spelling."

"Is it?"

"Usually spelled with an *i*, isn't it? That's the way that fighter 'Hurricane' Carter spelled his first name, didn't he?"

"I believe so." Was he really having this conversation?

"Mean anything different?"

"I have no idea. Maybe one is more the Jewish spelling." He'd been told this somewhere along the way. Wasn't it spelled that way in the Bible? Reuben, son of Jacob and Leah? And why hide that he was a Jew? He'd felt the need lately to pronounce himself one, despite his own ambivalent feelings about being observant.

"Well," said Chauncey, "I have the same problem."

He did? Were they about to make some improbable connection? There was a *Jewish* spelling of Chauncey too?

"You know that Indian tribe in Canada and Montana? I'm never sure whether to call them Blackfoot or Blackfeet." He looked at Reuben and waited.

"Me too," Reuben said. "Totally."

By the time he got back to the office it was almost five o'clock, and Rosa was getting ready to close up. She had her new project up and running. She wanted to make their website a cross between tradition and progress, between the folksiness of a recipe-sharing page and a "tech-watch" forum. One way or another this sixty-eight-year-old grandmother was determined to drag the *Sentinel* screaming and kicking into the digital age. He had only to bear the cost of such a venture, including the course Rosa was taking at the community college for advanced web communication. For all her fierce guardianship of the paper's traditions, a job to which she had given forty-five years of her life with the same soul investment his father had sweated over carcasses in his butcher shop, she had accepted the hard fact, which Reuben was reluctant to do, that they better start thinking of themselves less as a cozy newspaper and more as a data delivery service. In carrying out that goal, she had recruited an intern from the computer science department of Colorado State to come use his superpowers to update their site. Reuben, inspired to think big, doubled the website's video content, created a treasure hunt that involved local merchants, added live interviews as teasers for the print edition, and took Rosa up on her idea for the podcast, "Rosa Recalls," about Welton's pioneer history. And soon enough, more ad revenue transpired, and the paper against all odds was actually in the black, although just barely. Reuben had also tapped the university's journalism department for an intern, who relieved him and Jolie of covering every local fire, square dance festival, and peach jubilee. Sometimes he couldn't believe his own success or how to reconcile it with his fear of a lifelong Damoclean sword itching to drop.

"Our server went down for a while. We've been getting some good sticky on the site though."

He smiled as if he knew what the hell she was talking about.

"You have someone waiting in your office," Rosa said.

"Who?"

"She said her name was Marian."

He went into his office. From the back, he could see the woman sitting in the chair in front of his desk. She stood up when Reuben came in. With her long blonde hair parted crisply down the center, a thin, elegant nose, and a spray of ginger freckles on her cheeks, she looked in her early twenties and somehow familiar.

"I'm Marian Watkins. Tom's daughter."

Reuben stared at her. His ribs tightened. "How *are* you?"

"My uncle Jack was supposed to call by way of an introduction."

"He may have." Reuben looked at the pile of message slips. Rosa, distracted in her newfound capacity as digital czar, had stopped organizing his written messages for him. "I'm sorry."

He was dumbfounded to see her here. He shuffled through the messages so he could find Jack's slip. He felt frantic to find it, as if it would give him a moment to think. "We've been so busy with everything." He was struck by how much she looked like Tom, a slender model's version of the robust doctor. She had his same intense, unwavering blue eyes.

"I'm hoping you can help us get the word out about an event we're organizing."

Reuben stared at her, haunted by her face, by picturing Ardith's face mixed with hers, mixed with Tom's, all of it leading to the child. It was a dizzying thought. This poised young lady standing in front of him had a three-month-old baby sister she didn't know about.

"Please," he said, motioning for her to sit back down.

"Uncle Jack and I would like to start a yearly bike ride in Dad's name. The Tom Watkins Memorial Ride. The cycling club Dad was part of in town wants to be involved too. The goal is to increase awareness about rider safety, hopefully to prevent fatalities like what happened to Dad."

Reuben took out a notepad. He was trying not to look directly at her because he feared his face would show what couldn't be spoken. "Are you still out in California?"

"I'm at Boulder now. In law school there."

"Congratulations."

"Oh, right, like the world needs another lawyer." She laughed. "I'm not sure I even like it. My father's dying has made me rethink things. Part of the reason I applied to CU was thinking I'd be near him." She was silent for a moment. "Sorry, I don't mean to bend your ear about my career dilemmas."

"It does make you take stock." Who was he kidding? His own life had been turned upside down because of her father, and meanwhile, he was sitting here offering her blather about death and loss?

"I stopped in to see the police chief before I came here. I was hoping he might have some updates for us. It's been almost a year. He told me the investigation was still ongoing, but, no, there hasn't been a breakthrough. He was encouraging that the memorial ride might reawaken public interest in Dad's case. Of course, *we've* never lost interest."

"I know that Wade still wants it solved as much as anyone."

"Not more than I do, I'm sure." The shift in her tone was swift, decisive, dismissive of false reassurance. Reuben could hear Tom's voice in her, his authority.

"I can email you all the information about our plans. Uncle Jack has talked with your city officials already about logistics, so he can tell you more about things from that end."

"Your mother and sister, are they involved?"

Marian took a deep breath. "They prefer to remain uninvolved." She gave Reuben a quick smile that said end of subject. She stood up, hooked her slate-colored purse over her shoulder, and extended her hand. "Thank you so much for your time, Mr. Rosenfeld."

"Reuben."

"Yes, Reuben. Very nice to meet you."

After she left, he leaned back in his aged leather chair inherited from the venerable Brady Westcott and that still had the slightest redolence of cherry pipe tobacco, extended his arms in Christ-like surrender and just barely kept from falling over backwards.

23

She named her Olivia. It was a name she wished her parents would have given her. Ardith? How do you spell that? Is that American? *Arthur?* kids asked (or teased). *That's a boy's name!* For a while in high school she'd called herself Ar. But then a drunk boy at a party came after her pretending to be a pirate with a hook, *Argh, argh, I'm going to get you, Ar!* So that was the end of that phase. She grew tired of all the comments and just told people it was an old family name, although it wasn't: her mother had simply heard it one day and named her that. It sounded, to her mother, distinguished and substantial. A linguistics professor in college, versed in Anglo-Saxon derivations, had told her it was a variant of Edith, which, he added, as they began their short, doomed affair, meant rich, happy, and prosperous. Dropping her months later, he insisted he'd been honest about that, if not everything else, including the other teaching assistant he was seeing.

Though she'd had an amnio and two ultrasounds, she had asked Colleen not to tell her the sex, and when the baby did arrive, after an easy three-hour labor, with Ellen who had agreed to be her coach having little to do besides hold her hand through some very nasty, back-splitting final contractions, she reached down and touched the head and knew instantly it was a little girl, even before she was fully out. Colleen cut the cord—a moment of sadness remembering Reuben had done so for both Harry and Jamie—and placed the baby on her stomach. Ardith counted fingers and toes, studied the tiny face, the soft lashes and pursed pink mouth. Even all red and squished and covered with a healthy layer of pasty vernix, the baby's fine features shined through, and Ardith could not stop touching the perfectly round and rosy rims of her ears.

Six hours later, she brought Olivia home from the hospital.

They bundled her up in receiving blankets, blasted the heat in Ellen's car, and pulled snug her tiny knit hat, like a large thimble, that she'd been given in the hospital. It was December 27, a week beyond her due date. The snow on the roads had melted some during the day but turned to ice as the temperature dropped at night. Ellen drove even more slowly than they could have walked and what should have taken them only twenty minutes turned into a forty-five-minute drive.

At home, Reuben had a fire going and the house felt close and warm and smelled of spices. He'd been taking care of the boys. "What's her name?" he asked when Ardith carried her in. And again, it saddened her that her own husband was asking this question, an outsider.

"Olivia," said Ardith. He nodded.

"That's a pretty name." He went into the kitchen. Harry and Jamie were waiting too, and Jamie asked if he could hold her. He sat down on the floor next to the fireplace. At the hospital one Saturday afternoon, he had taken a course for brothers and sisters on how to care for newborns. He'd practiced changing a diaper on a life-size doll and had been instructed in how to support the baby's head. When Ardith placed Olivia in his lap, he held her with assurance, and Ardith's heart thudded with a sweet pain. He wanted to change her diapers and feed her and burp her, he told Ardith.

Harry said, "She's cute, I think," and left it at that. Their new dog, Charlotte, who Jamie had pleaded for, a corgi, fox-faced and with brown eyes that stuck out like Yoda, came over on her stubby legs and sniffed.

Ellen stayed around for a while. "It's probably going to be awkward," Ardith had warned her. But it hadn't turned out as badly as she feared.

Reuben busied himself in the kitchen, cooking up a big pan of lasagna. Everyone huddled around the fireplace until it was ready—the house was so drafty that Ardith kept Olivia swaddled in blankets. Finally, Reuben called them to sit down for dinner. Famished from having eaten nothing more than ice chips and Popsicles while in labor, Ardith devoured two full plates.

Exhausted—she'd been up for almost twenty-four hours—Ardith took Olivia upstairs to bed with her and lay down. She slept deeply for three hours until the baby woke to nurse. The clock said midnight. Ellen, who had stayed downstairs to talk with Reuben, had gone home. Later Ardith would find out that's when Reuben had asked if he could stay out at their farm for a while. With the baby here now, he felt the time had come.

As the birth had neared, the last couple of months, they'd fallen into a peaceful coexistence. He worked longer hours at the paper, so she hardly saw him. When he did come home, he slept on the couch for a few hours and then was up at five a.m. to exercise—she admired him for sticking to it—and then off to work. Because he often stayed late at the paper, he called from the office to say goodnight to the boys.

It was already as if they were living apart anyway. She imagined this was how a trial separation became permanent and eventually evolved into divorce. People wanted to get on with their lives. His decision to live out at Lyle and Ellen's was a first step in that direction. She felt moments of panic about his leaving and having to face how dependent she'd become on him. She worried about overcoming the despair of a failed marriage enough to get out of bed in the morning and this too worked her into a panic that she wouldn't be able to care for the baby. But once Olivia came, she could think of no one else. Instead of helplessness she felt an intense purpose; instead of self-doubt she enjoyed moments of surety close to bliss; instead of drifting into aimless despair she had focus. Reuben wasn't on her mind for large periods of time, something that felt foreign at first because he'd been so woven into the warp and woof of her consciousness for twenty years. Even when she'd been seeing Tom, Reuben had still been her "real" life with all its mundane, reassuring duties. At their most intimate moments she'd think: *I have to tell Reuben his glasses are ready at the optometrist.* Now they had separate lives except for the boys.

On weekends, he hung around the house or took the boys places. He wound up doing more with them than he had when he'd lived at home: bowling, ice skating, indoor swimming, museums, hiking, whatever he could persuade Harry to go along with. He took them up to the mountains for several nights where they learned to snowboard.

Before his brother Stan and his family visited back in early December, Reuben had explained on the phone that Ardith was having a child by another man and that neither of them wished to talk about it further. They were both committed to doing what was best for the boys, but the marriage was in trouble and he wasn't sure it would last and please don't tell Aunt Mildred any of this. He wished to be remembered well in her eyes. End of subject.

To their credit, they came out anyway. Though it was hard to face them, Ardith agreed to do so, fatigued, swaybacked, and unable to get her favorite black shoes on her swollen feet, much less tie them. They stayed at a bed and breakfast in town. The first thing Stan said to her was, "I don't care what happened. We still love you." Ardith held back tears and gave the girls their presents: miniature spinning wheels she'd found downtown in a gift shop.

They got through a fairly easy dinner at a Chinese restaurant filled with chitchat about the schools in Welton and the light snowpack so far this winter in the mountains and how the waves had frozen again this year on Lake Michigan and how the fish market on Devon Street next to their father's butcher shop, long gone, had burned down after seventy years, and not another word was mentioned about the baby, for which everybody was grateful.

As they were leaving for the ski resort, Stan hugged Ardith goodbye and said, "Please let me know if there's anything I can do." His two daughters, pretty as their mother, a former model, stared at Ardith's big belly. She let them feel the baby kick and then they drove off in their rented SUV. She had not heard from them since, and she imagined they had no idea what

to say after receiving a birth announcement, which she bravely
sent them.

Upstairs Ardith was bathing Olivia when she heard the front
door open and slam shut. "Harry?" she called. No one answered. She finished soaping Olivia in the plastic tub and rinsed
her off. "Up we go," Ardith said, lifting her out of the shallow
bath water and wrapping her in a huge purple towel.

Harry was sitting on the couch reading a snowboarding
magazine. Jamie had stayed after school for his first Boy Scout
meeting, a new activity he assured her he could fit in among his
various sports interests and still do well in school.

"Did you have a good day?" she asked Harry now.

She saw the top of his head move slightly behind the magazine. A nod? Affirmative? Charlotte had her chin on his lap.
She wasn't exactly the rough and tumble canine Jamie had in
mind when he begged for a dog, more like one that would enjoy
a good strong cup of tea and a chat with the queen. But with
Olivia, they formed a harmonious threesome during the day.
"Let's go, girls," Ardith would say. After years of testosterone
around the house, it felt wonderful to be free of such energy.
Putting Olivia in the stroller and attaching Charlotte's leash to
it, they would walk downtown and then over to Lake Finnegan.
Charlotte would stop to do her business in a most ladylike way,
and then they'd continue on the path that wove among the cot-
tonwoods and marshy shore.

Ardith clapped her hands to get Harry's attention now. "Put
your magazine down and talk to me, please."

He lowered the magazine.

"Oh my God. What happened!" His eyebrows...his eyebrows were gone, the empty white space covered with violent
slashes. "Harry, what—"

"Just take me to the doctor, okay? Don't make me tell you."

24

Reuben had stabbed himself in the eye. Putting on his sunglasses to leave, he'd forgotten that he had a pen in his hand. It hurt like hell, the poking.

Rosa had left for the day. He went into the bathroom and peered at himself in the mirror. In the hour since he'd poked himself, the eye had gotten much worse. The white of his eyeball looked as if Red Dye No. 2 had been injected into it.

He drove over to Dr. Stein's and parked in back of Tom's old office, a one-story brick building with a new doctor's sign out front. The inside had changed, a remodeled reception area with decorative glass block and an aquarium in the corner. It didn't look like Tom's personality anymore: mauve and marine colors, a large TV showing health videos, and recessed LED ceiling lights. Tom, Reuben remembered, had antique lamps on corner tables. "I accidentally poked myself," he said to the receptionist, who was new too. "I think I need to see someone."

"Dad?"

Reuben turned around. It was Jamie sitting by himself in a corner of the waiting room. He had on his Boy Scout uniform. "What are you doing here, Jamie?"

"Gross," Jamie said, scrunching up his face at Reuben's eye.

"Why are you sitting out here?"

"Mom's in there with Harry. He had a… I don't know exactly. Something weird happened to him. She picked me up from Scouts and brought me here with them."

Reuben turned back to the receptionist. "My son is back there?"

"Who's your son, sir?"

"Harry Rosenfeld."

"I'll take you back."

"Wait here, Jamie."

"I *am* waiting, Dad. I've *been* waiting. Did you punch yourself or something?"

He followed the receptionist back to the examining room. She knocked on the door and poked her head in. "Harry's father is here."

Ardith was sitting on a corner stool with Olivia asleep in her arms. Harry sat on the examining table, staring straight ahead.

"How did you know to come over?" Ardith said.

"I didn't. I hurt my eye." He peeled his hand away.

"Oh, Reuben!"

Dr. Stein turned around and nodded hello at him.

"What happened to Harry?"

"He got into some trouble," Ardith said. "His eyebrows are missing."

Harry hadn't looked at him since he'd come in, but now he turned toward Reuben. Where his eyebrows had once been was raw red skin and a filigree of scratches. "My God, Harry."

My God, yourself, Harry's expression seemed to say.

"I see we'll need to take a look at you too," Dr. Stein said, disposing of a cotton swab in the trash.

He had met Dr. Stein when she'd called to ask if he would place an announcement in the *Sentinel* about her practice opening. Wanting to settle out West—she'd done her residency at Johns Hopkins—she and her husband had researched small towns. They'd considered schools, crime, recreation, housing, climate, nearby colleges—her husband was a professor—and "all the intangibles" that make up quality of life, concluding Welton could offer them everything they wanted. She kept afternoon and evening hours, when her husband, Mark, who had found a position at Colorado State teaching biology, came home and could look after the baby and their three-year-old. As if he were not twisted up in the tragedy himself, Reuben had had a very nice talk with her about her predecessor, Tom, on the phone.

"It's good to finally meet you in person," Dr. Stein said. Tall, with crisp, efficient movements, she had sharp cheekbones and wore black rectangular glasses that had a decidedly hip look and might get her labeled avant-garde in Welton. She was in her early thirties, Reuben guessed, and had that fresh-faced eagerness of someone ready to contribute her energies to remote Himalayan villages or war zones or…Welton. After he had printed an announcement of her practice on page two in the *Sentinel*, she called again to thank him and mentioned that she and her husband would love to get together sometime with Reuben and his family. They were looking for a synagogue to join. Reuben made some remarks about there being one in Fort Collins and a rabbi over there he'd heard good things about, but that they hadn't had time to check it out themselves. He didn't mention that Harry had been kicked out of Hebrew school in Chicago when he was eleven for defacing his siddur and for general misconduct, which meant he refused to learn Hebrew and had no intention of being bar mitzvahed. With Jamie they'd just let the ball drop. Religion seemed like an option they'd never gotten around to signing up for out West. Mountains lulled one into complacency about the affairs of God and man. Nobody knew him (or his father, mother, grandfather, or Aunt Mildred) from Adam out here, as their friends in Chicago had warned them about moving. You could, in fact, take the shtetl out of the boy, for better or worse.

"We were just trying to find out what happened to Harry," Dr. Stein said. "It would help to treat the wound if I knew how you got this, Harry."

Harry looked down. Reuben walked over to him. Close up, he saw that where the eyebrows had been were now two angry red welts. He rested his hand on Harry's shoulder and hoped his son wouldn't bite his fingers off.

He didn't. He let Reuben's hand stay there. His son's shoulder felt like granite!

"What happened?" Harry said. He was looking at Reuben's eye. So was Dr. Stein. "I stabbed myself with a pen," Reuben said, answering the unspoken question. "I was putting on my sunglasses." Harry let out a muffled laugh, but it did the trick of breaking the tension. "Okay, I confessed. Now you tell me. It can't be any dumber," Reuben said, trying to introduce a self-deprecating, light-hearted note. "What happened, Harry?"

No answer. Stoic. His face had a faint constellation of pimples around the chin. His impenetrable green eyes. His hands in his lap.

"Well," said Dr. Stein, "I see no signs of burns, nor any infection. Did someone at school do this?"

Silence.

"Was it part of an initiation for a group?"

Reuben thought it was tactful to say "group" and not "gang."

"Answer her, Harry," he tried, commanded.

Finally, Harry spoke, "I'm not going to tell you."

Dr. Stein took a deep breath. "All right, Harry, but—"

"It's my business."

Dr. Stein looked at Reuben. She was patient, caring, and soft-spoken, a dedicated young doctor, but she was also learning about the Why of Harry. Reuben could see her reconsidering her offer of wanting to get together with them—a nice Jewish family recently transplanted here also. Or maybe she was just worried that her babies would grow up one day and refuse to talk to her too.

"I have to tell you," she said, "that eyebrows are the most difficult area to regrow hair. I'm going to prescribe some Rogaine to help the process. Other than that, it will just take time. You wouldn't be considering making this a permanent part of your appearance?"

"Not my style." Harry liked her, Reuben could tell, in spite of himself.

"Good." She dipped a sterilized swab in iodine and proceeded to clean the cuts. Harry winced. "Harry, was this done with a razor? Something else sharp? Can you tell me that at least? It would help me to know."

"A razor."

"Was it dirty or rusty?"

"I don't want to talk about it anymore. I don't want to make a big deal about it, okay?"

"I'm going to give you a tetanus shot."

While she prepared the syringe, she said to Ardith, "Let me know if there's any sign of infection—swelling or a fever. Bring him back in a week so I can check on him. When you're ready, Harry, I hope you'll tell your parents what happened," and she stuck the needle in his arm. She covered the spot with cotton and a Band-Aid, then said, "Harry, would you mind if I speak with your parents a moment? You can wait right outside." She extended her hand for him to shake. He did so and left without another word.

Dr. Stein smiled at them. Tom had once sat in this same office trying to understand Harry too, befriend him with kindness and jokes. Had he and Ardith already been fucking then? Reuben would have to drag the anchor-like chain of memories up from his consciousness and remember what day and month that was and whether Ardith was being unfaithful at that particular time. Just yesterday, summoned up by its own accord, an image floated before him: Ardith drinking a cold glass of water at the kitchen sink, her long taut throat, her hand on her hip, her elbow cocked with confidence—she'd just come back from running—her breasts snug in her black Lycra sports bra. Her cheeks were flushed, an alpenglow vigor, her chestnut hair pulled back from her forehead with a black cotton headband. He'd found himself savoring the image; she had looked, he remembered, so damn strong and healthy and mysterious. And now he realized this was during the affair; she had been thinking about Tom while she slaked her thirst and gazed out the back window.

Such moments on exhibit in one's private gallery of formerly innocent memories had to be scoured and banished for the fakes they had become.

"Let me take a look at you," Dr. Stein said. She shined a light into Reuben's eye. "You bruised your eyeball when you jabbed it and that caused a blood vessel to burst. There's not much to do, other than let time take care of the problem. But your eye is going to look very mean for a while."

"That's fine," said Reuben. Between Harry's missing eyebrows and his fiery eyeball, they'd make quite a pair. They'd both wear sunglasses and dark outfits and look mysterious instead of gouged. Men in Black—with eye problems.

Dr. Stein sat down on the stool at her small desk. "Has Harry been having trouble at school?"

"Not recently," Ardith said. "This all came out of the blue."

Reuben leaned back against the examination table. Ardith had sat down in Harry's chair across from the doctor. "I'm concerned," Dr. Stein said, "that he might be depressed. Has there been any change in his eating or sleeping habits? Any signs of increased irritability beyond the norm?"

"What's the norm?" Reuben asked.

"It's pretty wide. Still, you see the signs of something more troubling than adolescent moods. His secretiveness—is that typical of Harry?"

"He's always kept to himself," Ardith said. "We've had a hard time getting him to talk about his feelings or tell us what's going on with him. We usually have to infer it, and even then, we can't always tell whether he's had a good day or a bad one. He can act sweet but be miserable inside, or he can be pleased but jump down your throat for how good he feels. What you see isn't what you get with Harry. He's so hard to read. I don't know if other kids are like that as much, certainly our youngest, Jamie, isn't—he's wide open as a book with large print. Harry, on the other hand…" Ardith suddenly stopped, as if the wind had gone out of her. She seemed far off. Reuben knew that look of abstracted sadness. "Sometimes he'll talk to me."

Reuben felt as if he should say something. "He's seen a number of therapists. We had him on medication for depression, but he stopped taking the pills after three months."

"Was there any change in his behavior?"

"Some. He was a little more outgoing."

Ardith shook her head, disagreeing. "I'd say a lot."

Reuben shrugged. "I didn't see it as much as Ardith. In any case, he wouldn't keep taking it. He seemed intent on making it not work for him."

"Kids don't like a regimen," Dr. Stein said. "Getting them to wear a coat on a cold day is hard enough, let alone making them take a pill that reminds them they're different from other kids."

"I don't think Harry cares if he's different from other kids," Reuben said. "He just wants to go his own way."

"I think it's more complicated than that," Ardith said, with a note of irritation in her voice. "He won't let anybody in, and when he does, he gets very attached to the person. He's had a best friend, Ben, who recently backed off from him."

"When did this happen?" Reuben asked.

"I'm not sure exactly. I think it started earlier in the school year." Ardith gave him a weak smile, which could either be an apology for not telling him or a criticism of his not knowing (or forgetting). "Anyway, he was upset. This boy plays sports, has other friends, and stopped calling Harry. His mother, she's my midwife, said Ben wanted to have more friends once he got to high school, but she doesn't know herself what happened between them. I think it hurt Harry terribly, even though he won't show it or say a word. I don't know how much it matters now. I just found out he and his mother are moving to Boulder."

Reuben cleared his throat, trying again. He just wanted to get to the bottom of this. "You think this incident might have to do with Ben?"

Ardith stared at him a moment. "I don't know."

Dr. Stein turned around to her desk and withdrew a prescription pad from the drawer. "From all that you're saying it sounds as if he might be suffering in silence and needs some help. I know of a very good therapist for adolescents in Fort Collins. Would you be willing to try that again? And possibly medication?"

Reuben let out an audible sigh.

"I know it's hard."

"You can't reason with him," said Reuben. "He'll spit the pill out, hide it behind his tongue, or he'll take it for a while and then just when we're all getting comfortable with the idea, he'll insist on stopping. You can withdraw every privilege in the world or bribe him shamelessly, but if he's made up his mind about it, he won't take it."

"We still don't know how this happened," Dr. Stein said, writing down a name, "whether it was self-inflicted, a cry for help. In the worst possible case he might harm himself further trying to let you know how abnormal he feels."

"Harry doesn't want to be normal—"

Ardith cut him off. "We'll do it," she said. "He'll just have to try again. And so will we."

They went outside together after retrieving Harry and Jamie from the waiting room. Harry swung Olivia in her car seat. The little girl gazed at him with adoration—his teeniest fan. Harry made faces at her, carried her around the house like a football, though he was careful to support her head and not fumble. She'd cry when he'd leave the room. It somehow made Reuben feel better knowing Harry was capable of so much affection for children.

"Can I speak with you a minute?" Reuben asked her, once they were on the sidewalk. "We'll be right back," he told the boys. "Just wait here a moment, okay?"

He led her over to the edge of the parking lot. "What do you think happened?"

"I don't know," Ardith said, "but it scares me."

"He's protecting someone." The act seemed barbaric to him, vicious, not some schoolyard prank.

"Should we go to Wade? This is serious enough to warrant his involvement, isn't it? Somebody assaulted him, Reuben."

"What can we do if he won't give us any information? He's stonewalling us again, just like last time. He only confessed to you because crazy Vic had left town."

"That wasn't the only reason he didn't say anything." Ardith looked away.

Reuben nodded, embarrassed for them both at the memory. "Look, he's going to shut us down in any case. He's got a will of steel when he wants to. What's the point of going to Wade?"

"It just doesn't feel as if we should shrug our shoulders and say kids will be kids. You try to keep your distance and let them work things out, but there are some things that demand intervention. We could start with his teachers and the principal, asking them questions. They need to know about this."

It was odd that in the midst of the worst moments and crisis he could look at her and still be struck dumb. With her yellow windbreaker unzipped, her cotton blouse open two buttons at the throat, her own eyebrows intact and sleekly auburn, she seemed radiantly familiar, cut straight from their sad history and placed before him like a living ghost. His hands would go right through her. His heart, meanwhile, didn't know the difference. Nor his cock. "I have to tell you something."

"Oh no," said Ardith. "I can only take so much bad news in one day. Is it about money? I'm going to look for a job soon. I can always go back to teaching ESL, pick up some sections at the local colleges. I just want to have some time with Olivia first. Are we bankrupt?"

She wasn't joking, he could see. "No, we're not bankrupt and it's not about money. And you did your share anyway." She had sunk the entire inheritance from her mother into the paper. And he'd promised to make good on it.

"That's a relief. I'm sorry how much you have to work lately."

"Tom's daughter came to see me last week."

A half smile froze on Ardith's face. "What did you say?"

Neither of them had spoken Tom's name for many months and it hung in the air between them for a hard moment. "Which one?" Ardith asked.

"Marian."

"I thought she was in California."

"Well, now she's in law school at Boulder."

Ardith seemed far away; yearning and apprehension haunted her gaze. He hadn't thought about how bringing this up would make him feel. It was wrenching to watch this intimate, private moment, this turmoil and excitement swirl unchecked. She pulled the yellow windbreaker closed across her chest. The sun was dropping and the afternoon flush of a warmer March day disappearing with it. "I wondered if this would happen one day."

"You don't have to say anything."

"That doesn't seem right for a number of reasons. I think she knows about Olivia. Somehow she does."

"That's ridiculous," Reuben said. "How would she know? She hasn't even been around. And nobody besides Ellen and Lyle know."

"And Colleen. And Harry. And whoever else."

"You're getting paranoid."

"At one time…"

"What?" Reuben said.

"At one time, you wanted to punish me by making it as public as you could."

"I never wanted to punish you. Oh, who knows what I *wanted* to do. It doesn't matter now."

"It matters," she said. "It matters that you never did. You could have made things much harder for me. Instead you've been kind and generous." Her eyebrows knitted and her bottom lip jutted out a bit and she looked at him with such appreciation and even maybe affection that he felt his heart lurch.

His stomach growled.

"Are you eating more?" Ardith asked. "You shouldn't starve yourself."

Harry and Jamie walked over, swinging Olivia high by the handle of the car seat. "Be careful," Ardith said.

"Can we go to McDonalds?" Jamie asked. He looked as if he would soon be catching up to Harry in height. He was a square, rugged kid with quick feet, and Reuben secretly hoped he would one day put the name Rosenfeld on a Wheaties box. But then again, he was prone to such fantasies these days as an escape from getting his head whacked against reality, because right beside Jamie was his big brother with his eyebrows gone like a peeled onion.

"We can all go," Jamie said. But before Reuben had to make that decision or look Ardith in the eye to see if she wished them to be together, Harry said, "I don't want anybody to see me like this. You have to take me home."

25

Nothing was the same after that first day of high school. Harry had met Ben at Ben's house and they'd walked together to the school, board shorts past their knees, Volcom T-shirts, skate shoes, belts that could have gone around their waists twice, the ends hanging down like dogs' tongues on a hot day. They stopped on the way to check out their hair in the gas station mirror. Harry's was shorter, spiked with gel, little peaks—stalactite head, Ben called him. "Stalagmite," Harry corrected. "They're the ones that grow up from the ground."

"Whatever," said Ben. He ran water over his head at the sink faucet, then combed his hair straight back. "The tropical look."

"More like the flood-victim look." They stood side by side in the mirror.

Ben said, "You look like what happened after somebody put your head in a socket." He draped his arm over Harry's neck and squeezed.

"Don't touch the hair!" Harry yelled. Somebody knocked on the bathroom door, and both boys spilled out like smoke, a cloud of laughter, their first day of ninth grade and high school.

Everybody was waiting around outside the building; the bell hadn't rung yet. Harry recognized some kids from his junior high, but mostly there was a mob of faces he didn't know. The school pulled from all the surrounding small towns in the county. He stayed close to Ben. They didn't talk, just tried to look cool. A teacher, he seemed like a teacher, walked past them. A kid said to him, "Hey, Coach!" He waved, then gave Ben a double take on his way by, coming over to them and pointing straight at Ben: "I want to see you at tryouts, young man." He looked right through Harry. Ben had shot up over the summer and filled out.

"You're not going, are you?" Harry asked, after the coach left. "You don't want to be a jock, do you?"

Ben hesitated a moment. "Probably not."

They went to their separate homerooms, and Harry said he'd meet Ben at lunch. Harry went to English, art appreciation, and math, and then it was time to go to lunch, and he went down and searched for Ben. Finally, he showed up. "Why are you so late?" Harry asked him. "The bell rang ten minutes ago." He'd been talking to some other guys in his class who were going out for football, and Harry felt something go hollow in his stomach, some dead spot there he couldn't get air to. He breathed better again after they went through the lunch line—pizza— and found seats together.

Incredibly noisy and busy, the lunchroom looked like a free-for-all. Everybody was running around trying to find tables, shouting stuff at each other. There were cowboys sucking on wheat straws; there were the Addamses all dressed in black; there were the Jackets who never took their coats off in class; there were the wannabe gangstas in their chains and baggies; there were scenesters in skinny jeans and black eyeliner; there were the Retro-preps tooled out in khakis and plaid ties. They sat down next to a kid who said his name was Stewart Bledsoe. He was chubby and red-faced. He claimed to have played drums during the summer with some band named Donkey Hockers but had to give it up because he had a disease that made his hands sweat too much.

By the second week of school, Ben was sitting with the jocks and Harry was still eating with Bledsoe. Bledsoe said he was related to Drew Bledsoe, a former quarterback. Harry hardly listened. He watched Ben. He watched him eat; he watched him leave the lunchroom with his new buddies; he watched him practice after school. Sometimes, he followed him between classes. "I know what you're doing," Ben told him. He had jogged over to Harry after catching a pass. Wearing shoulder pads, his helmet and shorts, he was dressed for a light practice before the game tomorrow. Harry was going to the game. He didn't know where else to go.

"What am I doing?" Harry said.

Ben pointed his finger between Harry's eyes. It was a gesture he'd seen the coach make when he wanted to get a player's attention. "Stop hanging around. You're acting gay."

He wasn't gay; he ran home.

He was going to say something to his mother, tell her he couldn't help himself, and that maybe he needed help, but she was busy getting ready for the baby. His father worked all the time. Ricky Ryan was already talking about when he could drop out of school. Stewart Bledsoe told him he was a direct descendent of Abraham Lincoln. Harry went up to Ben one day at his locker to try to talk to him and Ben slammed the locker closed and hissed, "Stay the hell away from me!"

He tried to. Days, weeks, months passed. Halloween came. A kid knocked on their front door and asked if this was where the haunted house was? They hadn't even decorated. Then Thanksgiving at the dairy farm with Isadora who had raised the turkey they ate. Christmas/ Hanukkah/ Winter Solstice or whatever it was they celebrated. He got a new freestyle bike. Then December 27 and the baby was born. His father moved out. Ricky Ryan said, "Did your parents split because of that time we saw your mom?" He backed down from Harry's cold stare, his wordless threat. "I was just asking." He hated Ricky at that moment, more than usual. He wanted him exterminated.

In February, he joined the drama club at school to help make sets. It gave him something to do after school and he liked working on the production end. But every time he saw Ben strolling down the hall with his jock friends, his insides would twist, his face burn, his thoughts spin. He sent Ben a text asking if they could talk.

He heard nothing until one day walking home from school he was jumped from behind. They tackled him and held him on the frozen ground. He lay there in the field between school and the highway and didn't even move. He didn't fight back. All of them had caps on and bandanas pulled up over their faces like bank robbers; just their eyes showed. Even through their bandanas, Harry could tell which one was Ben, and he didn't take his eyes off him. Then he heard his old friend say, "*Do it.*"

26

Reuben sat at his desk listening to Jolie in the next room bend Rosa's ear. Generally, they got along, but whereas Jolie liked to gab, Rosa had limited patience for small talk or what Jolie called girl talk.

"Joe and I met when we were in high school. I'm not sure I'd recommend getting married so young. You miss out on a lot. I might have gone to college if things had been different."

"You can still go to college," Rosa said bluntly.

"I wish. No time for that now. 'Course, Joe doesn't seem to have much time for *anything* other than working at the asphalt plant and drinking beer in the evening. We haven't exactly been intimate lately, if you know what I mean." Jolie paused. "I found something the other night. While Joe was out. Have you ever heard of *Juggs*?"

"Pardon?" said Rosa

"I didn't know myself until I found a magazine. Well, I wouldn't exactly call it that. Some piece of filth rolled up in Joe's toolbox. I went looking for a hammer and found this, you know…it's got all big-breasted women in it. Veins and stretch marks—it's the grossest thing I've ever seen! Know what Joe said when I asked him about it?"

Rosa cleared her throat, which Jolie took as interest.

"Somebody had given it to him at work and he forgot to give it back."

"Hmm," said Rosa.

Jolie stood up abruptly. "Gotta go. *These* J-U-G-S have work to do. Bobby Mattson is with his grandma and won't take a bottle. Partly it's my fault, I mean the stuff with Joe, because I don't feel like having his big lips on me after Bobby's been there all day. You probably know all about this having your own kids. Need anything while I'm out?"

"I'm good here, thank you," Rosa said.

He was in agony. Listening to Jolie go on and on. It was some kind of sexual torture. *Juggs?* The combination of her singsong voice and talk about gargantuan tits. Right down to its reptilian stem, his brain ached listening to her—but once there it stopped, and his libido picked up and mortified him by pumping blood ("All hands on deck! Juggs ahoy!") to his dumbest of organs. He kept seeing the rose tattoo above her right breast that peeked out when she wore a low-cut blouse—had she gotten it to reinvigorate Joe's interest?—and imagined her writhing alone in bed, aroused and unsatisfied while the witless Joe rummaged in the garage for his *Juggs* collection. *Such a situation isn't uncommon after a woman has a baby,* Reuben envisioned sagely explaining. *Joe is withdrawing from you because he's jealous of the attention you're giving the baby. Men have a terrible time expressing their feelings. They'd rather sulk and take comfort in degrading materials featuring anonymous gargantuan-boobed women on top of fire trucks. Why, look at you, any man would...*

He had given himself a splitting headache, in addition to a hard-on. Maybe it was Jolie's combination of perkiness, small-town values, and uncensored blabbing that stirred him up. Or maybe he was affected by how much she seemed to respect him. She didn't see him as a massive failure or a cynical joke, an ineffectual galoot or a laughable cuckold, none of the things he assaulted himself with daily. She looked up to him, the boss, Mr. Rosenfeld, her mentor—Welton's very own H. L. Mencken! Her misguided admiration was the best proof yet that she was a simpleton. And all it did was swell his manhood more than anything he could find in a magazine of watermelon breasts. He went into the bathroom, not making eye contact with Rosa on the way, and splashed cold water on his face.

Harry had seen a therapist twice since the eyebrow incident, as they referred to it. Although they—Reuben, Harry, and Ardith—had had a meeting with the principal and been informed of the school's zero-tolerance policy for such behavior and that anyone responsible for such an action would face serious consequences, Harry had refused to give any names. The principal had tried to persuade him: "It's better for everyone if you tell us. What if this were to happen to someone else?" The principal, a youthful man in jeans and a sport shirt, wore an eye patch. He'd lost his eye as a child in a fireworks accident. They were like the three blind mice, Reuben with his bloodshot eye, Harry missing his eyebrows, and the principal with his eye patch. Reuben had hoped their common ocular afflictions might loosen Harry's tongue, but it was a no-go. Harry, loyal to an adolescent code of silence, would reveal nothing about how it happened or who did it—even apparently in confidence to Neil, Harry's therapist, whose full name was Neil Chesterfield.

"Harry has never had a real relationship and it's going to take a while," he had said to Ardith and Reuben in a consultation after the first session. One of those remarks that you swallow at the time but afterward sticks in your throat and makes you choke. Was he saying Harry had no "real" relationship with either of them? The statement had been provocative if anything, but Neil had no intention of backing away from it. Instead he'd suggested each parent come see him separately. Reuben's session had been spent not talking about Ardith and the affair but about Harry, his brother. He'd poured his heart out about missing him, resenting him, being jealous of him, loving him, hating him for dying. "Sometimes," Reuben admitted, "I wonder if Harry's death gave me a lifelong case of cynicism that I've just found a little too satisfying to get over."

And then it had been time to go.

In his next session with Chesterfield, who said there was nothing more he could share about Harry since he was a client too, Reuben confessed everything about Tom and Ardith. He couldn't help but wonder if Ardith still wanted him to be Olivia's father, whether because that was easier, less messy, or just because he was alive and Tom dead. And to be honest he wasn't so sure he was still against it. Olivia was seen as his daughter anyway and did use his name—Olivia Ley Rosenfeld.

It sounded classy to him, not upsetting or dishonest as he'd once feared; he could see it one day on a wedding invitation or a graduation announcement in fancy script. He'd taken one look at her when Ardith brought her home from the hospital and known he couldn't refuse her anything. He'd had no idea how a little girl would melt his heart. When he sat for her and the boys, those few times Ardith left for a quick errand, he handled her like a fragile vase, while Harry and Jamie moved her around the room like a FedEx package. "Loosen up, Dad," they would tell him. And he had over the months, putting funny hats on his head for her, making faces, barreling her through the house in her stroller with the dog hopping after them. Nothing could have prepared him for how he would feel about her—that he would stare at her with the fascination of a man beholding a new shore. He was her most frequent, large male visitor. Her alert eyes registered his importance whenever he came through the door. She would reach for his chin, the beard he had grown back, and tug on it, her gesture of hello. She knew him. Pure, unguarded delight lit up her face. It ripped at his heart.

Neil Chesterfield had listened without interrupting. Winded by giving voice to this psychic storm, Reuben slumped back on the therapist's couch. He waited for Chesterfield to impart some wisdom about the morass he'd just dumped on the man. Neil studied him a moment, smiled sympathetically as if Reuben had just disclosed either a heartwarming story or a terrible dream, put down his pen, and said, "Let's pick up again here next session."

27

Ardith watched her. Patient if bewildered, she sat with her hands in her lap, her long blonde hair across her shoulders. She wore a coffee-colored blouse, black leggings, and silver drop earrings. Ardith stared so hard at the resemblance to Tom that she failed to speak. Marian had no idea why she was here. Reuben had contacted her to say he'd like her to come up from Boulder and stop by whenever she had the time. Then he'd driven her over to the house, explaining, as he and Ardith had rehearsed, that his wife wanted to meet her. If that confused or deterred her, he was to say that it wouldn't take long but it was very important. Olivia had bridged any awkwardness. As far as Marian knew, the baby was just a new addition to this unfamiliar family. Olivia, with her round face and busy eyes, examined Marian, then reached up for her hair. Marian bent down and let her pull on it. Tiny white bubbles of saliva dribbled from Olivia's lips.

Ardith dabbed at her baby's mouth and sat her more upright facing Marian. Olivia gave her a flirting smile.

"She's showing off," Ardith said. "She won't do that trick for just anybody."

"How old is she?"

"Four months."

Marian nodded, then fluttered her lips at Olivia. Olivia's eye-lashes curled up elegantly, like a little doll from another century.

Her resemblance, next to her half-sister, was unmistakable, and made Ardith catch her breath. "You seem very comfortable around babies."

"I did a lot of babysitting when I was younger. I've always liked children. My sister not so much. Even though she wound up with three kids and I'm still single!" Marian looked at her watch. "I don't mean to be rude, but I don't really know why

I'm here. Your husband was very mysterious about my coming by."

"Sorry," said Ardith. "I just wanted to meet you, because of Tom."

"Because of my father?"

"Yes."

"Did you know him well?"

"I suppose I did."

"How so?"

Ardith smiled and looked away. They sat in silence for a moment, until Marian said, "I should be getting home." She looked around for Reuben, who would drive her back to her car. He had disappeared so Ardith could do this alone.

"She's your sister."

"What?"

"I'm sorry…"

"What did you say?"

"I planned to build up to it. I didn't mean to spring it on you like this—"

"What are you talking about?" Marian looked at the little baby and then at Ardith. She looked again at Olivia, her blue eyes and tiny thin mouth. "Oh my God…*shit*."

"I'll get us some cold water," Ardith said.

"It was anything but a fling for me. I had never seriously contemplated an affair in twenty years of marriage. Then your father came along, and I didn't even try to stop myself, as if I had no past at all to respect." A sign, Ardith thought now but didn't say outright, of how deeply and recklessly she'd fallen in love. "I was devastated when your father died. Finding out I was pregnant after his death made it possible for me to pull myself together, once I decided I would have the baby."

"This is like the greatest, saddest, most mind-blowing thing anybody has ever told me."

"Can you come visit again?" Ardith asked. "I'd like it if you…I don't know, it depends what *you* want. But I'd like you to come see us again."

"I just need time to wrap my brain around all this."

"You're handling it extremely well."

"Your husband. He...?"

"Yes, he knows. It's difficult, extremely. But we're trying to deal with it."

Marian studied her a moment. "I see why my father fell for you. You're his type, dark haired—he never liked my mother's dyed blonde hair. You're slim, a pretty smile, and you never take your eyes off people when they talk. My father would have enjoyed that."

"Thank you," said Ardith, but she wondered what she meant by *his type*. She suddenly felt uncomfortable talking about Tom with Reuben rumbling around the house; she could hear him going through boxes or pails in the garage, clanking around out there. His noise seemed to increase in proportion to how much deeper they got into the subject of Tom—or maybe that was just her conscience amplifying the racket. "Let me go see if Reuben can take you back."

"Can I hold her?" Marian asked.

"Sure," said Ardith. "As much as you like." Marian reached out her arms, her hands trembling, and Olivia fell into them without a peep.

28

Though Harry had gotten special permission to wear sunglasses to hide his missing eyebrows, it felt more conspicuous to have them on, so after the first day he stopped. Some snickering followed, but soon there was just indifference. He spent much of the school day with a sickening knot of pus-filled humiliation in his stomach. He had learned that Ben was moving to Boulder. His mother had found better-paying work there as a midwife. The whole situation felt too ugly to find any actual relief in Ben's moving away. He just tried not to think about it (let alone talk about it), which wasn't that hard until he looked in the mirror at his missing eyebrows.

One morning near the end of the school year, he was standing at his locker when a girl came up to him and asked if he wanted to contribute money for the wrestling team's trip to the regional tournament next month in Tempe, Arizona. The team had gone undefeated and had a good chance to win the Western regionals and go to nationals. This girl—her name was Brenva—pushed a Pringles potato chip can in front of him. A slit was in the plastic top to drop money. She was wearing a vest with buttons that said things like "The little voices talk to me" and "Be alert—we need more lerts!"

"Why are you doing this?" Harry asked her.

"For the wrestling team."

"But why?"

She gave him a crooked smile. Her own eyebrows were thick and sleek, dark brown like her eyes. She had a small chin and her mouth worked in funny ways while she spoke, more than just forming words—little half smiles and smirks and pouts, restless even in silence. She gave him a long explanation of why the team needed the money, everything from travel expenses to snacks to equipment. The school was providing some money but there wasn't enough, so they were doing bake sales and car washes and asking for sponsors. He was intrigued she was taking so much time with him, especially since he had no intention of contributing. Ben was friends with the wrestlers, and Harry didn't doubt that some of them had been among his attackers. He didn't watch Ben anymore; he didn't even look at him when they passed in the halls. Once, he heard Ben call his name, or thought he did, but he never stopped walking. He just kept his head down and went about his business.

"I mean," Harry said, when she stopped talking, "what's in this for you? Are you on the cheer squad or something?"

"Wrestlers don't have cheerleaders. I'm friends with them."

That's what he thought, the enemy. "I don't have any money."

"Even a quarter will help."

"Not even a quarter." He started to walk away.

"*Hey*," she said, "you're lying. Everybody has a quarter." She stood in front of him with her hands on her hips.

"You just called me a liar."

"Well…are you?"

He did have a quarter; he had thirty dollars in fact. He was going to buy some new pegs for his bike.

The bell had already rung. Still, she stood there. Classroom doors were closing. She showed no sign of budging. Her eyes narrowed at him. She wore a bright fuchsia off-the-shoulder sweater showing her smooth collar bones. Her legs in shorts were thin and bare as sticks on a cold day. He would have liked to draw her.

He blinked first. He took out his wallet and stuffed thirty dollars into the can. He wanted to see her big brown eyes get even wider, and they did, huge and bemused but not pitying. They didn't mock him or look at him like he was weird or say, *Gotcha, sucker!*

"You need some lessons in financial management," she informed him. "It's all or nothing with you." She took the money out and counted back twenty-nine dollars to him. "That's enough for today," she said, leaving open the possibility of more tomorrow.

29

When Ardith stopped to look around, it was as if she'd been transported back to Tom's house—the drawers of neatly folded clothes and shiny kitchen counters and clutter-free living. Her new mother's helper cooked healthy meals with green vegetables and made sure that Ardith had frequent naps. Ellen had recommended the girl, who turned out to be a classmate of Harry's. Luisa kept the house cleaned, as it had never been cleaned before: dishes put away; closets organized; towels folded and stacked in fluffy, fresh-smelling piles; the stove scrubbed of old grease; the checker pieces sorted from the Scrabble tiles; the refrigerator shelves adjusted so the liter soda bottles actually fit; the laundry put in drawers instead of on the stairs; the dirty bathroom windowpanes wiped spotless; the throw rugs with dog hair beat clean and aired on a clothesline.

A genie had come to help her.

"How do you know how to do all this?" Ardith gushed after the first week.

"My mother. She taught me. And she always gets on me when we clean together if I don't do things right, which means her way."

"I feel so guilty having you here. I wish I could pay you more."

"It's okay. I like being here. And honestly, it's easier than working with my mother."

"You have to make sure you have time for school and your own life."

"I have too much time to myself. I don't like sitting around just thinking. And high school is much easier than I thought."

"Harry said you were no longer helping with the theater productions. Is that my fault?"

"No, I was getting tired of it. And I wasn't making money doing it. Harry is…"

"What?" Ardith said, always tensing up when anyone had some opinion about Harry, usually unwelcomed.

"He's talented. All his painting of the sets. He doesn't even know how good he is."

"Do you see a lot of Harry at school?"

"We hang out. Sometimes. He has a girlfriend."

"What?"

"Um…I thought you knew."

"Harry has a girlfriend? What's her name?"

"Brenva."

"Brenda?"

"Bren-*va*."

"Oh." She was stunned. How could she not know this?

"I better go."

"Here," Ardith said, reaching into her purse. She handed Luisa a twenty-dollar bill. "Just a little extra."

"That's not necessary."

"Please. I want you to have it."

"Okay," she said. "Thank you." Ardith reached out to hug her and Luisa went soft in her arms. When she pulled away to look at her, she saw tears on Luisa's face.

"What's wrong, honey?" Ardith gave her a tissue from her bag and kept her hand on Luisa's shoulder.

"Nothing. I'm okay. I just get emotional sometimes when people are so nice to me."

"You're a gem," Ardith said. "You deserve every bit of kindness that comes your way."

It wasn't only Luisa who had come to her rescue. Marian too came up whenever she could from Boulder. They shopped together, went to matinees out at the new Cineplex and took turns walking Olivia in the lobby during her fussy times. They jogged around Lake Finnegan, as she once had with Tom. All the things she might have done with Tom, if tragedy hadn't intervened, she enjoyed with Marian, so much so that she had fallen back in love with him again through his daughter. "I feel as if I'm dreaming this part of my life," she told Marian, hugging her spontaneously in the produce section of the market. "Me too," Marian said. "It's everything I would like to do with my mother if I ever have a baby, but I know it will be far too complicated to ever happen with her."

Earlier in the evening, Reuben had taken the boys off to a basketball game in Denver. Harry had pulled all Bs and Cs on his latest report card, which they considered good for him because months ago, just about the time he'd had his eyebrows shaved off, he'd been flunking math and science. But going to see Neil and taking an antidepressant had turned him around. The change showed itself in subtle ways too: everything from offering to take Charlotte for a walk to his being interested in drawing more. The drawing in particular had become a regular activity. He had portraits of everyone in the house around his room, including Marian. Ardith resisted praising him too much, but she couldn't help offering a few compliments. She would go into his room while he was at school and sometimes just look at his pictures. Done in pen and ink, the drawings had long elliptical shapes, a little alien looking, and she was not surprised to find what they had in common were their missing eyebrows.

Her phone rang now. She expected Reuben back very soon with the boys from a basketball game in Denver. It was an out-of-state number, and she assumed a junk call, but some instinct told her to answer it. What if something had happened to Reuben and the boys?

"Is this Ardith?"

"Yes."

"My name is Patricia Grierson. I'm Tom Watkins's daughter."

She had never spoken to anyone else in Tom's family, and Marian would only say, despite Ardith's prodding for more, her sister had a different perspective on their father. No one else needed to know about Olivia. It was Ardith's decision if and to whom she would say anything. Olivia's existence was no one else's business, Marian had assured her. So why was her sister calling? And how did she get this number?

"Do you have a minute?" Patricia asked.

"Just a second." She wound up Olivia's mechanical swing. For an hour she would swing, with Charlotte watching in fascination. "Okay, just had to get the baby happy."

"That's what I wanted to speak with you about. Your baby," Patricia said.

"Olivia?"

"Is that her name?"

Ardith didn't like the shift in tone. "Yes, it is."

"I'm wondering if you plan on…how should I put this? Are you going to pursue this matter any further?"

"Pursue what?"

"Any action against us."

Action? "What do you mean exactly?"

"Well, if I have to spell it out…any attempt to bring a financial claim against our father's estate."

Ardith was speechless.

"My sister told me all about it when she was here. She's entitled, I suppose, to do whatever she chooses for you, but I just want you to know it won't be so easy getting help from us—"

"Wait…*wait.*"

"I'm just saying—"

"You're saying…" Her mind was going in so many directions at once she couldn't think what to say first.

"Look, I'm not the angel my sister tries to be. We have very different views about my father's actions. As far as I'm concerned, he ruined more than a few lives with his behavior. Do you think you're anything special?"

My God, help me, Ardith murmured. The voice was so hateful and condemning she felt as if she couldn't breathe.

"I'm sorry for you," Patricia said. "But don't expect anything from us. My mother or me. We don't want to be involved. My father put her through hell, and all the while she tried to hold us together as a family. She's the one I care about right now. She's the person that deserves my support." And she hung up.

"She's mad at me, she's trying to hurt me," Marian kept saying over and over. "I chose to side with him about the divorce and not with Mom. I shouldn't have told her. One thing just led to another. You can't imagine how they can grill me once I'm captive in their homes."

Ardith sat stunned. She had been unable to do anything more than pick Olivia up and clutch her. Marian had raced up from Boulder to talk in person, even though it was late. Reuben was still with the boys in Denver at a basketball game.

"Maybe I thought they had a right to know too, Ardith. My sister most of all. Olivia is Patricia's half-sister also."

"I thought we agreed you wouldn't tell anyone, for now anyway. She was just so hateful, Marian."

She hardly knew what had hit her. An assassination. What had she ever done to her?

"Look, Patricia is suffering from postpartum or something. That's all I can figure. She's usually not this bad, not like this."

"What does she mean exactly?"

"About what?"

"'Do you think you're anything special?'"

Marian looked away. "I don't know."

"How bad *was* he?" She felt as if she were speaking of a neighbor, or someone she'd heard about, not Tom. "I want to know."

Charlotte jumped up between them, as if to separate them. She settled herself against Ardith's leg. Ardith thought, *Let it go.* But she couldn't; she had to know everything. "Tell me, Marian."

"He had an affair with the wife of another doctor in a practice with Dad. They were good friends with our family. Their oldest girl, Mona, was Patricia's age and her best friend. My father was unhappy with my mother, and had been for some time, and so was Mona's mother in her marriage. It only lasted a short while before Dad ended it. But Mona's mother was far more invested and became wild after Dad tried to break it off. She became so depressed she had to be hospitalized and that's when everything blew up. Mona refused to speak to Patricia.

The practice broke up. Mona's mother and father eventually divorced, but her mother kept after my dad. It got so bad—her stalking him—he had to get a restraining order. Patricia was going through junior high at the time and felt really humiliated because everyone knew about it. I was only ten and mostly unaware of what was going on. It was a big, sick mess."

Ardith's stomach tightened. "And that's why she's so bitter at your father?"

Marian shook her head. "It got worse. Mona's mother committed suicide a year later. Everybody blamed my father. It all became so ugly, Ardith."

"But it wasn't your father's doing—the woman…she sounds disturbed." She had the strange sensation of defending Tom for an incident that would have shocked her if he'd told her himself. And why hadn't he?

Marian petted Charlotte slowly. "Look, it doesn't change anything," she said. "About Olivia. It's still a miracle."

"A miracle? Why a miracle?"

"He would have been so happy, Ardith. I know it."

"Did your father ever mention me? Do you remember my name coming up?" She felt desperate and pleading, but he might have given some sign to Marian that he was truly in love this time. It would have been safe to tell his daughter. That it wasn't just another appalling affair. That it meant more, much more.

"I've told you what he said. He said he had fallen in love with someone."

Yes, and it had shot her heart into the stratosphere when Marian mentioned it on one of their walks with Olivia. She'd placed so much faith and certainty in it, certainty that Tom had genuinely loved and not used her and she didn't have to flay herself with regret for the rest of her life. But now she questioned it.

"Did he say anything else?"

Marian's eyes were red-rimmed, and her nose was running. They were sharing a box of tissues between them. "No," she said, "he didn't say anything, and I can't ask him now or ever." She rested her hands on her knees. "All my life I've felt like both the prosecution and defense for him. It used to tear me apart, and the worst thing is that it's still tearing me in two."

Reuben walked in the front door. They'd just had the front porch fixed. There had been a little extra money, and he'd hired someone to rebuild both the front and back porches without the usual debate. Jamie followed, looking tired and hungry.

"What's wrong?" Reuben asked, glancing at each of them sitting on the couch, their eyes red.

"We're just having a good cry," Ardith said. "It's okay." But, for the first time in a long while, she wanted to get a hug, rest against him and just breathe as she sometimes used to do while he held her patiently, the familiar warmth of his skin. It started to make her cry again, and she caught herself. "Where's Harry?"

"He's in the car listening to a song finish," Jamie said. "By Disturbed or something like that. The Nuggets won," Jamie said, punching his fist in the air. "A buzzer shot by Jokic!"

Reuben put his cap on. Now that his hair was thinning, he wore it to keep the sun off. It touched her that he was going bald. "I'll say goodnight," he said.

"You want some coffee or something?"

"I'm fine."

"If you're tired you could stay here tonight."

"What?"

"Are you too tired to drive out to the farm?"

He hesitated. "I'm good," he said. "Automatic pilot." And he left through the front door of their new porch.

30

What was Ardith doing? Playing games? She'd never asked him if he wanted to stay over. Why did she look like that? Not only the crying but the openness in her face. And her voice!—solicitous, a gentle come hither. All warm cornbread and honey. The way she used to talk when they'd first been married. Or after sex when they'd satisfied each other. Now it confused the hell out of him. And what was Marian doing there? She had slipped into the family unit like a missing nail. But she only came up on weekends and never stayed late. He couldn't wait to leave so he could think about it all alone.

And about Jolie.

They'd been working late last Wednesday to put the paper to bed. He'd gone into the back of the vault to find a suitable piece from the archives for their "Looking Back and Forth" section and switched on the vault's single bare bulb. There she stood in the doorway, wearing snug jean shorts and a tight white blouse that seemed to glow. Her shapely calves were backlit by the bright workroom light, edging the flesh in silky incandescence. A halo of blue fluorescence circled the dark curls of her head. Her palms were pressed against the sides of the vault's narrow opening, as if she were posing in the entrance of a foamy, wave-swept sea cave. He could feel her waiting for him to do something—swim to her in their spelunking underwater adventure. And then, as fate would have it, her cell phone rang, and she vanished to answer it.

Her husband Joe. The baby was throwing up. She left.

He had sat in his office chair until one a.m. and thought about how stirred up he was, how foolish such a move would be, and how willing he would have been if she had come one step closer. But wasn't that always the story? Somebody had to move one step closer; otherwise, zip. Surely there were thousands of *almost* affairs that had *almost* happened by people *almost* moving one more step. Yet with Ardith and Tom...well, maybe it hadn't been such a big step. Or maybe someone took two steps to make up for the other person's hesitation. He never got into that with Ardith—who pursued whom, how equal it was. Such details faded in importance over time and left just the indisputable act and what it had produced. Olivia's existence plugged up all the hollows he might have wormed around in for the rest of his life searching for answers. The child was here. Either he would surrender to that fact, make peace with it, live with the outcome, or fight it forever. On some days he would have picked one answer; on others, like this evening, when he heard some long-lost yearning in Ardith's voice, he would have bet on acceptance, if not exactly reconciliation.

On his nightly drive back to Lyle's, he had to pass by the spot where Tom died. The same dark road. But now at least it had a white line designating a shoulder for bicycles. He suspected that was a result of Tom's death, one good thing to come out of the tragedy. Still, he couldn't pass the curve—someone had placed a small white wooden cross at the spot—without tensing up for all the heartache the place represented. He kept his hands tightly on the steering wheel until he drove safely by and arrived at the farm.

The milking-barn lights blazed as he pulled into the farm's gravel driveway. He'd watched Lyle and Ellen's milkers work. They'd spray the udders with disinfectant, wait a minute or so, wipe the disinfectant off with a rag, then hook up a machine that was linked to a computer. The light would go on when the cow finished, then the contraption would fall off automatically, and ten more cows would be led in. The work went on from five in the morning to ten at night, through three thousand gallons of milk that they shipped daily to their dairy co-op. Lyle did everything from cleaning up cow shit with a tractor to fixing fences destroyed by a wild bull to donning a huge prophylactic glove so he could insert his entire arm up a cow's rectum, palpating the animal to check for pregnancy.

He started up the stairs to his room but saw a light on in the kitchen and went in. Lyle was sitting at the table with a beer. He had on a Rockies cap and a bath towel around his neck, as if he'd just gotten out of the shower. At forty-nine, his shoulders were still well muscled and his waist lean. He kept in shape the old-fashioned way, by working.

"Eh, *patrón*, wassup?" he said when he saw Reuben in the doorway.

"Just came back from a Nuggets game in Denver with the boys."

"Any good?"

"They won."

Lyle nodded. "You want a beer?"

Reuben shook his head. "What are you still doing up?" Lyle was usually in bed by ten. He had a herdsman and a dozen employees to milk and feed the cows but things never ran smoothly by themselves.

"Just thinking."

"About anything important?"

"How much longer are you going to stay here?"

"Here?" Reuben said. It wasn't what he'd been expecting. "Should I be thinking about leaving?"

"I don't give a damn whether you leave. You think that's what I'm asking?"

"What *are* you asking?"

"Are you going to patch it up with Ardith or not? What the hell are you waiting for? You want to stay up in your little monk's cell above our garage for the rest of your life, fine. I'll stock up on toilet paper. But for Christ's sake, you can't hang on to this nonsense forever."

"Nonsense? Excuse me, but—"

"What's wrong with a little common sense, apologies all around. Shake hands and get out there and play ball."

"Spare me the World Series comparison! You think it's so simple that we can just say *no hard feelings, darling?* My wife had a child by another man. Another man she—" He couldn't even say it. He knew Lyle was thinking *fucked,* but it was *loved* that killed him. Only he knew in his gut how much. "Put yourself in my position." He felt pissed now. "You think you'd be any more magnanimous?"

"You don't know what family is."

"Pardon?"

"You heard me."

"What's that got to do with anything?"

Lyle leaned back, glassy-eyed. "I'll tell you a secret."

"Please don't."

He put up his hand for Reuben to relax. "Ellen and I were virgins."

"Virgins?"

"Virgins."

Reuben laughed. "Surely not."

"What's not to believe?"

"You never even married!"

"So what?"

"And what's this all have to do with Ardith and me? And by the way, what makes you think this is only *my* decision?"

"You're a stubborn bastard."

Lyle got up and opened the refrigerator to get another beer. He took one out for Reuben without asking and slid it across the table. It stopped, with perfect accuracy, halfway over the table's edge.

"Virgins? Are you out of your mind?" Ellen strolled around the kitchen the next morning, getting coffee for herself. Reuben looked at Lyle who was snickering. "Lyle slept with so many women he was a public health hazard. Including my friends."

"That all changed, babe. I mean we were *kinda* virgins because we hadn't slept with anyone for two weeks before we met."

Ellen snorted. Lyle had brought up the subject of their virginity ("I told our little secret about being virgins") as soon as Reuben sat down. After only a few hours of sleep, he found

Lyle still hunkered over the kitchen table. And still bare-chested, his eyes bloodshot and his hair matted to one side. It was clear he'd fallen asleep over his beer.

"You'd better go sleep it off," Ellen told him, then turned to Reuben. "He does this every few months. I think it's his way of telling himself, as his own boss, to take this job and shove it." She went over to Lyle and draped her hands across his bare chest, nuzzling his neck. "You stink too," she said, but kissed him anyway.

Sleepily, Isadora, one year older than Jamie, shuffled into the kitchen, wearing her pajamas. She hugged her mother's waist and gave Lyle a kick in the shins. "Dad, you look like a bum."

Lyle flicked his neck towel at her. She jumped back, screaming, then turned to Ellen. "*Estoy demasiado cansada para practicar piano.*"

"*Lo siento, mija. Te matriculamos porque pensamos que querías aprender a tocar el piano.*"

They had enrolled Isadora in a bilingual high school. Ellen would have long discussions with her in Spanish that left Reuben and Lyle, too, in the dust.

Lyle had planted some awful seed in his mind. Reckless, drunken remarks, with no knowledge of the facts. And what the hell was this about *you don't know what family is?*

"Miguel!" Isadora shouted and ran toward the doorway. She threw her arms around the man standing there in his rubber boots and work gloves. It was Miguel, their herdsman and Luisa's father. Reuben had first met him because his daughter helped Ardith. The girl just showed up one afternoon at Ardith's door saying she'd heard from her father's boss, Ellen, that Ardith might need help around the house and maybe some babysitting. She was also a friend of Harry's evidently, unbeknownst to them, because Harry never told Ardith and Reuben about his friends.

"I need to go into town to get some parts for one of the chillers," Miguel said.

Lyle nodded. "You want to use my truck?"

"I've got mine."

Isadora held on to his hand. He had evidently missed a lot of work and was having a hard time keeping it together. Reuben heard Ellen and Lyle arguing about him one night in raised voices, unusual since their disagreements typically took the form of friendly bickering. Lyle said Miguel had been given enough chances. Ellen maintained he'd been with them for years and was part of the family and whatever problems he had wouldn't be solved overnight. "And what are those problems exactly? That's never been clear to me. Meanwhile, I have a farm to run." "*We* have a farm to run," Ellen reminded him.

He only saw Miguel on weekend nights when he worked until ten, because usually Reuben stayed at the paper late, hating that his life had come to this necessity, an attic room with a twin bed, as if he were an impoverished college student again.

"Anything else?" Lyle said.

"I have to trim some hooves when I get back."

"I'll help you," Lyle said.

Miguel turned to Reuben. "Your family…everybody okay?"

"Yes, thank you." What else could he say? And what could this herdsman, with his own family intact, be thinking about why Reuben's wife and apparent new child lived apart from him.

"*¿Tienes hambre?*" Isadora asked. She held out her plate of toast to him.

"*No, coranzoncito,*" Miguel told her.

He left and Isadora went off too. Ellen turned to Lyle. "See? He's managing fine."

"Maybe. Maybe not."

"You have your mind made up regardless, evidently."

"I'd better get to work," Reuben said. He had enough tension in his own life.

"Me too," said Lyle, and winked at him.

He was late getting into the office. Jolie was wearing a floral dress of wild violets. She breezed across the room, doing something or other to the back of her hair. "Good morning, Mr.

Rosenfeld!" She was still doing that thing with her hair, sticking it with pins or something to get it off her neck. "Happy Friday!"

"You too," he said, and watched her wander off to get coffee.

He realized he was supposed to take Harry in for his therapy appointment this afternoon. Per Neil's suggestion, Reuben was to work on being more positive around Harry. They did best when they shared an activity—something to do, somewhere to go. So, as part of the program, Reuben made it a point to take Harry out once a week by himself and put on a happy face. The most successful outing had been to an exhibit of Toulouse Lautrec's work at the Denver Art Museum. Harry found it enthralling. Truly, Reuben had never seen him so interested in anything. Transfixed by the posters, by the sketches and lithographs of prostitutes, circus performers, and Moulin Rouge dancers that had brought Lautrec so much scorn as well as praise, he asked if they could go through the self-guided tour again.

But it was Toulouse Lautrec himself that fascinated Harry: the offspring of first cousins, he had a large head, huge dark eyes, and withered legs. He'd suffered a bone disease that had stunted his growth. In the gift shop, Harry looked through a biography of the painter. "Cool," Harry said, "redemption," and put the book down. He wandered off, and Reuben, curious—what an odd thing to say!—opened to the passage Harry had been reading:

> It was reported by the prostitutes that he had soft caressing hands and an exceptionally large penis.

Had Harry actually said "redemption?" He'd definitely mumbled something—maybe "rejection" or "gargantuan." But Reuben had heard it clearly in his own mind: *redemption.*

They purchased an art book of Lautrec's work, a poster, a T-shirt, and the biography. Harry wanted everything. Reuben had not remembered him getting so excited by a subject in years, so he'd bought out the gift shop.

He realized now he had an appointment and wouldn't be able to take Harry to therapy. He called Ardith and left a message when she didn't answer.

"Hi," Ardith said. "I saw you called."

"I was wondering if you could drive Harry to his therapy appointment this afternoon."

"All right," she said. "Jamie will be home, but Luisa will be coming over. He's saying he doesn't want anyone to babysit him anymore, even though I know he really likes her."

"He's twelve now. It's time. He especially doesn't need a teenage girl watching over him."

"She's such a help to me. I'm afraid to lose her. Even if she's not babysitting anymore. I feel guilty about just having her clean when she's so young."

"It's all relative."

"What?"

"Never mind." He stared at the invoice on his desk from the *Greeley Tribune* whose press the *Sentinel* used for their weekly edition. They had raised their prices. Next to it was an estimate to fix the clutch in the *Sentinel's* aging van that Calvin Ingle, eighty-two, had driven since his retirement as an accountant to deliver papers and keep busy. "Why was Marian at the house last night?"

"I'd rather not go into it."

"Okay."

A long pause, then: "It was about Tom. His older daughter, Patricia, called me."

"What did she want?"

"I don't need to trouble you with it."

"Okay. Thanks for taking Harry to—"

"She made me feel like a...like a tramp."

She didn't want to go into it? Then why was she telling him about it? Proceed with caution, she seemed to be signaling, but keep trying. "Did she call out of the blue?"

"Completely. She blindsided me."

"Was this right before I came back with the boys?"

"Yes."

"I knew something was wrong. I would have stayed if I'd known."

"What do you mean?"

"I wouldn't have rushed off."

"That's okay, you were tired. It had been a long day for you."

"What'd she say to make you feel like a tramp?"

"I've got to go."

"Okay," he said, staring at his feet. They were too large, too big for his own good. What had he said wrong? Never repeat the word "tramp" to your wife, for one.

31

Oh shit, Ardith thought, when she saw Harry with his arm around a girl at the Sugar Beet Parade. The girl, who had long brown hair, looked fourteen or fifteen. She was wearing a black tank top and an orange cap cocked sideways on her head. Her face was mostly hidden by her long hair and by pressing against Harry's shoulder. They stood on the curb across the street, watching the parade and eating snow cones. In between floats Ardith tried to look. Harry had told her he wanted to go to the parade by himself and that he'd meet everyone there. With his arm slung across the girl's shoulder, his fingers seemed dangerously close to her breast.

Harry caught Ardith's eye and immediately flipped his hand off the girl's shoulder.

Go away, the gesture said. *Stop watching me.* He glared at her.

Now she knew why he left the house every spare moment he got. He always told her he was just "hanging out," and though she pressed for more information about where and with whom, fearing it was Ricky Ryan, it was obviously to meet this girl.

Olivia pulled at her hair. "Okay," Ardith said, and started to walk. It was the only other place, besides the jogging stroller, that she liked to be: in her new back carrier, as long as Ardith kept moving like a pachyderm. She had a sudden stabbing longing for Tom to be with her at the parade carrying his almost five-month-old daughter. The question of *You think you're anything special?* from Patricia had not stopped drumming in her head. The damning words had curdled her usual trusting thoughts about Tom and turned them sour and ugly: alive, he probably would have demanded she have an abortion; alive, he would have dropped her for an affair with a different married woman. She was making herself sick with her doubts about a man who could never answer them now.

She slipped the back carrier off and took Olivia in her arms, stroking her soft head to quiet a rising fever of devouring judgment.

Last night Reuben had called to tell her he needed to borrow Harry's BMX bike for the parade; he was part of a bike brigade made up of his Rotary Club members. Unfortunately, his bike, he'd remembered at midnight, had a punctured inner tube he'd been meaning to fix. She had felt mildly annoyed with him for waiting until the last minute before "remembering" his own bike wouldn't work. What if Harry had wanted to use his bike today?

When she glanced across the street, Harry and his girlfriend weren't there anymore. Ardith walked along, looking at the booths and trying to keep Olivia's hands from grabbing the stained glass or yanking down the wind chimes. They paused at a booth with homemade cherry pies, and she thought about getting one but that would require stopping for more than a second.

Veterans groups carrying flags of the service branches marched past to loud applause. The high school color guard came next, twirling their flags to the beat of the Welton High School band behind them. A line of antique cars decorated with pennant flags and bunting drove in single file, tooting their *a-hooga* horns. Civil War soldiers, union uniforms she was glad to see, were followed by mountain men in buckskin and coonskin hats, and after them, adorned in a sparkling white gown and wearing a tiara, rode the Sugar Beet Queen, a tradition from the days when Welton once made its living producing sugar beets. Sitting atop a cherry-red Corvette convertible, the queen waved a white-gloved hand. Behind her, flipping and cartwheeling their way down the street, gymnasts and jugglers performed— and then the town's firefighters who tossed candies to kids in the crowd.

A cheer went up. It was Bud Ross on a fire truck. His ninety-fourth consecutive parade, having started when he was three. Ardith had read about it in the *Sentinel*. Reuben had led off the issue with a feature story on him. Ninety-seven years old and the last living member of the famous 1939 Wildcats, Welton's one and only national championship basketball team that had beat a team from Milwaukee. It was still the big news around here: little Welton, only six hundred people then, winning the national championship. The barbershop, where Bud Ross had worked until he retired and where Harry and Jamie got their haircuts, was covered with framed news articles of the triumph. Tall and thin, but not stooped, his white hair combed in a rolling wave, his cheeks sunken but tan, he offered a blazing smile and waved generously to the crowd. People clapped, yelled greetings back to him, waved little American flags on sticks. "Show us your set shot, Bud!" He obliged the crowd by bending his knees and pushing two hands out toward an invisible hoop.

What a town. You could still be cheered for an event that took place eighty-one years ago!

She saw Luisa standing with her brother and a friend on the other side and tried to get their attention and finally did, waving to her. Ardith had thought she had a crush on Harry and gently asked her about a boyfriend, but near tears, Luisa confessed she didn't think boys were her thing. She couldn't say anything to her parents. They'd be mortified. And they had enough problems. Ardith told her to please talk to her anytime about her feelings, assuring her the most important thing was her happiness. Her heart ached for the girl. Even in turning-blue Colorado, you weren't going to find a gay pride contingent marching in Welton's Sugar Beet Parade; no rodeo queens of that persuasion.

She had mentioned to Reuben about returning to Chicago. Did they really want to continue to raise the boys out here? They still had friends in Chicago, Ardith could get her old job back teaching ESL. Her skin would certainly look better from all the moisture. For all its open vistas, blue skies, snow-capped mountains, good schools, safe streets, fit people, and Western politeness—*you have a super day, ma'am*—maybe crustier Chicago was home. Much to her surprise, having staked his claim here, Reuben sounded more amenable than she thought.

She saw Jamie. Out in front in his Scout uniform, he carried, along with his friend Matthew, a banner that read TROOP 193 SALUTES AMERICA'S HEROES.

As she waved to him, Olivia yanked at her hair. "Will you please stop that?"

A woman turned around and smiled. "Is she giving you a hard time, Mrs. Rosenfeld?"

It was Jolie. Ardith hadn't recognized her. She'd grown her hair out and was wearing black Capri pants and a beige tank top, looking very fit. She had a camera around her neck.

"She thinks I'm a horse and my hair is the reins," Ardith said. Jolie was eating a hot dog. "Where are your two kids?"

"Joe has them down by the pony rides. Gives me a break— occasionally. Your husband gave me a job to do anyhow." She wiggled the camera. "Need to get some action shots of the parade for a spread."

"You're looking good, Jolie."

"So are you. Pregnancy must have agreed with you. I don't like being pregnant. Some women do, but I don't." Something in the way Jolie said it made Ardith think she was again.

"It's no picnic," Ardith said, an expression she would never have used in Chicago. "Especially in summer."

"Well, I'll escape that this time at least. This one's going to be a winter baby."

"Oh!" Ardith said, feigning surprise. "Congratulations."

Jolie shrugged.

"You don't look happy."

"I'm not sure we're doing it for all the right reasons. Anyway," she said, holding the hot dog up, "I might as well not worry about getting fat now."

"Eating for two," Ardith said, another folksy expression that sounded foreign to her. Was it the parade?

"I hope it's another girl this time. My little guy, whew…I don't know if I can take another fullback." Jolie smiled at Olivia, who had rested her chin on Ardith's shoulder. "She's got Tom's eyes all right."

For a second, Ardith thought she heard wrong—*Mom's eyes.* But when she saw Jolie's stricken face, she knew she hadn't.

"Oh my God," Jolie said, covering her mouth with a napkin stained with mustard. "I'm so sorry! I didn't mean—"

"How long?"

Jolie's eyes got wider. "I have such a big mouth!"

"How long have you known?"

"I just heard Mr. Rosenfeld talking on the phone to you one day. It wasn't anything specific he said. You just figure these things out from listening with a reporter's radar. I've kept it to myself! Honestly, I haven't told—"

Jolie's husband came over with their children. "Hi," he said to Ardith when Jolie didn't introduce him. Jolie stood with her hot dog in hand and the color drawn from her face, knowing she was the one. She'd spilled the beans. Another useful small-town expression. About your bastard child.

"Joe," he said, introducing himself.

"Ardith." She said hello to the little girl, dressed all in pink, the star of Jolie's former column that had morphed into an advice section for parents called "Quiz Maddy and Bobby's Mom!" The little boy, with his fat cheeks, squirmed in Joe's arms. "Nice to meet you all," Ardith said, excusing herself quickly. She could barely take in what she'd just heard.

Jamie and Matthew, a new boy the same age who had moved in across the street and become fast friends with Jamie, ran up in their Scout uniforms. "Did you see me?" Jamie asked

"I did, honey."

A group of men and women in electric blue Lycra came ahead with a banner in front of them that declared TOM WATKINS MEMORIAL RIDE. They received a huge round of applause. Marian's group had folded themselves into the pa-rade when time had been too short to pull off a separate event. Leading them slowly in his police car with its lights flashing was Wade.

"Marian!" Jamie called out. She waved to them. Earlier this morning, when she had driven up from Boulder for the parade, Marian had stopped by. She'd come bearing gifts, a one-piece romper stitched with bright lemons, a stack of cloth blocks, each as big as Olivia's head, and a bouquet of spring flowers for the house. She played with Olivia while Ardith made break-fast. Despite all the comfort Marian provided, she also brought Tom into the house. His rolling laugh that started as a roar and ended deep in a silent canyon was hers too. Both had the same fast walk that left Ardith practically running to keep up. Ardith had reveled in this likeness at first, as close as she could get to Tom again. But his presence had started to feel like a spirit that wouldn't leave the earth. She'd stopped being furious at him for riding his stupid bicycle that night. She had let go of the rage that consumed her knowing his perpetrator was still out there after having left Tom to die in a ditch. Now she just wanted to take a small step not to think about him every minute of the day without worrying she was forgetting about him and damning his memory.

"There's Dad!" Jamie shouted. A group of men all dressed alike in maroon polo shirts and white pants, Reuben's Rotary Club—no women in this branch—rode down the street on decorated bicycles, red and white streamers flowing from their handlebars. Reuben peddled awkwardly on Harry's BMX bike with its low-slung frame and high seat; he looked more as if he were trying to ride a unicycle. He was waving too. She could see that he was looking for her and the kids.

Then she saw Harry again, across the street. A crowd of boys stood a few feet away, their fists cocked, shouting things at him. She saw a bigger boy push Harry and the girl try to pull Harry away, and then Harry's fists balled up.

Ardith broke through the crowd. Olivia's mouth banged against the back of her skull and the baby shrieked. "Shh," Ardith pleaded.

Pushing and shoving broke out, and she saw Harry go down on the sidewalk wrapped up with another boy. Ardith got to the middle of the street just as a flash of maroon sped by her—Reuben. He'd fallen off his bike in front of Harry and the other boy, a huge crash.

32

At the house, Ardith told Reuben he should lie down in the bedroom. Exhausted from the day's ordeal, he was more than glad to do so. Somehow, he'd wound up in the middle of things, taking a splat in front of Harry and cutting up his hands. "Wash your hands well," she told him. "There's some Neosporin in the bathroom. I'm sorry."

"Not your fault."

"Were you trying to help?"

"In my graceless way."

Jamie passed by holding Olivia upside down by the backs of her legs.

"Is she all right?" Reuben asked. "Be careful!"

"Uh-huh," said Jamie. "It helps her spine grow. I Googled it."

"You're going to drain all the blood out of her."

"She likes it," said Ardith. At least she didn't complain. She only complained when Ardith stood still. She was dying to bypass crawling and get right to walking—or driving. Ardith had a glimpse of the strong-willed, if not outright wild, teenager she would become. "I'm going to talk to Harry."

"You want some help?"

"I'll be fine. Just rest." She wanted to handle this herself, not gang up on him.

In the garage, Harry was fixing the handlebars on his freestyle bike that had been thrown out of whack in Reuben's fall. He went around to the high seat and adjusted it. "What happened today?" Ardith asked.

"Nothing worth mentioning."

"That's not my impression. So, this girl…Brenva? She's the cause of this fight?"

"I suppose so. She used to be the girlfriend of the guy who jumped me, Rol—"

"Raoul?"

"*Rol.* None of those guys have ever liked me. Not since the first day of school. When Ben turned."

"Turned? You mean—?"

"I mean, he went over to them. He wouldn't sit with me at the lunch table and didn't want me hanging around him any-more." Harry looked away. "I sort of followed him around too much after that. Anyway, that was then."

"I'm sorry about that, Harry. I wish you would have talked to us at the time. Those boys today, were they the ones who shaved your eyebrows?"

"Maybe."

"And Ben was part of that group before he and his mother moved to Boulder?"

"Yes."

"Why didn't you tell us about them? Were you afraid they would retaliate?"

"I wasn't afraid."

"Were you ashamed?"

"Dad really smashed this up bad. I can fix it, though."

She looked at the way he was studying each link of the chain, and it suddenly hit her. "You were protecting Ben, weren't you? Even after what he and his friends did to you." She could see his shoulders tense up. "Is that it?"

"What's it?"

"Your devotion to Ben in spite of his behavior is commend-able, Harry, but you could have told me." He dug into a toolbox and retrieved a wrench. "Is this all because of our situation?"

"Which *situation* is that?"

Ardith took the wrench out of his hands. "Were you follow-ing Ben around at school because you needed my attention?"

"If that's what you want to believe."

"I want to know the truth."

"I got carried away. I'm not like that anymore."

"You know I'm not saying any of this explains what those boys did to you. Their behavior was abhorrent and cruel."

"Glad you see it that way." He had picked some soda cans out of the recycling bucket and was stomping them into wafers.

"You wouldn't do this with Brenva, would you?"

"Do what?"

"Follow her if she didn't want you to."

"I told you. I don't do that anymore."

"I just want to make sure."

"If you say so."

Ardith glared at him a moment. He went back to fiddling with his bike. "Are you being careful with this girl? Do you know about safe sex?"

He looked straight at her, his cool green eyes. "I'm not going to make that mistake." She had no question about what "that mistake" meant. She thought of Olivia's blue eyes. Ardith's were hazel, Reuben's brown—how could she ever imagine people wouldn't guess? "I'm thinking about us going back to Chicago, Harry. How would you feel about that?"

"I want to stay here. I like it here now."

It's the girl, Ardith thought. "Dad said he might consider moving back too. Eventually I want to return to work. I'm not going to find a job so easily out here. I worry about the culture too—this fight today, those boys. I don't know, Harry."

"If you say so."

"Stop saying that."

"If you say so."

"Stop it! *Stop it!* Damn you, Harry!" She had tears in her eyes. He stared at her. "Why do you act like this? I'm on your side. Don't you know that?"

"Are you? I didn't know you were on anybody's side, besides your own."

"What's that mean?"

"It's great that you have all these super plans. *I'm thinking about going back to Chicago, Harry. I worry about the culture out here.*" His voice was sneering. "You think you can just start over with a new baby and have everything come out okay? My other family is all fucked up, so I'll just make me a brand new one. Get Marian to help and toss the loser one away."

"Marian's become part of the family—"

"She's not *our* family. If he had lived, you would have moved into his mega home by now with Olivia and thrown us away."

"That's not true—"

"Yes, you would have. Don't tell me that wasn't the plan."

"I know you feel that way, Harry, but I'm not throwing anybody away."

"You *are*. You're still cheating on us."

She felt slapped. She had to close her eyes a moment before she could speak again. "I think about you all the time—I worry about you."

"Worry isn't about *me*. It's about you. You suffer. You hurt. You cry. You worry. *You* made a mistake. It's all about you even when it's about us."

"A new baby takes over your life—"

"I'm not jealous of Olivia. You know that's not it."

"Then what is it?"

"There's nothing of you left. There's nothing of the *old* you."

She tried to touch his bare arm, marked with a bruise from the fight, but he pulled away. What could she tell him? He wasn't wrong, but he wasn't right either. "I can't go back to that other person, Harry. I'm sorry that I hurt you and you can't imagine what a torment that is…" How *did* she say any of this without referring to herself? "Maybe I chose the hardest way to go through this when I decided to keep Olivia, I don't know. And, yes, I've been selfish and self-absorbed. But I'm not finished, Harry. I'm not finished with loving you. You try to tell me that's not true."

"Are you finished with Dad?" His voice wobbled with emotion.

"You're asking a question I can't answer right now, Harry."

"And one you don't think about anymore."

"I didn't say that."

He squeezed his bike's hand brake and looked at her.

"You're scared," he told her. "And you're still not listening."

She climbed up the stairs afterward, feeling as if she'd been ground up and spit out from the fleet of tractors that had pulled up the rear of the parade. No, they hadn't been the last group. It had been a phalanx of street sweepers cleaning up the horseshit from the Golden Trails Riding Club. More like that. Worthless.

She went into Jamie's room to retrieve Olivia. She would lie down with her and take a nap, if Olivia would let her. The baby was sacked out next to Jamie on his bed, her back curled against his thigh, her small fists in front of her face like tiny binoculars. He was listening to hip-hop that blared through his ear buds. Ardith pointed to her ears. "Turn down the volume. You're going to ruin your hearing!" He pumped his fist at her, not hearing a word.

She walked into her bedroom. Their once bedroom. His arms folded across his chest, Reuben lay with his eyes closed. Raw scratches raked the backs of his hands. Somehow, he had gotten the brunt of the fight without even being in it. "Are you sleeping?" Ardith asked.

"Fast asleep."

"Do you want me to go away?"

"No. I keep seeing pavement in front of my face."

"Did you put Neosporin on?"

"Not yet. What happened with Harry?"

"It did not go well. He's so angry at me."

"We can only try. Maybe one day all our sins will be forgiven."

"Real convincing there, Reb Rosenfeld."

She went into the bathroom to grab the Neosporin and stood a moment studying herself in the mirror. The breast feeding had actually helped her lose weight, but her body had been devoted to Olivia for so long she had only recently started to hunger for another's touch, one that would leave her empty of want. It had been over a year since she'd even hugged Reuben. She tried to imagine his hands on her breasts and his mouth near her ear, but there was always static in the picture, his anger, her confusion, and now Harry's voice: *There's nothing of the old you.*

In the bedroom, she opened the ointment to apply it. Seeing an angry welt on his left hand, she lifted his hand and without thinking kissed it.

"Ardith?"

"Close your eyes." She bent down and kissed him: the familiar feel of his full bottom lip, the sweet taste of him she had forgotten. He cupped his hand around the back of her neck.

"Wait," she said. "Let me close the door."

"Where are the boys?"

"Jamie's in his room. Harry is walking Charlotte."

She locked the door.

Afterward, they lay in silence, just as they had silently and hurriedly gone about removing their clothes. At any moment Jamie might appear with a hungry Olivia or Harry return heavy-footed—his size 12 feet having shot ahead of the rest of his growth—clomping up the stairs. But she'd forgotten all that with Reuben's weight upon her, his slimmer, exercised body, its unexpected contours and sensation of lightened comfort. She had wanted him on top. Certain she wouldn't be able to come, she urged him on, gripping his buttocks, but in the throes of directing his thrusting, she felt a sudden, insistent surge of desire, her skin alive to his heat and tensed muscles. At his cessation, she touched herself and came instantly, a breaking wave of unspoiled release. It had been months, light years.

A slight embarrassment came over her, and she pulled the sheet up to her neck, as if she'd just seen a new lover's face for the first time in daylight. Turned on his side, Reuben studied her while she stared up at the overhead light fixture with its yellowing plastic cover. Here they were again. Together. Not together. Reconciled. A mistake? He started to speak, and she put a finger on his lips. She wasn't so much afraid of what he would say as what she would say back, and how unready she was to hear her own words.

Reaching for the Neosporin, she rubbed the ointment on his scratches. She examined his nails. They needed attention, too, the cuticles peeling and cracked from the dry Colorado air. No rain in weeks. She could only imagine that his stifling attic bedroom at Lyle and Ellen's punished his skin further. He never complained to her, which made her feel all the crueler not to invite him home for good.

"Just rest," she said. She went into the bathroom and showered. When she came out, he was gone. A note on the bed said he had left for work to check on some things. He'd drawn both a smiley and frowny face at the bottom. *Check one*, he had written. Obviously, he was just as confused as she was.

She looked in on Olivia, still asleep next to Jamie, her pacifier lolling halfway out of her mouth like a drunken sailor with a cigarette.

"What are you watching?" He was bent over his phone, peering at the small screen that strained her eyes when she tried to watch a video for any length.

"Boxing."

God forbid, his latest interest. "Is it okay she's still here?"

Jamie looked down at his sister. "Yeah, I like it. I changed her earlier, by the way."

"Thank you, darling. And please don't take up boxing. I can't stand the thought of your beautiful face bruised."

"Don't worry, Mom. Nobody will get close enough to hit me."

"That's not the answer I was looking for."

Her phone rang. Luisa, whose voice was so hushed Ardith could barely make out the words. "What's wrong, honey?"

"I need to speak with you." Her voice grew even softer. "I can't talk over the phone."

"Are you all right?"

"Can we meet somewhere?"

"Why don't you come here?"

"Is anyone else there?"

"Jamie and Olivia. Harry will be back soon. He's walking Charlotte."

"Can you meet me in the park by the playground?"

Too much was happening: she'd slept with her estranged husband; her son, after almost getting beat up, had just let her know she was a self-indulgent waste of a mother; and Jolie's infallible reporter's nose had sniffed out her infidelity. The least she could do was be a decent grown-up friend to Luisa who sounded deeply distressed.

Then again, Olivia would wake up and be famished.

She would tell Jamie to bring her to the park if she did wake. "I'll be there in fifteen minutes."

"Thank you, Ardith. Thank you so much."

She checked one more time on Olivia. There'd be hell to pay tonight for letting her sleep this long: a late-night shift of watching hair-extension infomercials (which riveted Olivia like no other program), until her daughter got tired enough to sleep. But the day was already lost so she might as well give it up altogether. She gathered her purse and keys and went out the door.

Was this all about Luisa coming out? She'd just joined the Gay-Straight Alliance at high school but was afraid to tell her parents. To test the waters, she'd casually mentioned to her mother how some people (meaning Luisa's friends in the Alliance) want to be known as "they." *¿Cómo?* her mother had said.

"It's different today, Mami. Some people consider themselves neither male nor female. More like neutral."

"*¡Los hermafroditas!*"

Luisa pointed to her head. "No, up here."

Her mother nodded and winked. "Yes, smart girl."

"You can see why I'm afraid to say anything," she'd confided to Ardith.

"I think you're looking for excuses not to be yourself."

"I know. I'm so messed up."

"No, you're not. But you have to find more support than me." She would drive Luisa to Fort Collins where there was free counseling for LGBTQ teenagers. And Ardith would go with her when she finally did come out to her parents.

Luisa was sitting on a park bench. The parade had dispersed, and residents were back in their homes at the dinner hour. Ardith wondered what, if anything, Reuben was thinking. Why hadn't he called or texted? For that matter, why had he jumped up and left? On the other hand, *she* hadn't texted him an answer to his note, mainly because picking a sad or happy face felt absurd in the face of their situation. What did love even mean for her these days? Was there such a thing as reborn love or just old love you settled for and made peace with? Could she even love Reuben out of anything more than wanting his forgiveness? What were the chances of two people with a gaping fissure running down the middle of their marriage ever having that scar heal over enough to ignore its ugliness?

She waved to Luisa to wait just a moment and took out her phone. She texted Reuben an upside-down smiley face. As honest as she could be. And if this—whatever *this* was—were to become more, she needed above all never to be dishonest with him again.

"What's going on?" Luisa looked pale. She gripped her hands together so hard that Ardith gently took them in hers to comfort her. The wind had come up and blown through the cottonwood trees and tufts had settled on the girl's lush dark hair. The tufts, with their downy fibers, looked like small translucent snow creatures. Ardith felt reluctant to let go of the girl's shaking hands long enough to brush them off.

"Swear to me you won't tell anyone."

"We'll deal with it, whatever it is. I promise."

"But you have to promise not to say anything to anyone. I trust you, Ardith. You're the only person I can trust now."

"Luisa, if anyone has harmed you, I can't—"

"It's not that."

Off in the distance, Jamie hurried toward them with Olivia in his arms, famished no doubt. A good block away and yet her breasts had started to leak. She turned back to Luisa. "What is it then, honey?"

"My father…"

PART 3

33

Carla was back from Las Vegas, where she'd sneaked off for the weekend with Donny. She had wound up spending most of her time alone in the hotel room while Donny gambled and drank downstairs in the casino. Her fake ID didn't fool anyone, especially casino security. A guard examined the ID, flexed it, shined a flashlight on it, and told her, "This doesn't even come close. Please step away from the gaming area." Donny slid out of sight during the episode so he wouldn't get arrested for even being with her in the first place.

"On the second night," Carla told Luisa, "he completely disappeared. I went downstairs to search for him. Nowhere. And he wasn't answering his phone. I was getting worried but also angry. Meanwhile, *my* phone was going nuts because my parents thought I was having a weekend sleepover at my cousin's until they found out I wasn't. When Donny finally came back, it was six a.m., and he stunk of booze, cigarettes, and perfume. He tried to convince me he'd run into some old army buddies and that they'd gone to another hotel for drinks and then lost track of time. Yeah, right."

"What did you do?" Luisa asked. They were at Luisa's house in the basement, trying to stay cool on the hot spring day. School would be out in a few weeks.

"I had to call my parents. I didn't have a choice. Donny threatened that if I called them I'd be in big trouble. 'Not as much as you,' I told him. So he stormed out of our hotel room. That was the last I saw of him. He left me there without any money. My parents drove the twelve hours to get me. I'm, like, grounded for two years. They're talking about bringing charges against Donny, who isn't even in the state anymore. I don't think he owned his house after all. I'm not sure his Camaro wasn't stolen either. And, no, you don't have to say it."

216 STEVEN SCHWARTZ

Luisa wasn't going to. She was just glad Carla was back, and they were friends again. She could use a friend. "You're not… pregnant or anything, are you?"

Carla shook her head. "I was stupid but not *that* stupid. Although as stupid goes, I pretty much get a big participation trophy." Carla stretched over her head and then dropped her arms and shoulders heavily, sighing. "I have a question for you. Does that mother you help know anyone else who's looking for someone? I need a job. My parents are insisting I pay them back for everything it cost to come get me. They're calling it 'restitution.'"

"I can ask her," Luisa said. She thought of Ardith and how kind she'd been and how she could tell her anything.

"Does she pay well?"

"Very well. I'm not sure they can afford it. I make as much as my mother does cleaning a house, which I do for them also. Her husband doesn't live there anymore. I don't know why. Ardith said it's temporary until they figure things out."

"Well, they have that weird kid, after all."

"Harry's not weird. He's been a good friend to me."

"What about that other lady? Your dad's boss? Does she still come around?"

"Ellen? Sometimes. When she does, my father and she always go into the TV room and shut the door."

"Your mother, where is she then?"

"She goes in there, too, but she's not always around."

"Not around?"

"I mean, she's working."

"Why does she come to the house to talk to him? She could talk to him at work. She's his boss."

"I asked my mother that. She just shrugged, like she does when she doesn't want to be bothered. Then she went back to making tamales. They always say it's 'business' when I ask them what's going on."

"I'm sorry about what I said before about your father. I was pissed at you for calling out Donny."

"That's okay. I'm just glad you're here." She reached out and brushed Carla's cheek with her fingers, letting them linger there for a moment before pulling away in embarrassment.

"What was that for?"

"I—"

Carla's phone rang. "Yes. I know. I said I would. I'm coming, *okay?*" She hung up and rolled her eyes. "My mother. They might as well make me wear an ankle monitor. What were you saying?"

"Nothing."

"Are you going to that stupid parade next week?"

"I suppose." Luisa jammed her hand deep in the front pocket of her jean shorts, afraid it might reach out and stroke Carla's cheek again.

"We should go together." Carla threw her arms around Luisa. "I love you, girl. Let's not ever mess this up again, yeah?"

And then it happened, a week before the Sugar Beet Parade. She found her mother sitting in the corner on a straw bottom chair in the living room, as if for an appointment. She was wearing the shapeless floral dress she put on every morning. She had an empty coffee mug in her right hand. Her other hand lay palm up in her lap like a child waiting for a shiny coin. The blinds were drawn. Luisa couldn't remember the last time her mother, who always rose before she did, had forgotten to open the blinds first thing. "Where is everybody?" Luisa asked.

Her mother stared into space.

It would take almost an hour before her mother told her everything. A policeman had come to the house very early that morning while Luisa and Marcos were asleep and after their father had left for work. She didn't open the door at first because she thought it was someone from ICE.

"Why would you be worried about that?" Luisa asked. "You're a citizen."

Her mother nodded but said you still have to be careful. When it became clear he wanted to speak to Miguel, her mother said through the door that he wasn't here. When will he be back? the officer asked. She wasn't sure, though she knew of course. She also knew not to say anything more. To make him go away, she lapsed into Spanish, pretending not to understand. The officer had some questions for Mr. Rojas. He slipped his card under the door.

As soon as he left, her mother called her father at the dairy. He came home right away and packed a suitcase.

"He left us? He didn't even say goodbye?" Luisa said, stunned. "*Why*? What did he do?"

Marcos came down the stairs, rubbing his eyes. It was Saturday. Luisa told him to go into the den and turn on the TV. He looked at his mother. She nodded for him to do so too. "What's going on?" he said.

"Just *go*," Luisa said, barely able to control herself. She wanted to scream at her mother for everything: Why had she acted so suspicious when the police came? How could she just let their father run off?

Marcos left and turned on the television.

"What did Daddy do?"

Her mother's face, scored with new lines that weren't there yesterday, collapsed. Tears were pouring down her face. She never cried—her expression always showed the same determination to get on with things no matter what. Luisa kneeled down in front of her. "Please, Mommy. Tell me."

"*Mató a un hombre.*"

He had killed a man. It was an accident. He hadn't known it. He'd been driving home from the dairy and gotten a text from...

"From who?" Luisa asked.

She nodded toward the den.

"Marcos?"

"Yes. He wasn't paying attention."

He'd looked down at his phone and then felt a thud but thought it was an animal. He was already late getting home because there had been a party at the dairy, and the boss man who usually helped him wasn't available.

"Did he get out to look?" Luisa asked.

Her mother took the tissue Luisa had gotten her and dabbed at her eyes. She shook her head.

"Why not?"

"*No sé.*"

Two days later, it was all over town. The doctor who had died. Her father had driven that road to work so many times he knew exactly the spot where the doctor had been hit and knew, too, he'd killed him. He told no one at first, not even Luisa's mother. Then when he couldn't stand it anymore, he confessed everything to her.

"Why didn't he turn himself into the police?"

"*Intranquilo.* Scared for us."

"Why for us?"

Her mother buried her face in her hands. "*No más.*"

"You have to tell me where he is. Running away makes everything so much worse!"

Her mother got up. She glanced at the den where Marcos had the television turned up loud. She started to walk upstairs, but collapsed on the bottom step and hugged herself, sobbing and rocking back and forth.

Luisa ran over to her. "It will be okay, Mommy. I'll fix it. I promise. I'll make it better."

She had never felt less sure of anything.

They heard nothing from their father. Ellen had gone away for spring break with her daughter on an eco-tour to Patagonia and was out of contact. Lyle called wanting to know where his herdsman was. Luisa had always been afraid of him. He could be gruff, unlike Ellen who was sweet to everyone. He wanted to know why her father wasn't answering his phone. Luisa said there had been a family emergency, and her father had to go out of town and was too busy to talk.

"A family emergency? Why didn't he tell us?"

"I don't know," she said. She was lying through her teeth.

There was a long pause and then he said, "Tell him to call me ASAP."

ASAP. ASAP. She just kept repeating the letters to herself. Her mother was off cleaning houses. She wouldn't talk about it anymore. He would be home soon, she claimed. He had gone to talk with some people he could trust.

"What people?" Luisa had asked.

"Men he knows."

"Which men? What do they do? Are they lawyers?"

"*No sé.*" What her mother said all the time now.

"What are we supposed to do in the meantime? What if he never comes back?" They owed money to everyone. They had bills and car payments. Who would fix all the things her father always took care of? Her mother couldn't support them on what she made. Why had he deserted them like this? "Stop pretending you don't hear me!" Luisa shouted.

Her mother shook Luisa by the shoulders. "*Prison.* They capture him, he is a criminal." Then she got her cleaning supplies and walked out the door.

She had forgotten all about the parade. When Carla showed up, she was still in her pajamas. Her father's absence, other than Marcos's whining about when Daddy was coming home from his business trip, had started to feel normal. It had been seven days. No further visits from the police. Ellen still gone. The bills kept coming but the lights worked, unlike years ago when their electricity had been turned off. But that had been before her father found steady work at the dairy and when her mother was too pregnant with Marcos to do her houses. They'd lit candles and made a picnic in the living room and soon the lights and fans came back on and it was just brushed off as a funny episode. Still, Luisa remembered how her father had to borrow money from his brother in California, her uncle who she had visited only once. Was that where he was now? In California at their uncle's, begging for money?

Her mother said, "When it is safe, he will come back."

What did that mean? How would it *ever* be safe? Even if he made it across the border to Mexico he could be sent back. He had to know this. Or was he planning to stay away until the statute of limitations expired? She'd Googled it. Five years. But that was only if you didn't leave the state. Leave and you had to stay away another five years. Was he planning to hide out for *ten* years? She'd be twenty-five by that time and out of college. But, no, she *wouldn't* be in college because there wouldn't be any money for her.

At least she wouldn't have to tell him she was gay.

She couldn't sleep, sickening herself with terrible thoughts about what people would say or do when they found out. If you leave an accident, it wasn't an accident anymore. It was a crime. You were a coward. People hated you. They thought you were evil. She never understood how anyone could do that—how heartless you'd have to be. But her father said he'd hit a racoon that had then run off in the bushes. Would anyone believe him? Did she?

She buried her face in the pillow, weeping, wanting him to come home and terrified of what would happen if he did. By the time Carla rang the bell that morning, she had forgotten it was the day of the Sugar Beet Parade. She wasn't sure she'd slept at all.

They dragged Marcos with them to the parade. What did all this cheering and waving and celebrating old people and old times have to do with them? She felt dizzy. Then she saw the group with a sign that said Tom Watkins Memorial Ride. And all the bicyclists ride past and the cheers that went up for them, for the doctor, the man her father had killed. She squeezed Marcos's hand tight. She felt as if she were going to faint.

Across the way, Ardith, holding Olivia, caught her eye and waved. So friendly, so happy to find Luisa in the crowd. Hardly aware of doing so, Luisa mouthed the word *Help*.

34

At the park, Ardith calmed herself while waiting for Ellen by thinking about the weather, the most mundane subject she could contemplate without her heart pounding in anger. Or was it fear? What did *she* have to be afraid of? And yet she'd practically had a panic attack on her walk here. Ellen was just back from exploring the southernmost point of South America, evidently enjoying her time with Isadora, while Ardith had been sweating out the last week, picking up the phone to call Wade and then putting it down every time she thought of Luisa.

Luisa had besieged her with questions. Should she go talk to a lawyer? But she didn't have money for one. How about a public defender? You had to already have a court date for that. And her father hadn't even been arrested yet. What did it mean that the police hadn't come back to the house since that first day? Should her father come home then? Had he overreacted, fled out of fear alone?

She had a thousand questions for Ardith and not a clue that Tom was Olivia's father. Luisa's mother, meanwhile, had collapsed into herself, and Luisa didn't know what to do. Was her father going to be sent to prison and her mother deported, even though she was legal? What would happen to her and Marcos? She was hysterical, and Ardith that day in the park, trying to calm her down, held her through heaving sobs.

From the very first, when Luisa told her everything, it had been an out-of-body experience. Only Olivia's ravenous nursing had anchored her to the earth. She heard Luisa's words—*My father killed Dr. Watkins*—but they were enveloped in a great smothering silence in her brain that stifled every sensible response. She should have dragged Luisa to the police and made her repeat what she just confessed. She should not have said another word in front of Luisa. Instead, with Olivia on her breast, she comforted Luisa with her free arm.

Her inaction during the following week made her feel as if she were just shoveling more dirt on Tom's grave. She jumped at the slightest noise, dropped plates, forgot a wellness visit for Olivia, and dented the car's bumper pulling too far forward to a high curb. Zeroing in as only he could, Harry pounced. "You're not yourself. What's wrong?" And Reuben asked if they could talk about what happened. For a moment, she thought he meant with Luisa. She had almost forgotten they'd slept together, and that it was supposed to elicit some discussion about their future. To Harry, she answered, "I'm just busy." To Reuben: "Yes, we should do that soon," a mediocre response that she knew baffled him. Meanwhile her brain pleaded for some answer to miraculously appear.

And then Ellen came home.

She watched Ellen from a distance walking toward her across the park grass. It had been months since they'd seen each other. Ardith had tried—sent text messages about getting together for lunch. Just really, really busy, Ellen texted back. Ardith had missed her, her closest friend here, but how many text messages could you send before you had to take a hint? Now, however, the reason Ellen had been putting her off became clearer.

Last night, Ardith had texted Ellen that they needed to talk about Tom and Miguel. Evidently Ellen got *that* message, because she texted right back. They could meet tomorrow. Ardith had picked a secluded spot on a bench in the park, not far from where a week ago she'd consoled Luisa about her father.

"Hello, Ardith."

Ellen wore pale-green drawstring pants and a T-shirt that had a picture of a small ship, maybe the one she'd been on with Isadora in Patagonia. Her face and arms were deeply tan and Ardith pictured the two of them in a Zodiac sighting orca whales and sea lions, penguins and albatrosses. So much freedom.

"I wanted to tell you, Ardith. I'm sorry that I couldn't."

She'd memorized a list of questions with which to confront Ellen, but now her mind went blank. An enormous fatigue threatened to overtake her, thoughts of Tom sucking her under.

"I know it's difficult to understand. I thought I could manage the situation for a better outcome. Obviously, I haven't. And now we—"

"How could you do that to me? You were at Olivia's birth. Tom's her father. Did you even think about what it would mean to me?"

"I'm sorry."

"Sorry?"

"I had hoped to persuade Miguel, at the right time, to turn himself in."

"What right time? What does that even mean, Ellen? The right time was when he first told you."

"He was trying to get things in order. He was afraid of what would happen to his family if he went to jail."

"And what about Tom? Was that supposed to be at the right time also? When do you care about what happened to him?"

"Ardith, I wish it were that simple."

"Does Lyle know about any of this?"

"No."

"So it's all your deceit."

"Do you know why I didn't tell you, Ardith?"

"Because I would have gone straight to Wade."

"Maybe. But that's not the only reason. There would be no justice for Miguel. If I believed there would have been, I would have tried to persuade him to confess."

"You've made it worse, Ellen. He could have gotten a fair trial. Instead you and your so-called advice heightened his crime."

"You think he would have gotten a fair trial? A brown-skinned man who kills a white doctor who's a paragon of the community? You think anyone would believe Miguel that he didn't realize what he'd done? You don't. Half this country is waiting to take out their rage on a man like him."

"This isn't about social justice, it's about Tom, Olivia's *father*, an innocent man who was hit and left for dead! And what? Miguel doesn't have to face any consequences because *you* get to be judge and jury and decide what the greater good is?"

"There have been plenty of consequences. He's wretched. His wife is terrified. He's talked about killing himself. I believe he would do it if he didn't think it would only make things worse."

"If he's so wretched, why doesn't he turn himself in? That has to be better than living with the guilt. Instead he's run away. It's wrong, Ellen, and you know it. Rationalize it any way you want, but with your help or whatever you call it, you've kept him from taking responsibility. That's all that matters." Ardith leaned toward her. "I don't think you ever had any intent of persuading Miguel to turn himself in, did you? It's only because the police have started closing in on him that you're here. You must have thought he could get away with it."

"God, Ardith, if you believe that then why are you even talking to me? There are no good guys here. Not you, not me, not Miguel. Only ways people survive—some of us, at least. Morality has a stick up its ass until it comes to actual decisions about people you know. But now it's your call. You know everything I do. Make the decision you have to."

"I just have one more question. You told Luisa I needed someone to help me with Olivia, right?"

"Yes."

"Why?"

"Because you needed help."

"Who told you?"

"You, I suppose."

"I didn't tell you."

"Maybe it was Reuben. I don't remember. Someone."

"No, it wasn't Reuben. Luisa just appeared one day at my door and said she heard I might be looking for a mother's helper."

"Because you were. She practically lives next door to you. It was perfect for you both."

"I think you sent her there as insurance."

"What do you mean?"

"You knew if she was there, I'd feel torn about reporting her father."

Ellen took off her glasses and wiped the lenses on her T-shirt. "You must really hate me even more than I thought to believe there's a conspiracy here. Did you ever consider that we're all responsible for what happened to Tom? That any one of us might have stopped him if we'd paid more attention to how he was getting home? You especially, Ardith. And yet none of us did." She touched Ardith's hand and then stood up. "I hope one day you'll forgive me. And yourself."

35

The morning light slanted through the open windows, filling Luisa's classroom with a golden-rose color. She could imagine an angel floating in on the rays. Or instead, all of them, her fellow students, her teacher, Mr. Mazur, with his humorous algebra posters around the room, everybody dying in a nuclear flash. She had never felt less safe.

"Luisa?" Mr. Mazur said.

She looked up at her teacher. The other students had turned around to stare at her. She had taken a seat in the furthest corner of the back row for the last two days of the semester.

"You're wanted in the office, Luisa."

She shut down her laptop and slipped it into her backpack.

"I'm sure you'll be back before class ends," Mr. Mazur said.

How would he know? Why was he trying to reassure her? Her heart started pounding. She walked between the rows of silent staring faces to the front of the classroom and out the door. Each shaky step must have looked obvious to her classmates. Ever since her father left, she hadn't felt right in her body. Not eating, she'd lost weight. Her clothes hardly fit, but she couldn't ask her mother for money for new ones with her father gone. She got distracted so much that Carla had asked if she was okay. "I'm fine," she said. When in fact each word she managed to get out was a like a small bead that she had to examine for its color, shape, and familiarity to make sure it fit into a sentence.

The administrative assistant, Mrs. Nichols, told Luisa to have a seat. Mr. LaSalle, the school resource officer, would be with her in a minute. Though always friendly, greeting kids with a big smile in the morning, Mr. LaSalle was mainly there to break up fights, confiscate weapons, and conduct active-shooter drills. Luisa had never spoken directly to him in her life.

"Luisa," he said, standing before her. His gun, she couldn't help noticing, bulged on his hip. "Would you follow me, please?"

He led her into a small office. An overweight policeman stood there next to a woman holding a briefcase.

"Hello, Luisa," the man said. "I'm Wade Mitchell, Welton's chief of police. We appreciate your coming to talk with us."

"I don't understand why I'm here."

"Detective Janice," the woman said, introducing herself. Was that her first or last name, like Judge Judy on TV? She wore a black suit with black flats and a white blouse. "We'll get you back to class right away so you can be with your friends." She smiled encouragingly. "I promise. We'd just like to ask you a few questions."

Luisa looked around. Mr. LaSalle had already faded behind a small desk, which seemed far away from where Luisa pressed herself against the back wall of his office.

"Please sit down," the police chief said. She sat down in front of Mr. LaSalle's desk. The police chief and the detective pulled up chairs on either side of her. She clutched her backpack to her chest and stared straight ahead at the clock on the wall behind Mr. Lasalle.

"You don't mind answering a few questions, do you?" the detective said. Luisa wished they were sitting in front of her. On either side like this, it felt as if they were squeezing her in a vice.

"I know my rights," she said. "My mother should be here with me." Her mother would be even more intimidated, but Luisa had seen enough movies to know a parent had to be in the room with you.

"You haven't done anything wrong," the detective said. "This isn't a formal meeting that requires your mother be here. We just hope you can help us understand some things."

"What sort of things?"

"When was the last time you saw your father?"

"He's on a trip. A business trip."

"Well, Luisa," the detective said, "we know that's not true. Your mother told us otherwise."

"You spoke to my mother? When? What did she say?"

"Would you like some water?" the police chief asked her.

Luisa looked at him, trying to focus.

"I'll get you a cup. Officer LaSalle will stay here with you while you speak with Detective Janice."

"My mother doesn't speak English well. When did you talk with her?"

"Your mother is fine," Detective Janice said, ignoring the question. "We know you're concerned about your father, Luisa. We'd like to help him." Luisa looked at Officer LaSalle. He smiled at her, but then he looked down at his desk.

"I want to call my mother."

"Of course. But we just spoke to your mother. She knows we're speaking with you. You're not in trouble," the detective said again.

"If I'm not in trouble, why can't I leave?"

"You're free to leave anytime you want, Luisa."

The police chief came back and handed her a cup of water. She took a long while drinking it, because she needed time to think. When she turned around, she saw he had placed himself with his back against the door.

"I don't know anything about my father. I told you, he's away on a business trip."

Detective Janice pulled her chair closer. She had long legs; her pant cuffs rose above her ankles, and her knees almost touched Luisa's when she leaned toward her. "I'm sure you've ridden in your father's truck before. Probably plenty of times, right?"

"Why are you asking about my dad's truck?"

"Has it ever been in a wreck?"

"No."

"Never gotten a scratch?"

"I don't know. Yes, probably—it's an old truck!"

"Before your father took the truck with him, did you see any damage to the headlight?"

"No."

"Do you want to help your father, Luisa?"

"I want to go back to class."

"Of course. You want to be with your friends. You're in no trouble, Luisa. We're just having a conversation. Does your father drink a lot?"

"Mr. LaSalle," Luisa pleaded, "can I please leave?"

He stood up. "Okay. That's enough. I'll walk you out, Luisa."

"I'll take that," the police chief said about the paper cup in her hand. She'd crushed it into the size of a gumball. He smiled at her as she unclenched her fist and handed it over.

36

Brenva expected success from other people, which was one of the reasons she wasn't with Rol anymore; he was lazy. Harry had to fake it sometimes to meet her standards, but she had gotten him thinking about himself in terms he'd never seriously considered before, a guy with a job, a family one day, people—kids, relatives, friends—in his life. She made normal sound less like poison. Before, he'd pictured himself living the existence of a Toulouse Lautrec, a freakish outcast with art as his soul, burning up every minute of his doomed life. "You can do that on the side," Brenva said, ever practical. Then she'd kiss him with an open mouth, her tongue circling his, and he'd forget even how to spell Toulouse Lautrec's name. He'd just feel her lips brushing his and hear her telling him how she loved kissing him, and that he couldn't pay attention to mean, sucky people. If she was bothered by Rol and his friends coughing *fuckfaceslut-losers* as they walked past, she didn't show it, except to take his hand or pull his arm tighter.

When she came over to the house for the first time to have lunch, he could see his mother was a little shocked, which pleased him. Brenva had an eyebrow piercing and wore a spaghetti-strap lime dress with a black bra and a studded leather black choker. Still, she was the one who unfolded her napkin, kept her hand in her lap, said please and thank you, and jumped up to do the dishes afterward. Once, in front of his mother, she told Harry not to mumble—it was a sign of poor self-esteem.

When school let out at the end of May, his father said he was old enough to work. And, yes, he could bring Brenva, as long as she was willing to work too. So, they came in every morning from nine to twelve; he cleaned up, ran errands, filled paper bins, answered phones, and helped eighty-two-year-old Calvin Ingle deliver newspapers on Thursdays. Brenva learned how to summarize press releases: announcements of horse shows, weddings, church dinners, food drives. Jolie showed her how to write them: date, time, place in the first line—who, what, when, where, and why in the first paragraph. Harry watched Brenva's fingers fly across the computer keyboard; somewhere she'd learned to type at warp speed. He felt both jealous and proud of her. She set a good example (as his father had complimented her) and made it harder for him. She was only too happy to get anyone coffee, deposit checks at the bank, or even tidy up the bathroom. The daughter of a single mother, she'd always been independent.

One afternoon Harry had been looking down at ad copy on his father's desk for Luigi's, an Italian restaurant that had opened in town and advertised in the *Sentinel*. His father had been using the boring clip art, a picture of a fat chef in an apron holding a pizza that looked like every other fat chef in an apron. Harry drew the front of the restaurant from memory in pen and ink. It was an old building whose façade had been re-stored. He worked for two hours getting the bricks right, the tin cornices cleanly etched, and the pediment at the proper angle to the roof. He examined it, felt satisfied, and was about to rip it up when his father looked over his shoulder. "What's this?"

"It's a duck."

"What?"

"Never mind," said Harry.

"That's Luigi's," his father said. "You drew this? What are you going to do with it?"

"Destroy it," Harry said calmly.

"No, you're not. I'm not going to let you exercise your per-petual instinct for aesthetic annihilation."

"Jesus, Dad, speak English."

"This is too good," his father said. Jolie came over to look, then Brenva, and Rosa, and the journalism intern from the uni-versity. He wanted to die. They all agreed the restaurant owner should see it. Two weeks later it was framed and hanging in the restaurant's entry and Harry got a check for two hundred dollars. Brenva kissed him on the cheek when his father handed the money to him at the paper. "Your first sale!" she cheered. She was thrilled for him, everyone was; Jolie got chocolate cupcakes to celebrate. Rosa said he should talk with one of her sons who made a nice living as a graphic artist. He didn't know what to do other than wait out the attention and feel pleasure's bite.

"What's wrong with me?" he asked Neil one afternoon. "What's my condition? Am I depressed, schizo, OCD—in what way am I sick?" He wanted to know. He thought if he knew, and he could take hearing it now because he was with Brenva, he could stop loathing everything that should be good in his life.

"You don't feel love," Neil said.

"I'm not loved?"

"No," Neil said, "you can't feel it."

"Are you saying I have no heart or anything?"

"Just the opposite," Neil told him, pulling his chair closer to where Harry sat on the couch. He pointed straight at Harry's chest. "It doesn't get in there. You're like someone who has an allergic reaction, a little makes a lot of trouble. You're so sensitive in fact that you can't take love in, so you've fought it off all your life. Now you don't want to do so anymore. And it's a problem. That's why we're here."

Brenva was coming home today. She and her mother and older sister had rented an RV for a trip out to Utah, to Canyonlands National Park. Harry had exchanged texts with her the first two days and then nothing, until three postcards came (Brenva's mother had insisted the vacation be about nature, not devices), all postmarked from Moab, as if she'd been saving them up. Along the way, they had hiked beneath plunging waterfalls and camped high above gorges, rafted a river and explored cliff dwellings, rode packhorses and fished right outside their camper. *We live in the most beautiful part of the country*, she'd written to him, and signed her messages with *love*. At least the first two postcards. The third one, she just wrote, *See you soon!*

He was waiting at her house the minute she arrived. He thought she'd pinned her hair up off her neck and then realized she'd cut it very short. She and her sister stumbled from the camper talking loudly. And then she saw him, sitting on her porch step, and she waved, only it wasn't much of a wave for not having seen him in ten days, more a surprised wave than an ecstatic one, and he knew something was wrong. Gone was the heavy eye makeup and eyebrow stud. She wore a short jean jacket with a plain white T-shirt underneath.

"Harry, hi!" she said, and gave him a one-armed hug because a sleeping bag was draped over her other arm. "How long have you been waiting here?"

He'd been waiting since three this afternoon. It was now eight at night.

He helped them unpack the RV, lugging out bags of uneaten groceries, board games, movies, yoga mats, water bottles, sheets, and towels. When the RV was cleaned out, Brenva's mother said she was going to drive it back to the rental lot before it closed, and Brenva's sister should follow in the car. That left Harry and Brenva, and he tried to kiss her as soon as her mother and sister turned the corner. She pulled away. "Hey, give me a chance to catch my breath. Let's talk a minute."

So they sat outside and talked about her trip and about whether his mother still wanted everyone to go back to Chicago, which she did. He thought Brenva would be more upset to hear this, but she didn't look as concerned as he imagined. She didn't look like she wanted to run away with him or hide him under her bed or make her mother adopt him or any of the other desperate ways he pictured they would stay together. She said, "When would you leave? Not soon I hope." He knew then that being apart had been a mistake.

Her mother and sister came back with the car. "We got up at six this morning," Brenva told Harry. "I'd better get to bed. I'll call you tomorrow, okay?" He felt punched by the cool tone of her voice, its politeness, how casually she said goodnight, giving him a kiss on the cheek, how tan she had gotten, how much older she looked with her hair cut short, how she linked arms with both her mother and her sister, walking in between them to the house. She did turn to wave, but it was a guilty fast wave. The lights went off downstairs. He waited by the trees across the street to see if she would come out as she had on other nights and let him put his hands underneath her shirt, caress her small breasts while she said his name and kissed his neck and the line of his jaw and touched him in front of his jeans so that warmth exploded inside him. He had gone home sticky and full of wonder, full of her, fuller than he'd ever been in his life, wanting her sweet breath and eager hands on him again— her eyes shining up at him under the linden tree, its smell of honey and lemon peel, that he couldn't seem to leave now.

He didn't remember how or when he went home that night. He stayed up all night listening to music and drawing. Once, his mother came in, wanting to know why the light was still on—he said he couldn't sleep—and she asked if anything was wrong. He could feel himself slipping back into a crushing space in a disintegrating skin. He said no, he just had insomnia, and then it was the next morning, and he was standing outside her house again at seven a.m. Waiting. But no one came out.

He took a long walk around the neighborhood, and when he came back, Brenva was standing on her lawn watering the plants, the same ones that he'd taken care of while they'd been gone. He went over to her.

"Harry!" She splashed him once with the hose. "You look terrible. What's wrong?"

"Are we through?" he asked. He didn't know how else to ask, what he should say to hint around.

"What do you mean? I just got back."

"Something's wrong."

She whipped the hose up and down making silver arcs of cascading water that splashed the irises. "I just think we should be friends for a while." She avoided his eyes. "What do you think?"

"I think—"

PART 4

37

But, yes, the summer, Reuben mulled, sitting in the courtroom awaiting Miguel's sentencing. Where had it gone? It was almost October. Or more to the point, *how* did it go. One minute, Harry and his girlfriend were an industrious twosome at the *Sentinel*, and the next Harry had fainted outside the girl's house. Dehydration, Dr. Stein had diagnosed after Reuben rushed him over there. And exhaustion. Once again, she probed Harry as to what was up. Hadn't they just been here months ago, minus his eyebrows that had finally grown back, when she asked the same question? At least Harry was more forthcoming this time. Strikingly so. And Reuben, having learned his silent place, sat and listened to Harry unburden himself to the good doctor. Brenva had dumped him. They were over as a couple. He didn't know why. "I'm so sorry," Dr. Stein told him. "I know how that hurts. But you need to take care of yourself. When was the last time you ate, Harry?" He didn't know. He couldn't remember either, how long he'd been standing outside Brenva's house. Only that, like a human sundial, the rays had gone from shining on his feet to beaming in his eyes.

Reuben had driven him home, insisting he drink the full bottle of water he'd been given at the clinic. Taking a chance, he'd reached over and squeezed Harry's shoulder. He knew better than to say everything would be okay. It probably wouldn't. And who was he to promise such sentiments when he had to rake out the muck from his own stall of pessimism every day? Then again, he hadn't expected that his hand on his son's shoulder would result in spontaneous and explosive sobs from his firstborn. So forceful in fact that Reuben pulled into a remote corner of the Gas Mart and just let Harry cry himself out. When it had subsided, Reuben drove carefully home, as though protecting the fragility of his son depended on not exceeding

the speed limit. Nobody was home, and he walked Harry upstairs and said he would make him a peanut butter and honey
sandwich with a glass of milk and bring it to him. By the time
he came back, Harry was asleep. Reuben had sat at the boy's
desk and watched over his grieving son until Ardith returned
with Olivia from the market.

"All rise."

Funny thing. (Especially considering nothing was at all *funny*
about the present circumstances and such an expression only
served to point out the opposite.) Nevertheless, it bore some
ironic consideration that Ardith was sitting right next to Luisa
and her mother, the family of the accused. Now *that* would take
some explaining. Were Reuben to print the unexpurgated story,
he'd have to point out that Marian, daughter of Tom, run down
by Miguel, and half-sister to Olivia, resided on the opposite and
adversarial side of the courtroom with her mother. Her sister,
Patricia, had declined to attend.

Ardith wasn't talking to Ellen. And Marian wasn't talking to
either of them. Ellen sat in the very back of the courtroom,
apart from everyone. Lyle, who had washed his hands of the
whole business, wasn't talking to anybody, including Reuben
who couldn't get a word out of his friend other than, "I'm
sorry, buddy. Given everything that's come down, Ellen and I
need to spend time alone sorting out this shitstorm. I think you
should go home."

And for a while, until everything blew up again, Reuben *was*
back home sleeping in the marital bed, though not, since the
single previous time, sleeping *with* Ardith. They woke in the
morning and greeted the children, who, with the malleability or
just the survival instinct of offspring accepting abrupt parental
reversals, asked no questions, not even Harry, who had taken
up kayaking, paddling with solitary resignation on the placid
waters of Lake Finnegan. He had even gotten Reuben interested, and it wasn't long before they were out on the lake together
amidst the changing aspens, circumnavigating the small body
of water, passing by various waterfowl—honking geese and

preening swans—as well as (Reuben couldn't help recalling) the country club where Ardith commenced her affair with Dr. Tom. Nevertheless, given kayaking had replaced running due to his recent plantar fasciitis, Reuben became quite adept at meditatively paddling across the glassy surface of the lake and, after a while, unseeing Ardith in her tennis romper bouncing around the court to return Tom's serves.

How he could run those movies back.

"This has been a difficult case and before the court imposes sentence, I will call upon each of the attorneys for the parties. Is there anything you wish to add for the prosecution, Ms. Rivera?

"No, your honor."

"And, Mr. Gertz, for the defense?"

"I do not, your honor."

"I've received many letters about this case, as well as the victim's impact statement by extended family. Given the widespread community interest, I want to allow ample time for response from all concerned parties. I wish to call upon members of the victim's family at this time to step forward for comment."

The plea deal, as Reuben had covered it for the paper, had outraged the town, if the emails he'd received were any indication. *Shameful. Sickening.* And less printable words. Some of them directed at him, as if he had anything to do with the arrangement between the parties.

Once Miguel had returned, after being confronted with extradition from California, the case against him proved weaker than the facts initially presumed. A piece of a headlight found at the scene and matching Miguel's truck had, after much investigation, become a critical part of evidence. And Miguel's own admission that he realized he was culpable after reading about the accident in the paper incriminated him. On the other hand, his subsequent knowledge didn't disprove that he believed he'd struck a small animal like a racoon at the time of the event.

More worrisome for the prosecution was evidence that Tom had been in the middle of the road when he'd been struck. The traffic reconstructionist had identified a tire skid mark as belonging to Tom's bike. The implication followed that Tom had either lost sight of where he was on the dark road or the doctor was intoxicated and had strayed from the roadside, as the defense would surely claim if the case went to trial. Was it not better to settle on a plea than besmirch Tom's honorable reputation and make him liable to a degree for his own death?

Marian thought not. It was worth the risk of whatever would come out at a trial if there was a chance it could put Tom's killer behind bars for years. She insisted the plea bargain was not proportionate to the crime. She assumed Ardith would agree and together they could persuade the reluctant prosecutor to go to trial or at least push for years in a state prison. That was until Marian found out from investigators that Ellen, who had been questioned as Miguel's employer, had been shielding her father's killer, and Ardith herself had known for weeks and had taken no action, leaving it to investigators to follow through on their own. It was of no use for Ardith to explain about Luisa and her brother and that she was trying to think out the best way to proceed. "*Six* weeks, Ardith," Marian had said. "You needed *six* weeks to report the man who killed Dad? That's a pathetic excuse for inaction. Didn't my father, *Olivia's* father, require more urgency than your own confusion?"

The prosecutor argued that pleading guilty to careless driving resulting in injury or loss, a class one misdemeanor, with a penalty of ten days to one year in a county jail and a fine of three hundred to one thousand dollars, was the best deal they could get. She'd strongly recommend at least a year in jail, but the actual penalty was up to the judge at sentencing.

Reuben hadn't known that Luisa had confessed everything to Ardith. He hadn't known that Ellen had been advising, protecting, and essentially abetting Miguel. He hadn't known throughout the time he and Ardith lay side by side in bed after he'd moved back that Tom, deceased or not, was again at the center of his wife's thoughts. "I didn't want to drag you into this," she explained, when everything finally came out. "And if you knew…you might feel obligated to publish what you did."

He was stunned. Amazed that she thought he would betray her confidence and that she had kept this information, so central to their lives, from him because she didn't trust him. It was more of the same. More deceit. More withholding. More… cheating. An undeniable pattern. "I can't be here," he said. He moved into a motel the next day. Ardith had pleaded, "You don't understand. I was trying to protect you."

Reuben shook his head. "No, you haven't stopped being this secretive person, and it's not good for us, for me. I don't know if you can be any other way now. You're so used to hiding things from me that it feels natural to do so."

So. He moved out a second time. The saddest part was that Harry and Jamie barely seemed to notice.

Not until today, when Ardith came into the courtroom, where Reuben happened to be sitting on the defendant's side, because the other side was so crowded with Tom's supporters—Marian, her uncle Jack, the bicycle advocacy group, Tom's former patients—had Reuben sat this near Ardith. "Is it okay if I sit next to you?" Ardith asked him, as if they were strangers at a lunch counter.

It was sad, really, how you could become a stranger in your own marriage. You could never imagine such a thing during the promise of the beginning amidst that heady scramble to know everything about each other. It was all hunger back then. Tell me *all*. Show me where you grew up, the corner where that mean kid threw a rock at you, where the weird babysitter lived, the alcove in the attic where you went to be alone, how you danced in your underwear in front of the mirror, yes, the exact way, I want to know, so I'll never not know that I didn't always know. I want every holy piece of you that I missed.

"I understand that the victim's daughter wishes to make a statement."

He could feel Ardith go rigid beside him, and, oh hell, who knows why…he took her hand. She looked down at it, and for a moment he thought she would shake it off like a bug. But she squeezed his hand back, and they listened.

"My father was fifty-three years old and the healthiest, happiest, kindest man I knew. He was run down and left to die in a ditch. He lay there until the next morning. Picture him in that ditch. Picture him in the dark alone. Picture him dying without anyone to hold or comfort him—he who as a doctor always comforted others. I never had the chance to say goodbye and tell him how much I loved him. I was robbed of that. I don't understand how there can be leniency for the person who did this to him. My father deserves better than that. I am begging you, your honor, to apply the maximum punishment. Every day I miss my father. Every day I have to make believe I'm more okay about his death than I am. The legal system is supposed to help me with that, not open a gaping wound further. Please grant us the justice we deserve."

Marian sat down. Ardith withdrew her hand from Reuben's, bent forward, and wrapped her arms around herself, as if to keep from blowing into pieces.

"Thank you, Ms. Watkins. Rest assured that I take your heartfelt words under consideration. I can only imagine what it's like for you to lose a father at your age. I thank you for your courage in coming forward to speak."

Not good for defendant, Reuben jotted in his notebook. *Judge praises courage of daughter of victim with backhanded slap at defendant's cowardice.*

"My name is Fenton Taylor and I'd like to speak on behalf of the cycling community."

Fenton, a retired forest and conservation technician, headed up the bicycle advocacy coalition. When the story broke about Miguel being the hit-and-run driver, Fenton organized a meeting at the community center demanding action on behalf of vulnerable riders. As he told Reuben in an interview for the *Sentinel*, he was mad as hell about perpetrators getting off too easily. This case was where it was going to stop.

"Tom Watkins was a founding member of our group. If the streets of Welton are at all safer for riders, it's because of him. Tom pushed hard to make Welton the bicycle-friendly town it has become. He loved getting others interested in cycling and believed that the benefits to individuals and the environment were second to none. Tom simply wanted people to get outside, ride, and enjoy the freedom of cycling. As a caring community, we must send a message to reckless drivers who flee the scene of an accident. This man"—Fenton turned around and pointed to Miguel at the defense table—"failed to give assistance when he might have saved a life. Your honor, please send a strong message."

"Your frank thoughts are duly noted, Mr. Fenton, and the court appreciates the cycling community's considerable interest in this difficult case. Does anyone else wish to make a statement from the victim's family?"

Marian stood up. "No, your honor."

"Does the defendant wish to make a statement before sentencing?"

Miguel's lawyer leaned over to him, and they whispered together. Miguel stood up slowly and cleared his throat. "I want to apologize to the doctor's family. I cannot defend my actions and I accept whatever punishment the court sees fit. Anything I could say for myself at this point I realize will sound like an excuse. I know you will find it hard to forgive me. I only hope one day you can, because I don't believe I can ever forgive myself." He turned around to Luisa and her mother. "*Mis amores, por favor perdóname.*"

He sat down.

Defendant made little effort to appeal for lighter sentence.

"If there are no further statements—"

"I wish to address the court, your honor."

"You are…?"

"Ardith Ley, your honor."

The judge looked down at the papers on his desk. Reuben, blindsided, said, "Ardith?"

"I'm sorry," she whispered to him. "I love you." She walked to the front of the courtroom. "Thank you, your honor. In some ways I have no right to speak. I am not a member of the victim's family, nor am I part of the defendant's. The consequence of these proceedings will not affect me legally or directly impact me. I am, however, an involved party with the deepest connection possible to the deceased. He is the father of my daughter."

Reuben's head dropped.

"Tom Watkins cared about everyone in this community. He didn't make distinctions between rich and poor. He didn't treat anyone differently because of the color of their skin. He loved his patients, all of them. He especially loved children and young people who had their lives ahead of them. He wanted to make a difference to them in any way he could. His humanity showed through in every patient he treated. I believe if he were here right now he would ask for mercy for the man who caused his death. He would wish compassion over punishment. He would not want a father to be taken away from his children. He would not want a husband to leave his wife with no support for the family. I cannot help that I fell in love with Tom Watkins." Ardith's voice broke. She hesitated, took a breath, and then continued. "I betrayed my husband, my children, and my own values by doing so. I'm the last person, perhaps, who should stand up here and plead for the man who killed the father of my daughter. But I believe in my heart it's the right thing to do, and I believe that Tom would want me to."

Ardith walked back to her seat. She sat down next to Reuben and didn't look at him, though he could feel her face burning, or he believed so. His own certainly did. He opened his notebook.

He closed it.

"I thank everyone for their statements. I am now ready to impose sentencing."

38

Harry thought he heard Olivia crying. She slept in her own room now—his old room since he had moved down to the basement. He walked up the two flights of stairs to check on her. Charlotte, at the foot of the crib, increasingly more protective of Olivia so she hardly left her side, lifted her head when he opened the door. Olivia was sound asleep with her thumb in her mouth.

He checked on Jamie—now James. Ever since his brother learned there was a girl in his seventh-grade class named Jamie, he demanded everyone call him James. If you slipped up, he'd go to his room and slam the door. His little brother—not so little anymore—had grown sullen and shed his so-called "sunny disposition." He complained about chores, snapped at you for no reason, and spent a lot of time in his room with the door locked. "Be careful you don't pull it off," Harry had teased him. Big mistake. Jamie threw his bike helmet at him, leaving a dent in the doorframe after Harry ducked. "Fuck off!" he yelled. Whew. He'd never heard his brother curse, let alone be violent. It was such a goddamn relief. Someone else in the family could be the crazy one. Harry stood there a moment. He wanted to say something consoling. *Welcome to adolescent hell.* Or: *It will get worse before it gets better, but it will get better.* Or: *It's okay to whack off.* "Sorry, James," he said, and left it at that.

He couldn't sleep through the night. He would hear phantom cries from his little sister or imagine he smelled smoke and the house was on fire. He'd have to drag himself out of bed and go through the same ritual every night: check on Olivia, then James, then listen at his mother's door. He was like a night watchman, without anyone ever knowing he was on duty. Then he'd sit at the kitchen table and drink a glass of milk like his father used to do when he lived with them.

It was so calm at three in the morning. Their creaky old house seemed to be holding its breath. Even the cat clock left behind by the former house owners with its annoying, ticking tail had finally died. He didn't know why he had such insomnia. He'd been dreaming of Brenva tonight. Her slim fingers were stroking the back of another kid's neck like she used to do for him. He stood there watching and frozen, but nobody noticed him. It was torture. Why was he dreaming bad things about her? Just before school started, she'd dropped off a package of comics and Oreos at his doorstep, along with a note insisting she really meant what she said about wanting to stay friends. And they should hang out again! He must have read the note twenty times. He even took out a piece of paper and rewrote it in the calligraphy that he'd taught himself. Then he wrote it over again, until he had twenty separate index cards that were supposed to be for his public-speaking project. He examined the flaws on each card—too much flourish in the lettering; too thick a serif; too blotchy from using the wrong nib—and then tied a silver ribbon around the stack. *Can we be imperfect together?* he wrote on a separate card in front.

But he didn't bring the stack to Brenva as planned. It would be too close to what he'd come to think of as his Ben behavior. She would see it as creepy. And even if not, she wouldn't understand what he was trying to tell her anyway.

He finished his glass of milk and rinsed it out in the sink. Maybe he *would* get a job one day as a night watchman. Something about the vacancy of the hour suited his nature. Despite everything Neil had told him, he couldn't help wondering if he was just one of those people meant to be alone in life and not feel ashamed of it.

This afternoon, his mother had come home from the sentencing looking wiped out.

"What happened?" Harry asked her. He had wanted to go, knowing Luisa would be there, but his mother said he needed to be in school. It wasn't a circus. He'd never said it was. If she didn't know by now that he cared what happened, he'd never convince her. Where did she think he'd been the last year? He'd watched her go through hell and now she was telling him he thought the whole thing was for his amusement?

"Luisa's father received supervised probation."

"No jail time?"

"No."

"That's really good then, right? Good for Luisa and her mom! Isn't that what you wanted, for him not to go to jail?"

"Yes."

"Then why…you don't seem very happy about it."

"I'm just tired. It was…an ordeal."

"What did Dad say?"

"I haven't spoken to him about it. I left right away. I need to lie down now—" Olivia cried out from upstairs. Harry had been watching her since after school when Mrs. Olsen, their elderly neighbor, had left after babysitting. Charlotte barked at the top of the stairs. "I need to feed Olivia and then lie down. Okay? I'll talk to you more later. It's been hard. You may hear some things. You'll just have to ignore them."

"What kind of things?"

His mother pinched her temples between her thumb and forefinger. Olivia cried louder. Charlotte barked insistently. The racket was deafening. "I promise I'll talk to you later."

That was the last he heard from her today. He'd heated up some leftover spaghetti when his brother came home and told him not to bother Mom. She was resting. He didn't see her for the remainder of the evening, isolating herself with Olivia. His father texted that he was going to work late at the office and wouldn't be stopping by tonight. *Whatever*, Harry had texted back. He didn't know why he ever thought he wanted to marry Brenva. Marriage turned people into lunatics.

Now he could swear he did smell smoke. He went to the base of the stairs, sniffed but smelled nothing up there. He went into the den. A window was open. The smoke was coming from outside.

He opened the front door and could smell it more strongly.

Luisa had finally fallen asleep. The sentencing had wrung them all out. They'd been stunned, surprised, and beyond grateful when the judge announced that after careful deliberation, the sentence would be probation and a five-hundred-dollar fine. A one-year jail sentence was suspended subject to fulfilling the terms of probation. A dazed moment of silence followed, then the courtroom erupted. The judge banged his gavel for order to continue, and Luisa leaned forward, her mother clutching her arm so tightly it would leave a bruise later on. "Given the first-time offense, the promise of continued employment for the defendant at his place of work, and the remorse shown by the defendant for his act, I've come to this difficult decision. I understand it will neither address in the entirety the wounds of the victim's family nor fully appease the community. But it is my belief that justice will be done more by allowing the defendant to make restitution and redeem his place in society than by sending him away for this tragic offense." The judge exited the courtroom to a mix of protesting voices.

Luisa hugged her mother, then Ardith. She could not believe what Ardith had done for them. She had watched Ardith leave the podium and walk back to her seat. She put her hand on Ardith's shoulder, whispered, "Thank you," but Ardith sat like a statue staring straight ahead, her face frozen.

As soon as the judge finished sentencing, Ardith walked quickly out of the courtroom. Luisa stared after her. She wondered about Mr. Rosenfeld. Did he know? Did Harry? She felt utterly torn between her appreciation for what Ardith had done and her shock that she had done it.

To avoid the crowd outside, they left through a side door of the courthouse. Pressed together, with Luisa in the middle, a small knot unto themselves as if afraid to allow any opening between their bodies, they quickly went inside their house and locked the door behind them. Her father said everything would be better now. He'd be better. He'd stop drinking. "I'm making a pledge," he told them. "I've been given a second chance. I won't take it for granted. I'm blessed." Luisa thought he was talking to himself as much as them. Her mother had not stopped thanking God since they left the courtroom.

They'd let Marcos go to school rather than the sentencing, best for him, even with the possibility of their father being taken into custody and Marcos unable to say goodbye. Her little brother wouldn't stop asking questions about whether Daddy was going to jail. Now they could tell him it was all right. But was it? Marcos had gotten into a fight at school when someone called their father a murderer. Luisa had buried herself in schoolwork to avoid interacting with any of her classmates, even Carla. Her mother had lost three cleaning jobs, supposedly because they didn't need her anymore, but Luisa knew that wasn't why. And her father, who Ellen had told could have his job back…well, Luisa worried whether he was in any shape to work and whether the boss man, as her father referred to Lyle, was as understanding as his wife. In the meantime, waiting to hear his sentence, he had kept busy fixing things around the house, but he had also sat around a lot staring into space, as if just waiting for his fate. He stuttered now when he talked. He had become a meek man, and Luisa wondered if he had lost his soul. And even if he didn't go to jail would he ever get out of the jail he had put himself in? Sometimes she thought he wanted to be imprisoned, not only to be punished but because he didn't want to think for himself anymore. Sometimes, too, she heard him talking aloud and when she asked him who he was speaking to, he quickly said no one and went out to work in the shed. But Luisa feared those were the same voices she heard in her head, especially when the house was silent in the middle of the night like now, voices screaming with hate.

Smoke.

She got out of bed and opened her bedroom door. A blast of heat and smoke forced her back. She went into her bathroom and wet a washcloth and put it over her nose and mouth. She got on her hands and knees and crawled along the floor, taking the wet washcloth from her face only to scream for help. She kept touching the wall, trying to estimate how far she was from the stairway, until the wall felt too hot and she crawled blindly forward. A voice called from below and she shouted in its direction, "Up here!" A figure moved toward her, a firefighter who picked her up and put her over his shoulder and brought her downstairs and outside to the cool air that she gulped down. Bent over, coughing, her eyes stinging and watering so much she couldn't focus, she caught her first full breath and expelled a cry for her family.

"They're safe," the fireman said. He put a blanket around her shoulders and led her over to where they were huddled, her father, mother, and brother. Fiercely, they wrapped her in their arms. And then like someone who had just stepped out of a dream, there was Harry Rosenfeld, standing barefoot in jeans and no shirt, as if he had just dropped by.

THE TENDEREST OF STRINGS

39

Reuben bought a new suit for the funeral. After all his exercising and dropped pounds his two older suits no longer fit. He stood at the gravesite on this cold December day with Wade's entire department in front of him. Wade's sister was present and his ex-wife, but he saw no other family members. No children. No living parents.

Mike Uphoff delivered a eulogy extolling what Wade meant to the town, praising his dedication to "a community made safe for the many people of Welton, who will dearly miss his gentle strength on behalf of us all."

Reuben hadn't seen it coming. Oh yes, he had. But perhaps like Wade himself he refused to believe that another heart attack was imminent. His last conversation at Wade's cabin an hour away in Red Feather had been about Wade's retirement six months hence. He'd put thirty-five years into the job, and he was ready to let it go, fish at the lake near his cabin, watch the aspens turn color and the elk migrate, and try to keep up with his two Labradors. Did he have any regrets? Reuben waited with his pen poised and his recorder on. "Turn that off a sec," Wade said. He was still angry about the Watkins case. He didn't think justice had been served. He thought it sent a terrible message to all the drunks out there who didn't give a damn about who they ran down.

Reuben had let him go on. He didn't know what it was about the case that drove Wade mad. Surely, he'd had plenty of other cases that didn't get the convictions he wanted.

Then again, Reuben could not stop working the case for all its enduring private affliction. Months after the sentencing he was both amazed and appalled that in this small town no one had said one word to him about what had happened in court. It was as if his wife had simply stood up there and recited a holiday poem. Could it be that the entire town pitied him to the point of widespread conspiratorial silence?

Well, there was one person. Rosa. Sort of. She'd laid her hands on his shoulders with ministerial succoring and looked him directly in his eyes for a long moment before she spoke: "For all those who exalt themselves will be humbled, and those who humble themselves will be exalted. Luke 14:11." Then she went back to calculating the *Sentinel's* algorithmic presence on the web. Aside from her mixing up humility with humiliation in his case, he appreciated the sentiment.

"No need to stir up the whole business again by printing any of this," Wade had said during the interview. "I wouldn't want to give anybody more fuel to do what those kids did already."

Those "kids" were the ones who had set fire to Miguel's garage. The smoke had seeped into the main house, and if it hadn't been for Harry—

"It just hit me hard," Wade continued, "that's all I can say. Tom and his family deserved better. I don't know where you stand on any of this. I know it's been… Look, I *do* have something to say on that subject. The thing about Tom, and though I know I shouldn't be bringing him up to you of all people, but maybe this will help, is that he was every man's bad comparison. He was a specimen of health, for instance, and you can imagine how that made me feel. But for all that, for *all* his attributes, I never felt like I actually knew the guy. Not like I know you, Reuben. That counts for a whole lot more in my book." He nodded at Reuben's recorder. "You can turn that thing on again. I got some people to thank for their years of service with me that I'd like to get into the article, if you give me the space."

Two weeks later, Wade put his head down on his office desk and never woke up.

At the gravesite, Wade's sister accepted a folded department flag from two of Wade's officers. A third officer took out his radio and spoke into it, making the final ceremonial call: *Radio number 3-1 is out of service after thirty-five years and four months of police service. Although you are gone, you will never be forgotten. Rest in peace, our friend. The time is elevn p.m., December 27.*

And then it was over. Reuben hung back. Mike Uphoff came up to him and patted his arm. "Good remembrance in the paper," Mike said. Dennis Olberg gave a stiff nod as he passed. Dot Myers wiped her eyes. Chauncey Griggs approached, opening his arms wide, and Reuben flinched, fearing an awkward hug. But it was for an elderly lady standing behind him.

He made his way over to Wade's ex-wife, Joan, and expressed his condolences. What was the protocol for extending your sympathies to an ex-wife? Bereavement etiquette with exes was complicated—though, as usual, much of this question resided largely in his head, because Joan hugged him and said, "You were a good friend to Wade. You're a good man." It took him aback. Of all the things he might have prepared for at Wade's funeral least of all was to be told he was a good man.

He waited until almost everyone had left and then walked up to the grave. He picked up a handful of dirt and threw it on the coffin. It was a Jewish custom, but he was sure Wade, his lost friend, would understand.

Afterward, he drove to the house. He could see guests had already started arriving for Olivia's first birthday party. Ardith had asked him to give her regrets for not being at the funeral. "And I'm sorry I can't be there for you. I know you really cared about him." It was true. He'd made very few friends since he came to Welton. Lyle, yes, but Lyle was mostly incommunicado since all the trouble. They'd talk occasionally, but the easy banter and crusty fondness he'd felt from Lyle was gone. Reuben couldn't bring himself to ask how things were with Ellen. He was the last person to be discussing matters of trust in a marriage. Despite the promise of gainful employment, Miguel no longer worked at the dairy farm. The family had moved to Greeley after the fire. It was too dangerous to stay in a town when people—three juveniles who decided to take their dislike of the justice system's decision into their own hands—wanted to burn your home down with you in it. Reuben would have been happy to print their names in the paper if they'd been eighteen. As it was, he had to report that the three had gotten off with community service. No one suggested it was a hate crime, though the police, that being Wade when he'd been alive, did find one of the boy's phones that had been dropped at the scene—clumsy arsonists that they were—with racist tweets. No, Wade told him, he couldn't put that in the paper. It was inadmissible evidence for a trial that was not to be. The whole town just needed to put the whole business aside. Not that Wade himself ever could.

Despite the bad blood between them, Ardith had invited Ellen to the party. She was trying to use Olivia's first birthday as a chance for rapprochement. She'd even invited Marian, knowing full well that Marian had filed a wrongful death suit against Miguel and was unlikely to come. Not that there was anything to get from the penniless family, other than a judgment hanging over them for the rest of their lives if Marian and her family succeeded. Blood was thicker than water or at least half-blood. Reuben had thought surely this would affect Ardith as the most bitter of acts, and yet it had not stopped her from employing Harry with his impressive calligraphic skills to pen an invitation to Olivia's half-sister.

Harry. Harry the hero, Reuben had taken to calling him. "Don't tease him," Ardith scolded. "It embarrasses him." But he wasn't teasing. He was serious. He would have gladly put Harry's name in the paper if there was any way he could have managed it without appearing biased. He'd played a critical role in what happened—or hadn't happen. If not for Harry's pounding on the front door, would the family have escaped? If he hadn't woken up the neighbor to call 911 would Luisa, the last member in the house and closest to the garage where the fire had started, been rescued in time? "Stop asking me why I was awake at that hour," however, was all he said to Reuben. As usual, his son abhorred praise, all the pricklier and more dismissive when it came from his father. But should he not be proud of his firstborn? Was it so bad after the facts came out about the incident that Reuben started every conversation with "My boy Harry who saved those people's lives..."

Nah, he didn't. That was the voice of his long dead father who *would* start practically every sentence with *My boy Harry*, about Reuben's brother, the pride and hope of the family. What a burden the dead carry for the living, not vice versa. Poor Harry in heaven. If such a place existed, he was surely looking down on Reuben and saying, *Sorry, bro. My death was supposed to make things easier for you, not harder.*

He walked up the steps of their house. He no longer looked at the pile of two-by-fours covered with a blue tarp like a monument to his lassitude. Ardith had managed to start a garden at least, dormant in the frozen ground now. There had been money for a new furnace and a replaced roof, thanks to hail damage insurance. They'd get there, they would. Or Ardith would. He had his studio apartment not far from the paper. He slept there, cooked for himself, spent as much time as he could with the boys, and filled the days with passing hours that offered no answer other than to keep going and fill more days. It was not hope but it wasn't despair either. This was the Why of Them and no explanation sufficed more than another. You kept on because you had done so a minute, a second, a wish before. They were a fractured family, kept together by the tenderest of strings, but they were still here.

"Reuben, hello!" It was Dr. Stein. "Nice to see you," she said.

"You too," said Reuben, making his way into the party, after hanging up his coat.

"You wore a suit. Super!" Dr. Stein said.

"Thank you. It was actually for—"

But Dr. Stein was swiftly commandeered by a mom Reuben didn't know and whose panicky eyes said, *I'm a first-time mother and I have a question that only you can tell me it's nothing to worry about.* At his annual physical, when Jamie announced with a newly cultivated assertiveness that he wished to be called James—he'd printed up business cards to make the point—Dr. Stein brought up an organization called Adventure Judaism. James could go on local hikes and backpacking trips in canyon lands, climb mountains and snowshoe, all the while learning about his heritage and how to take care of the environment. During the process he would study to become a bar mitzvah. Was he interested? He jumped at the chance, and Reuben would hear him practicing his Torah reading in his room. Judaism goes wilderness. And why not? He pictured his son making the blessings over bread and wine witnessed by curious bighorn sheep. Good for him. Ardith was delighted, and frankly, so was he.

Babies were everywhere. He wasn't sure where they all came from, Olivia's playgroup, perhaps. He saw Jolie, eight months pregnant, tireless in her dedication to the paper even in her condition, chatting in a corner with a tall woman who Reuben realized was Ellen. And standing just at the entrance to the kitchen and talking with Harry was Luisa, whom Reuben hadn't seen since they moved to Greeley.

An arm went around his shoulder. "You're full of crap." Lyle. Without any preliminaries, Lyle proceeded to harangue him about why he wasn't living at home with his family. Still! The same old stuff, as if they'd never stopped having this conversation. "If I can make up with her"—he nodded at Ellen—"you can get your butt back here."

"Jesus, Lyle, hello, I think."

Jamie came out of the kitchen carrying a sheet cake with a single lit candle. Right behind him was Ardith, holding Olivia in a ruffled pink dress and a white hairbow. Her cheeks red and her lips pursed in concentration, Olivia leaned out from Ardith's arms—way out—trying to get to the cake. Everyone began singing "Happy Birthday." Ardith whispered something to Olivia and then took a big breath and blew out the candle. Applause. A nimbus of rose light fell around the two of them. Ardith looked as pink as Olivia, her face flushed with a mother's joy. Glancing up, she saw Reuben across the room and smiled, her eyes, he thought, welcoming. She waved for him to come get a piece of cake and be with—he believed so, he did—their daughter.

He remained at a distance.

Then suddenly Harry was next to him. He had been filming the party with his cell phone. As tall as Reuben now, he rested his hand on his father's shoulder. His son's touch, the implicit compassion and perhaps forgiveness, struck him with unexpected force, and Reuben's eyes welled up.

"It's okay, Dad," Harry said. "We're good here. We're all good."

And they stood there for an eternity, watching the rest of their family just steps away.

ACKNOWLEDGEMENTS

For their friendship, readings, and support, I would like to thank Charles Baxter, Robert Boswell, John Calderazzo, Robert Cohen, Ann Cummins, Elena Engel, Andy Konigsberg, Deanna and Gary Ludwin, Toni Nelson, Jerry Roselle, Jenny Wortman, and Jaynie Royal and Pam Van Dyk at Regal House.

A special thanks to Stephanie G'Schwind for her unerring editorial judgment and warmest friendship.

I can't count, nor would she want to remember, how many drafts my wife, Emily Hammond, read of this novel and, despite my own flagging will at times, refused to give up on it. I owe its existence as much to her as my own efforts. And finally, my children, Zach and Elena, younger when I started, now grown, my deepest love for their belief in me.